EDGE

EDGE

Nick Oldham

Severn House Large Print

London & New York

This first large print edition published 2015
in Great Britain and the USA by
SEVERN HOUSE PUBLISHERS LTD of
19 Cedar Road, Sutton, Surrey, England, SM2 5DA.
First world regular print edition published 2014 by
Severn House Publishers Ltd., London and New York.

British Library Cataloguing in Publication Data

Oldham, Nick, 1956– author.
  Edge. – (A Henry Christie thriller)
  1. Christie, Henry (Fictitious character)–Fiction.
  2. Recidivists–Fiction. 3. Police–England–Blackpool–
  Fiction. 4. Detective and mystery stories. 5. Large type
  books.
  I. Title II. Series
  823.9'2-dc23

  ISBN-13: 9780727872678

Severn House Publishers support the Forest Stewardship Council™
[FSC™], the leading international forest certification organisation. All
our titles that are printed on FSC certified paper carry the FSC logo.

Typeset by Palimpsest Book Production Ltd.,
Falkirk, Stirlingshire, Scotland.
Printed and bound in Great Britain by
T J International, Padstow, Cornwall.

For Belinda

AUTHOR'S NOTE

This is a work of fiction, and any historical, geographical or factual errors are entirely my doing.

One

Charlie Wilder was dreaming about a sawn-off shotgun. It was one of those slow motion, technicolour dreams in which he could see the fingers of his left hand supporting and encircling the side-by-side double barrels, and the forefinger of his right hand curling around the double triggers that had been specially modified and aligned so he could put the tip of his finger across both of them in order to fire both barrels at once.

Next in the dream, he saw himself bringing the weapon up and shoving it into someone's face. The features of the face were indistinguishable, pixelated out, because it did not matter who the gun was pointed at. Whoever it was, they were just nobody to Charlie Wilder.

In the dream he felt his lips curve into a genuine smile and the tip of his finger apply only light pressure on the triggers, which he pulled at the same moment he heard that bastard of a prison officer start to walk along the cell block landing at exactly seven a.m., clattering his baton on every cell door, bawling insults at each of the inmates.

Charlie jerked awake, physically experiencing the recoil of the weapon in his dream, and opened his eyes. Now he smiled grimly as he listened to the screw called Dawson hurl his abuse. His

1

words were not general, but specific to each and every prisoner, based on the intimate, personal knowledge he had accrued of each man, gleaned from his interactions with them and his continual poring over personal files.

Charlie waited on his bunk until Prison Officer Dawson reached his cell door and whacked the tip of the baton against it. Charlie blinked as he listened to the tirade of insults aimed at himself and the other prisoner in the cell, an old thief and drunk called Victor, a guy who had done more harm to himself than to others in his miserable life.

Charlie occupied the lower bunk. He could have had the upper one, but didn't care where he slept. He had gladly given the privilege to Victor, who rewarded him with a continuous supply of chocolate and tobacco.

'And as for you, you dim-witted hillbilly,' Dawson yelled, dropping the inspection hatch and angling his face into the gap, keeping up his nasty tirade against Charlie with gusto.

Charlie let it all ride over him, unaffected, but seething with anger for other people who had really suffered from Dawson's abusive tactics that often carried on beyond the cells and sometimes became physical. He was an old-fashioned screw, but his bullying and aggression and overbearing personality ensured that his inappropriate behaviour was never tackled by his colleagues or bosses, many of whom secretly liked to see him getting away with it.

Charlie had witnessed one weak boy, nothing more than a kid, a stupid lad in for burglary,

2

being browbeaten and battered into submission by Dawson's unremitting, horrible name calling, until he eventually went over the edge.

The lad had been found one morning, dead, hanging by the neck from a shoelace tied to the end of his bed.

The smirk of victory on Dawson's face had been fixed there for days afterwards as he revelled in the power he had to drive others to suicide.

'No response, you chicken-shit?' Dawson demanded of Charlie.

This time the smile of victory was on Charlie's face as he tilted it to the door and said, 'Last time you say that to me, sir.'

'Yeah, I know. That's why it was a good one, numpty-head.'

The two locked eyes for a moment, then Dawson slammed the hatch shut, was gone, moving along to the next cell.

'Bastard,' Victor the drunk whispered hoarsely from the top bunk. He had also been subjected to a lot of Dawson's cruel antics.

'Mm,' Charlie agreed, adding, 'but he won't be doing it for much longer.'

He sat up, allowed his eyes to roam the cell, taking it all in for the very last time. Today was going to be a special day and Charlie Wilder was going to make it all happen.

At 9.05 a.m., the prison doors still hadn't opened.

Luke Wilder, Charlie's brother, was pacing anxiously along Ribbleton Avenue at the point where it joined Church Street on the outer rim

3

of Preston city centre. The rain, so far, had not started to fall, but glancing up into the dark, low, angry clouds above, Luke knew it wouldn't be long before the storm began. It had been forecasted to last for a long, long time.

Which was good.

Luke knew Charlie liked bad weather.

It drained people, made them weary, put them off their guard and made them slow-witted and miserable; all helpful traits for the second part of the day's events that Charlie had planned and Luke had set up.

'C'mon,' Luke muttered irritably. He stopped sharply just as the huge front gates of Preston Prison opened. A GuardSec prison van crept out on to Church Street, turned left towards the main set of traffic lights on Ring Way, the dual carriageway that half-encircled Preston, one of England's newest cities. Luke saw the face of a man crushed grotesquely up against the window of one of the inner cells in the vehicle and their eyes met momentarily, but without meaning. 'Remand prisoners,' Luke said to himself as the prison gates closed and the establishment behind became secure once more.

Luke spun three-sixty degrees on his heels so the bricks of the high and intimidating prison walls were on his right. He walked back up to the small annexe through which prisoners were now released back into society. In the not too distant past, inmates were let out through the Judas gate set within the main gate, which was how leaving a prison should be. A statement. A

4

moment. Like something from the beginning of a movie.

Now it was boring, lacking drama.

They were all now released through an internal door that opened into a dull, tiled foyer within the annexe. It was more like leaving an office than exiting to liberty after a period of incarceration.

Luke stood at the foot of the ramp leading up to the foyer door behind a queue of other people, all sullenly waiting for the appearance of loved ones. Two stereotypical council estate girls with babes in prams (one also with a babe in her stomach) waited in the queue, chain-smoking, the cigarettes held between nicotine-stained fingers. They constantly swept back their bleached blonde hair, the black roots showing, both dressed in gruesomely coloured velour tracksuits.

One of them, the un-pregnant one, kept slyly appraising Luke, who knew he was a decent enough looking young man.

He eyed her back confidently, liking the look of her neck tattoos and multi-pierced ears, nose and lower lip. But he didn't like the look of the kid in the pram, which was of mixed race. Kids were not on Luke's agenda. He hated the little bastards.

She pushed out her generous breasts with little subtlety. They wobbled whitely, exposed by the low cut of her T-shirt and undersized bra, which accentuated their fullness. Luke gave her a grin and shook his head.

He took a thin cigarette from his tin of self-prepared roll-ups and lit it, inhaling the bitter smoke, getting bits of tobacco caught between his teeth which he picked out and flicked away.

'C'mon,' he muttered again.

There was a lot to get through today.

Then the door opened and the first of the day's released came out.

The man went straight to the girl who had been eyeing Luke, the one with the slinky neck tattoos. They greeted each other with lustful greed whilst Luke wondered who the kid in the pushchair belonged to. It certainly wasn't the man's. Luke chuckled mirthlessly to himself. Some people lead such complicated lives, he thought.

A dribble of other prisoners followed but not the one Luke was here to greet, making him fret that he had turned up on the wrong day, which would have been a bit of a disaster bearing in mind what lay ahead. Even though he knew he was right, he pulled out the official paper from his jacket pocket and did a quick double-check.

He was correct. Today was the day his big brother Charlie Wilder was going to be released.

As he stuffed the letter back into his pocket, the door opened again and Charlie stepped out a free man. Almost.

Luke grinned and watched Charlie saunter cockily down the slope towards him.

Charlie was the older brother by a year, better looking in a harsh sort of way, taller, leaner than Luke, but two years of being banged up, though having taken a lot of excess weight off him, had

6

replaced it by building muscles in his arms and legs. That said, his face looked hollowed now, to Luke, in the true light of day. And he seemed more haunted, his eyes deep in their sockets. In fact, Luke thought, Charlie looked even scarier than he had before he was sent down. His hair was quite long and unkempt – purposely – and he wore jeans, a short jacket and trainers, and carried a rolled-up plastic bag under his arm in which all his belongings had been placed. Still, the brothers did look broadly similar and in bad light they could easily have been mistaken for each other.

Luke was a little alarmed by the sight of Charlie. He had only seen him at visiting times over the last couple of years and though he had noticed changes in his brother, it was only seeing him in the flesh, full length, face to face, that he completely realized what the changes were.

The weight loss, yes. The muscle, sure.

But there was more to it than those things. His aura was different. Even scarier. He looked like a wild animal and Luke swallowed drily . . . *as today will no doubt demonstrate*, he thought.

Charlie stood a few feet from him, a grin spreading. He reached out and took the roll-up from Luke's lips and put it between his own, drawing in the last remaining smoke from it, then flicking it away into the road.

Not much of a gesture but one which clearly defined the pecking order in this relationship: Charlie boss, Luke underling.

'Hi, bro,' Charlie said.

Luke nodded awkwardly.

Then neither of them could hold back their brotherly emotions any longer. It had been a very long time since they'd been so close without any sort of barrier between them – a table, a screen, a cop or a screw. They embraced clumsily – showing feelings wasn't something they were familiar with, as much as they loved each other – but they back-slapped and were on the edge of tears.

'Two years, two damn years,' Charlie almost sobbed.

'Yeah, but you're out now.' Luke held him at arm's-length and scrutinized him.

'Yuh, yuh – and a busy day ahead – if you've done what I asked you to do?'

'I have, mate, I have,' Luke said, reacting to the slight hint of threat in Charlie's voice.

'Good, then it'll be an effin' great day, right back in the saddle is what I want. Now then, business to do,' he concluded seriously.

'But a bit of pleasure first.'

'Oh yeah.'

Luke led Charlie up past the prison to a side street outside an electrical warehouse where he had parked up some transport for them, an old but clean Vauxhall Chevette.

'Hell's this?' Charlie sneered, surveying the rust bucket.

'Just get in, bro. If anybody's watching us I want 'em to see us getting into a straight motor, yeah?'

'Got it,' Charlie said, clicking on to his brother's train of thought. Even though he had only just stepped out of prison, he would not have been surprised to have the law on his trail already, and you could not be careful enough. Being sloppy was what had landed him in the dock last time. Charlie ripped open the ill-fitting passenger door and dropped heavily on to the battered seat.

Luke climbed in after checking for a moment they hadn't been followed or watched. He couldn't spot anything obvious, but it was hard to say for certain.

As Luke slid in behind the wheel, Charlie raised his right leg and tugged up his jeans, pointing to the tracking device fitted around his ankle. It was like the 1960s idea of how a space-age wristwatch might have looked. Charlie was out of prison on licence, having only completed half of his sentence, and one of the conditions of his release was that he had to wear an electronic tag and was therefore subject to constant surveillance and curfew.

Luke nodded. 'I know – sorted.'

'Good.'

Luke fired up the car which coughed out a cloud of dirty, blue-grey exhaust smoke.

'Are all the cars fixed up, like I wanted?' Charlie asked.

'Yeah – Johnny's been busy on that score, so they're sorted, too.'

'Good.'

Luke drove the short distance to the city centre, parking on a back street in the Avenham area behind Church Street, leaving the car keys underneath the driver's seat. The car would not be here when they returned. He and Charlie then walked up to and along Church Street and Luke steered his brother into a hairdressing salon at the top of Fishergate, Preston's main shopping street.

Charlie hesitated at the door.

'First job,' Luke said, 'a bit of pampering. Get a good haircut, which is why I told you to let it grow for a few weeks.'

Charlie relented and was treated to a nice trim from a heavily made-up hairdresser with large boobs which constantly brushed against the back of his head, causing a surge of blood within him. It was all he could do not to slice his hand up between the young girl's legs. He fought the urge and sat back to enjoy the session, feeling he was being eased back into the civilized world – or at least the world he inhabited. The prison barbers he had encountered over the last two years had been butchers.

Luke also had a similar haircut.

Next up was a set of new clothes. Jeans, trainers, a Metallica T-shirt and a zip-up top, and they felt good. Charlie left Next bouncing on his toes, wearing his new gear and binning the old.

'Now let's grab a coffee,' Luke suggested.

They strolled down to Costa Coffee on Fishergate and had an Americano and an all-day breakfast panini each. Charlie scoffed his as if he had not eaten for a week.

'Feel good to be out?' Luke asked.

'Oh yeah – ain't going back there in a hurry.'

'Good, good.' Luke nodded. 'I fixed up the other thing like you asked, yeah?' He sounded a little unsure.

'Good – let's do it.'

They left the café and walked down one of the side streets that ran at right angles off Fishergate to a nondescript door adjacent to a florist's shop. Nothing on the sturdy door indicated what lay beyond, but Charlie did not hesitate, rang the bell and stepped back so he and Luke could be seen by the discreet lens of the CCTV camera fitted in the brickwork a few feet above the door. Their wait lasted a minute, then the door was opened by a dark-skinned middle-aged woman, quite stunning, with jet black hair pulled tightly back and large brown eyes. She stood aside and indicated that the brothers should step inside the vestibule. They were expected.

She closed and bolted the door and led them upstairs, both brothers mesmerized by her Lycra-clad legs and shapely bottom that swayed provocatively in front of their eyes. They could see the line of the thong looped through her buttocks and Charlie's mouth twitched. She showed them into a plushly furnished waiting area: two sofas, a coffee table and several potted plants that could have been plastic. The window blinds were drawn, the lighting subdued.

'I got another guy coming before anything else,' Charlie told the woman. She nodded – she knew this – and disappeared behind a door marked private.

Charlie and Luke sat on one of the sofas and

the woman emerged a short time later with a wireless credit card machine; after entering a figure, she held out the machine. Luke took it, swiped a credit card and entered a PIN number after a slight hesitation on seeing the amount: £600. Not that he was too concerned. The card wasn't his and by lunchtime it would be destroyed.

'What are we getting for that?' he asked, handing the machine back.

The woman tore off the printed receipt and gave it to Luke together with the stolen card. 'I'll show you,' she said.

She went back into the private office, came back out, then went through another door beyond which the brothers managed to see a long corridor, with doors either side.

'What did this place used to be?' Luke asked.

'A club of some sort, I think.' Charlie stuck out his right leg and again showed Luke the electronic tag around his ankle. 'This comes off before anything else.'

'I know – all arranged.'

As if on cue the doorbell chimed and the woman reappeared – alone – and went down to answer it. She came back up followed by a man in his forties, his grey hair cropped in a military way. He was carrying a small tool box. Luke stood up and shook his hand and turned to Charlie who was watching through hooded eyes.

'This is the guy who's gonna take that off.' He pointed to Charlie's ankle.

'They told me you can't get 'em off without detection.'

The man, whose name was Dibney, said confidently, 'I can,' then wrinkled his nose. 'Let's have a gander.'

Charlie sat back and laid his ankle on the coffee table, tugged up his jeans leg. The man smiled knowledgeably as he recognized the make and model of the tag. He put his tool kit on the table and squatted next to Charlie's leg, inspecting the device carefully, smirking.

'OM247PID electronic tag,' he said. 'Know it well.'

'You know it?' Charlie asked incredulously.

'Used to fit 'em for a living; used to take 'em off, too. Piece of piss if you know what you're doing,' he sniffed. 'Bit like bypassing a burglar alarm system, if you know what I mean? If you keep the connection, you fool it.'

'You used to be a screw?'

'In the private sector.' He opened his tool kit and took out a slim device that resembled an iPhone. He switched it on.

'What's that do?' Luke asked, watching the process.

'Two things. Finds the frequency the tag is emitting . . .' He dragged and tapped icons on the touch screen, opened various apps.

'Then what?'

'Then – and this is the really clever part – once it's locked on to the frequency I then press another button and this little thing—' he waggled the device – 'pretends to be the tag. I can then remove

13

it, reset it, and then voila! It starts to send out its signals again and the tracking centre still thinks it's round your ankle.'

'Fuckin' 'ell,' Charlie beamed. 'And they're none the wiser?'

'Exactly.'

'How much was it, that?' Luke asked about the device.

'A lot.'

'And why don't you work for them any more?'

The man gave him a withering glance. 'Guess,' he said, but rubbed his thumb and forefinger together: cash. 'I got four more lined up today.' The device buzzed. 'Got the frequency,' he said.

A minute later he had removed the tag, reconnected it, reset it and then handed it back to Charlie. 'When you want it refitted, gimme a bell. He has my number.' He nodded at Luke.

'Two hundred as agreed?' Luke said and handed the man a bundle of notes.

Then he was gone.

The brothers eyed each other with amusement, then turned to look as the woman who had let them in appeared from the corridor. This time she was not alone. Behind her were two slim, dark-skinned girls, late teens, dressed in skimpy clothes. Both were doe-eyed, had an air of vagueness about them.

'These are your ladies,' she said.

Charlie rubbed his hands together gleefully, smiled wickedly. 'Gonna be a good, good day,' he half-sang. 'Feel it in my bones.'

* * *

'First day of rest of us lives,' Charlie enthused as he and Luke tumbled out of the brothel and made back to Fishergate about thirty minutes later. He was buzzing, but sanguine after his encounter with the prostitute who, it had transpired, spoke not a word of English and was from Brazil. 'Today is revenge and set-up day.'

The brothers shared a knowing glance.

'Going to make a killing today, amass some cash with the guys, get one big adrenalin rush, then we all move forward into an easy, new line of business.' He continued to chatter enthusiastically, his head still spinning from the sex, his blood syrupy in his veins.

'How are we going to do that?' Luke asked. Nothing had really been shared with him. He had been tasked to do things, fix things up, but without ever really knowing or understanding the reason why he was doing these things. He was just following Charlie's orders, like he had done all his life.

'Let me introduce you to a guy first.'

'You not want to get home, chill, see the bird?'

Charlie glanced sidelong, his eyes narrowing. 'Yuh, later, business first, then party.'

'KK.'

They walked up Fishergate, then across to the Guild Hall and went into a bar behind the Harris Museum which at night became a club but during the day offered a trendy spot to stop for coffees and light lunches. It was just beginning to fill with mid-morning trade.

They sat at a window table, ordered coffee.

15

'Who is this guy?' Luke asked. 'You've told me nowt so far, just do this, do that—'

He was stopped abruptly in mid-sentence as Charlie's right hand shot out and grabbed his face, squeezing tight, twisting it out of shape. Luke jerked back and Charlie let go.

'I been in prison two years, boyo,' he hissed, leaning over his latte. 'A lot of time to consider, a lot of time to meet people, to listen . . . so all you need to do for the moment is keep doing just that, OK? Do what I say and I'll look after you and the boys like I always do.'

Luke rubbed his face back into shape.

'I'm the boss, yeah?' Charlie said quietly. 'Nowt's changed. I'm in charge and we're going to move into the modern world after today – one last day in the past – and all I ask you to do is stick with me.'

Luke nodded. 'Course, didn't mean anything.'

Two years had dulled Luke's memory somewhat. He had half-forgotten what a volatile temper Charlie possessed, one which could be ignited by almost anything – a wrong look, complete innocence . . . anything.

Charlie, like Luke, wasn't a huge young man, but what he lacked in physical presence he made up for in his ability to attack without remorse, to beat people down. Luke had once seen him stomp a man's face into a bloody unrecognizable pulp just because the man had brushed past him in a pub and not apologized. It had been nothing, instantly forgettable to most people, but Charlie had seethed all night, then lain in wait for him and half-slaughtered him.

Charlie nodded. 'So how are the guys?' he asked.

'Good, good, yeah,' Luke said vaguely.

'Looking forward to me coming home?'

'Oh yeah,' Luke said with just a hint of hesitation. He sensed that Charlie picked up on this, so he quickly said, 'What are we doing here, then? Who is this guy?'

'Just wait and see, OK? We meet him, we bang out a deal . . . I do what I have to do around here,' he said, looking past Luke's shoulder, imagining something, then continued, 'then we go on the rob – if you've sorted everything, that is?'

'I have,' Luke said defensively.

'That's all right, then.'

'So, come on . . . who is he? Why the mystery?'

'Just wait, OK?' Seeing his brother's expression, Charlie relented slightly. 'We meet him, we bang out a deal—'

'What sort of deal?' Luke interrupted irritably, but clammed up when Charlie shot him a death stare.

'We bang out a deal,' he continued, 'we do what I have to do around here, then we get on home, go on the rob big style, then we celebrate at the farm. Then tomorrow we check out those properties I asked you to look at—'

'That's something else I don't get—'

Charlie stared at him to be quiet. 'Then we eff off to Spain for a week and leave my tag at home, yeah? How does that sound?' he purred.

17

'Good, sounds good.'

'Like I said, today's gonna be a good day. I'm out of clink, we lay the foundations of a new business, we celebrate until we're shit-faced, then tomorrow – big silver bird to Malaga. It's all started good, hasn't it? Haircut, clothes, fuckyducky, new business.' He gave Luke one of his best winning smiles. 'Brilliant.'

Two

A small, very nondescript Asian man in his midthirties arrived ten minutes later and sat with the two brothers.

'Mr Hassan, please meet Luke, my brother,' Charlie said. They shook hands and Luke felt Hassan's palm, which was dry and smooth.

Hassan asked Luke, 'How do you like my girls?'

Luke frowned at him, then the penny clanged. 'That was your place? That knocking shop?'

Hassan nodded. 'One of many, but I call them houses of pleasure, not knocking shops.'

'I met Hassan in clink,' Charlie explained. 'We got talking . . . he opened my eyes.'

'To what?' asked Luke.

'Big possibilities.'

Hassan eyed the two brothers, a sly grin on his face.

'We thought we could do some business,'

Charlie said. Luke waited. Charlie went on, 'What we did before to make a living . . . fraught with danger, old style. What Hassan has on offer is an easier way ahead.'

Luke hesitated, narrowed his eyes, then said doubtfully, 'Start talking.'

'OK, OK,' Charlie said, 'but I promise you, this will set us up for life. We've been farting around, dealing drugs, pulling armed jobs, but it's been all over the show, bit here, bit there . . . not good business, no focus and far too friggin' easy to get caught.'

'What I suggest is a life with a lot less hassle,' Hassan picked up quickly. 'It's not easy, you cannot make that mistake, no business is. It requires commitment and time and energy . . . but it is safe and no one gets hurt.'

'It's like we'll be offerin' a commodity,' Charlie said, using words that were not really part of his vocabulary, something that Luke noticed. 'And it's something that every guy wants.' His eyes glistened with possibility. He turned to Hassan and urged, 'Go on, tell him.'

Hassan leaned towards Luke. 'Let me tell you this – and I'm only telling you because I've checked you both out – that place you've just been to? I own ten more like it. *Ten,*' he stressed.

Luke blinked and said, 'Right,' drawing out the syllable uncertainly.

'Each place has an average of ten girls. Each girl does fifteen tricks per day – as an average,' Hassan shrugged. 'Usually more. I even have to book them all appointments because demand is

19

so high and it's the only way to keep control. I also have another ten girls set up in exclusive apartments near MediaCity in Manchester and they deal with just five regular clients each day, from the TV. These are high-class girls.' He arched his thick, black eyebrows at Luke. 'I want to expand. I have expertise, I have the commodities, but I need help to franchise the brand, shall we say?'

'Commodities?' Luke asked.

'Girls are queuing up to come to this country.'

'Talk money,' Charlie urged him impatiently.

Hassan eyed him, then Luke. 'How much did you pay for Katrina this morning?'

'Was that her name?'

Hassan nodded.

'Three hundred,' he said. Even though it wasn't his credit card.

'So you have lived the example,' Hassan said. 'Now work it out. One girl, fifteen clients per day. That equals four thousand five hundred pounds per day. Ten girls, therefore, is forty-five thousand. *Each day*,' he stressed. 'Six days a week. Two hundred and seventy thousand pounds each week. Gross figure, admittedly, but in ten weeks the figure is around two and a half million.'

'Get to fuck!' Luke snorted.

'The high-class girls get a thousand pounds per visit . . . five each day, thirty grand a week.'

Luke looked disbelievingly at Charlie. 'Is this right, or bollocks?'

'It's right,' Charlie assured him.

'So where do the girls come from? What do

20

they get? Who looks after them?' Luke demanded.

'All businesses have overheads. The girls get twenty per cent, another ten goes in costs – but most costs are minimal – and I will provide the girls for you.'

'How?'

'I have a line from Brazil, via Portugal to Blackpool, Manchester, Liverpool and Leeds Bradford airports. I have ten girls arriving each day.' He laughed harshly. 'Obviously they all think they're going to end up as nannies or waitresses, and hope to send money back to their families – but confiscate their passports, lock them in a room, and they start to comply with my requirements easily enough.' He could have been discussing the importation of coffee beans or corned beef, and his perspective on them was soon confirmed. 'They're just commodities, as we have already mentioned,' he said heartlessly.

'And what do you get from us?' Luke asked.

'I need money up front first, say fifteen thousand, and then I'll take ten per cent once you're up and running. Like I said, a franchise. You'll have my expertise, my know-how, my girls, and I'll even put clients your way. You need to provide suitable premises, security, staff . . . but I'll talk you through that. It's just like running a Spar shop.'

'No-brainer,' declared Charlie, sitting back, clasping his hands behind his head.

Luke crunched it all over, then said, 'So that's why I've been looking at property in Rochdale.'

'Duh – yeah,' Charlie said.

'And fixed up the job for this afternoon.'

'Duh – yeah,' Charlie said again.

A smile crept on to Luke's face. 'I like it.'

Hassan grinned and slowly rubbed his hands together so they looked like two snakes doing a dance of death.

'It's the same every Friday that he's on an early shift.'

Charlie and Luke were sitting in a Toyota Land Cruiser fitted with bull bars and false registration plates.

'He takes his break at eleven thirty a.m.'

'Yeah, I noticed he disappeared at that time,' Charlie said.

'I've watched him for the last four months.'

Charlie glanced at Luke and half-smiled. He knew Luke wasn't dumb, even if he wasn't the sharpest knife in the drawer, and when he was given a job to do, he sorted it.

Such as this one.

The Toyota – which had been swapped for the Chevette which had been taken away together with Charlie's electronic tag – was parked at the end of a narrow cobbled street in the Deepdale area of Preston, one of many similar streets in that location, dating back to Victorian times. The brothers were looking at a terraced house about halfway along, the front door of which opened directly on to the pavement.

'Is it a prostitute or just some bint he's shagging?' Charlie asked.

'Don't know . . . haven't actually knocked on the door,' Luke said, 'but he walks here, goes in, gets his rocks off and he's out, walking back maybe half an hour later. Takes him five minutes to get here, five to get back. Time enough for a brew when he gets back.'

Charlie nodded.

The Toyota was ticking over nicely, its engine sounding nice, purring.

'And you reckon he's in there now?' Charlie said.

Luke checked his watch. 'Yep.'

'And my tag's halfway home now,' Charlie grinned, 'so everybody thinks I'm on the other side of Lancashire.' He was at the wheel, his hands in latex gloves and a white surgical face mask hanging around his neck, ready to be fitted. His baseball cap was twisted around so the peak faced backwards. The same applied to Luke, who checked his watch again.

'Vinegar strokes done, cock wiped off, underpants and uniform back on,' Luke predicted. 'If he's on schedule, that is. Time to mask up.'

They fitted their masks which covered the lower halves of their faces, just below the eyes.

Charlie slipped the automatic gearbox into drive, keeping his foot on the brake as the transmission connected and the vehicle tried to move forward slightly as all the power linked up. His fingers tightened on the wheel, his gaze concentrated on the front door that Luke had identified.

It opened.

The man stepped out directly on to the pavement.

Charlie's heart surged. That bitter taste of adrenalin that he loved so much slushed on to the sides of his tongue.

The man turned back to the door and hugged the woman, gave her one last kiss. She was in a dressing gown, pulled tightly around her body.

'Not a hooker,' Charlie whispered, 'just a shag.'

'Yeah, you're right.'

'You don't kiss prossies goodbye.'

'Cheating on his wife,' Luke said.

'Yeah – bastard,' Charlie said, teeth gritted. 'On the firm's time, too.'

'All-round bastard,' Luke said.

'You're right there.'

When the couple separated, Charlie and Luke got a glimpse of her breasts before she could pull her robe back tight, but then the gap was closed and the man walked away as she blew him a kiss and kept the door open an inch to watch him.

He had a spring in his step.

'How touching,' Charlie snarled. 'Let's get this over with.'

He slammed down the accelerator.

The big car lumbered forward at first, then surged powerfully. The engine roared as the vehicle picked up speed, narrowing the gap quickly.

The man did not even look around.

Not until Charlie swerved on to the pavement between the lamp posts and the Toyota was almost on him.

Then he looked.

His head ripped round, and his eyes almost burst out of his skull as he twisted and saw the huge car almost on him, like a Pamplona bull thundering down a narrow street.

There was one moment there. Just the tiny nanosecond when the man's eyes locked into those of the driver, Charlie Wilder, and despite the mask worn by Charlie, the man knew in that instant who he was – but then the moment was over and the bull bars of the four by four rammed into him. He didn't even have time to throw up his arms. He was simply flattened.

There was the dull thud of connection.

Then the man disappeared under the front radiator grille of the car and there was a rumble as he went underneath and the vehicle drove over him, catching his right arm and clothing in the chassis, ripping off his arm at the shoulder and dragging him for ten metres before he rolled free.

Charlie stomped on the brakes, almost upending the car.

He looked back through the rear window to see the man trying to push himself up on his one remaining arm, a trail of blood from where he lay all the way to the car where his torn-off limb jerked gruesomely.

With an expression of grim determination, keeping his eyes on the badly injured figure, and without looking at the gear lever, Charlie found reverse and floored the accelerator again.

The car roared backwards.

The man's face turned towards it and although

he was stunned from the first blow, almost unable to comprehend what had happened and experiencing awful pain throughout his body, he realized that a second helping was on its way.

The rear bumper smashed into his face and the car went over him again, rising and falling with a lurch as his body went under the back wheels, then the front.

Charlie stopped and looked. The man was not moving.

Even so, he had to go forwards, whatever.

'Hold on, bro,' he said. He flicked the gear back into drive, pulled the steering wheel slightly down to the right and pressed the accelerator. The car rose at an angle as the front offside wheel crushed the man's head.

Charlie drove on, over him again, and then gunned the car off the pavement and away.

Doors opened on the street, shocked inhabitants emerged and, as Charlie sped away, he glanced into the rear-view mirror and saw the woman step out of her front door, still wrapped in her dressing gown.

He skidded around the corner, punching the air delightedly.

And the prison officer called Dawson was dead on the pavement, his head crushed into a horrific mess of blood, bone and brain and an arm torn off.

Three

In some respects it was an easy scene to cordon off – a street of terraced houses, simple to block off at either end. The problem was keeping people in their houses, but no crime scene was ever as protected as the cops would have wished.

A life might have ended, but life also went on. And the public still wanted to go about their business.

The first officer on the scene was a uniformed patrol constable who was just turning out of the police operating centre just off the A6, close to the city centre. Geographically, therefore, he was not too far away from the street where Tony Dawson, the prison officer, had been mown down. It had initially been reported as a road traffic accident, a pedestrian injured, believed fatally. A traffic car from a little further afield had also been called up to attend, as had other mobiles.

But it was the cop from the nick who arrived first, maybe within three minutes of the call. On his arrival the PC found a cluster of shock-faced people milling around the body, over which some well-meaning soul had draped a white sheet that had quickly soaked up blood and was stained red.

The constable alighted from his car and asked

everyone to step back. He squatted down on his haunches and gingerly drew back the sheet.

How he managed to stifle a cry he didn't know, but after that first shock he controlled himself and re-covered the body, noticing the prison officer's uniform underneath the anorak the man was wearing. The man's head was crushed beyond recognition and the PC already knew that at some stage in the next few moments he would have to face the unpleasant task of delving into the man's pockets for an ID of some sort.

He was relieved when the flashing blue lights of a traffic car turned into the street and behind that came the patrol sergeant's car, then another patrol car, and the police began to take proper charge of everything.

It was only a matter of time before a call was put through, via the local CID office, to the Force Major Investigation Team (FMIT), inviting a senior detective to come and take charge of what was quickly established to be much more than a simple hit and run.

DCI Rik Dean was the FMIT officer who took the call. He rose from his desk in his office at police headquarters, hunched himself into his jacket and set off down the corridor. He swung into Detective Superintendent Henry Christie's office to find the incumbent surrounded by towers of paperwork that were, bit by bit, becoming a file for a major inquest. Henry, tie discarded, sleeves rolled up, concentrating on the work, didn't notice Rik at the door; he had to knock gently to attract his boss's attention.

Henry glanced up, focused on Rik.

'Job on,' Rik said. 'Fatal hit and run in Preston – with more to it by the sounds.'

Henry gave a dismissive wave and said, 'Keep me in the loop.'

Rik nodded, understanding: the job was his. He pulled on his outer coat and said, 'Will do.' He made his way out of the block in which the FMIT team were housed and jumped into his Vauxhall Insignia, noting how dark the skies had become. The rain had not started yet, but it would. The FMIT headquarters office was situated in what had once been student accommodation at the police training centre at Hutton Hall, about four miles south of Preston, and Rik was soon motoring down the dual carriageway through Penwortham towards the city. He had said that he would be fifteen minutes, but arrived three minutes short of this ETA.

He was pleased to see the street had been cordoned off and a screen had been erected around the body, though judging by the heavy sky, this would soon have to be replaced by a proper tent to protect the scene. A Crime Scene Investigation van was parked nearby and it was from the back of here that Rik collected and stepped into a forensic suit, shoes, face mask and gloves.

He then ducked under the tape and made for the actual scene.

He was briefed by the still ashen-faced PC who had been first to arrive, then he himself contorted around the screen surrounding the body.

Normally FMIT would not have anything to do with road deaths. Traffic cops were well trained in dealing with fatalities but Rik had been assured this one was no accident. The guy had been deliberately run over, reversed over, run over again. Clearly some thought and intent had gone into it.

When Rik lifted the blood-soaked sheet, he too was shaken by the terrible sight underneath. He had seen death in many forms, but it was instantly clear that this was one of the worst he had encountered. He wasn't sure he'd ever seen such a crushed head since he had once attended an industrial accident on a building site when he'd been in uniform.

'Not a nice one,' a voice behind Rik's shoulder observed.

Rik replaced the sheet carefully and turned to face the officer who had spoken these dour but true words. It was the patrol sergeant, someone he recognized but did not know personally.

'Who would do something like this?' the sergeant asked.

'A psychopath?' Rik ventured.

The sergeant shrugged his shoulders in acceptance of such an assessment.

'What do we know?' Rik asked him.

The sergeant pouted. 'Not a lot at the moment. We've banged on a few doors but we've only got one actual eyewitness so far, a man sitting in the back of a panda car round the corner.' He jerked his thumb. He was referring to a marked patrol car. Though it was many years since the demise of the actual 'panda cars' made famous by Lancashire Constabulary – those blue Ford Escorts with the white stripes – 'panda' was a term still used by many officers. 'He's a window cleaner who watched the whole thing from up high. He's still spewing.'

'Are we looking after him?'

'Oh yeah.'

'Anybody else see anything?'

'Not so far.'

'And do we know who the deceased is?'

'Think so.' The sergeant explained what he had found out so far.

'What was he doing here, on this street? Does he live here?'

'That we don't know yet.'

'Sarge?' The first PC on the scene poked his head through the gap in the screen. 'Just knocked on a door across the road—' the PC pointed – 'and the old guy in there said we should speak to the woman at number thirty-three. I've knocked, but no reply . . . but I kinda think someone is in, just not answering.'

Rik said, 'I'll have a look.'

There was no answer at the front door so Rik made his way to the alley at the back and counted down until he reached the back yard of number thirty-three. The walls were high, brick built, and the gates were basically full-sized doors with latches. Rik tried thirty-three and found it to be locked, but it felt rickety and weak, so he pretended it wasn't locked and put his shoulder

31

to it, forcing the corroded screws holding the bolt in the rotted frame to give easily. As he stepped into the concreted yard he just caught sight of movement at the back window as someone ducked quickly out of view. But not quickly enough.

With a cynical twist on his lips he went to the window and tapped gently on it with his finger-nails and held his warrant card up to the glass.

'I saw you,' he said, speaking through the glass. He tapped again. 'Please answer the door. It's important.'

After a short pause, a woman rose from her hiding position behind the sink and pulled her dressing gown tight around herself.

Rik smiled. 'I'm a police officer,' he said through the glass and pointed at his warrant card.

The door opened to reveal a middle-aged lady whose face was racked with grief.

'It's just an arrangement we have,' she said, swallowing back a choking sob. 'He's married, I'm married . . . we're never going to get divorces, shit as it all is.' She stopped talking and looked more melancholy than grief-stricken for a moment, as though her whole life was one big disappointment.

'OK,' Rik said. 'Big question: did you see the . . . incident . . . happen?'

She screwed up her face. 'No, not really. He'd literally just gone, going back to work. I'd closed the door, but just as I closed it I heard a car's engine rev, then I saw this big black four-wheel drive thing hurtle past the window. Er,' she thought, trying to focus, 'then I just had a feeling and I opened the front door again . . .' Her eyes started to water and blink rapidly as she tried to hold herself together. 'I looked out and Tony was lying there on the pavement and the car was deliberately reversing back over him.' She relived the vision with a shudder. 'Then it shot forwards over him again and sped off and his . . . his head was crushed. They must have been waiting for him, otherwise how else would they have known he was here? His arm was torn off,' she concluded with a shudder.

'So no accident?'

A tremor rattled her chest and she shook her head vehemently. 'He was murdered.'

'Did he have any enemies?'

'Yeah – six hundred in Preston Prison . . . and all the prisoners who've ever been released in the last ten years, probably.' She frowned and said, 'Will my husband have to know about this?'

Rik almost sniggered at this but held back the cynical response that went through his mind. *You're having an affair. Your lover is mown down outside your house. Answer, yes, of course your husband will have to know, you silly selfish person. Not least because your hubby's already high on my list of suspects, followed by the dead man's wife. I'm afraid your life will never be the same again, love.*

Rik's face gave its best sympathetic facade and he responded in a more subtle, professional manner than he would really have liked.

33

The other two were waiting for Charlie and Luke when they arrived back home. They drew up in their third car of the morning, a ten-year-old Fiat Punto, not stolen and quite legit, but another car in terrible condition, similar to the Chevette. Luke had driven this one and on the journey Charlie had asked how everything really was at home.

The big problem for Luke was the moment when Charlie asked him why Annabel's visits had become less frequent, almost non-existent. Annabel being Charlie's long-standing girlfriend.

Luke coughed uncomfortably, hesitated. 'I don't really know, bud, not seen all that much of her to be honest.'

Charlie had scrutinized him closely as he spoke and clocked his brother's discomfort, noted it, then leaned back in his seat, head against the rest, his lips puckering thoughtfully. But he didn't press the issue. He would find out soon enough what she'd been up to. His hands bunched into tight fists.

Until that moment came, there were still things to do that day. Throughout the remainder of the journey across Lancashire, Luke briefed him on what was planned for the afternoon and Charlie soon forgot about Annabel as the prospect of some real, visceral excitement made his blood pulse.

The other two, Johnny and Jake, were waiting for Charlie's return in the front room of a council house on the Wallbank estate in Whitworth. The house belonged to Johnny's sister, Monica, but she was out for the day, making herself scarce, even though this was the address that Charlie had declared as his home address for the Probation Service. The two greeted Charlie effusively, glad to see him back in the land of the living, and Jake swung Charlie's electronic tag around his fingers.

'What d'you want me to do with this?'

'Leave it here. As far as the Probies know, this is where I've been since you dropped off the Land Cruiser and this is where I'm staying, 'cept I'm not. Now then, guys,' Charlie said, 'down to business.'

'It's an easy target.' Luke was chewing fast, nervously, on gum.

He and Charlie were in their fourth vehicle of the day, a good quality nine-year-old Ford Mondeo, stolen, on false plates, with a half-decent turn of speed. They were on a street in Rochdale with an eye-line view of a busy convenience store further down the street, set back from the housing line with half a dozen customer parking bays outside the front.

'And a double whammy,' Luke added.

'How's that?' Charlie asked.

They were dressed in their normal working gear: blue overalls with the name of a fictitious company embossed between the shoulder blades, light boots, latex gloves. The other two, Jake and Johnny, were dressed exactly the same, but they were sitting further down the street in another nondescript car, a stolen Nissan of some sort, facing up towards Luke and Charlie's car, so that the shop was halfway between them.

'Asians – and money,' Luke smirked.

A quick smile scudded across Charlie's face. It always felt good to point a shotgun at a dark-skinned face, he thought. 'Nice,' he said.

'Mind you, that Hassan guy's an Asian.'

'He's different,' Charlie said, and glanced down into the footwell where, at his feet, a sawn-off shotgun lay diagonally across the floor mat . . . the gun of his dreams.

Charlie Wilder's heart pulsed strongly in a way it had not done for over two years.

There was no doubt that armed robbery was a crime on the wane because it was far too dangerous for the perpetrators these days, with armed cops roaming everywhere, not afraid to shoot back, and because other forms of criminality were much safer and more lucrative, something Charlie had learned well whilst in prison. But to get grubby mitts on a bundle of cash quick, which was what he needed to do, the excitement of a robbery could not be bettered.

He reached down between his feet for the shotgun, slid his fingers around the barrel and lifted the weapon on to his lap.

His mouth went dry. The weapon, sourced by Johnny, was exactly like the one in his dream, right down to the alignment of the triggers, making it easy to fire both barrels at once.

'This guy,' Luke explained, 'only banks once a week – on a Friday. Been watching him now for four months and we reckon there's fifteen gs in the bag. Thinks he's being cute sending his daughter to the bank, but he isn't. We've followed her and watched her pay in . . . just easy.' He checked his watch. 'Not long now . . . hell, we're glad you're back out, man,' he told Charlie.

'Yeah,' his brother said, throat dry. 'But this is the last one . . . and it's where the money is all going, to new ventures.'

Luke's head cricked sharply around. 'All the money from this robbery?'

'Yes.'

'To Hassan? I don't know if the guys're gonna totally like that.'

'They'll have to. Anyway, Hassan's going to bring a couple of samples over tonight; that'll soothe their savage hearts,' Charlie said. 'They can screw themselves into oblivion. They'll be happy enough.'

The door to the convenience store they were watching opened and a customer came out.

Luke held back his response to Charlie. He knew the other two would not be happy. They didn't know anything was going to change. They were both eager to resume the lifestyle they'd led before Charlie had been sent down. The last two years had been horribly boring for them, mostly, and they needed Charlie's leadership to motivate them out of the lethargy that had seeped into them. And they were desperate for some money. Benefits, and a bit of dope dealing and some petty thieving, didn't bring in much.

Luke kept his mouth shut. Instead he said confidently, 'He'll have counted up by now. It'll all be bagged up, a full week's takings. Then he'll give it to his daughter who works for him in the shop.'

'Good.' Charlie's eyes were glued to the shop as his fingertips stroked the shotgun.

Rain began to splatter heavily on the windscreen, big blobs. It looked as though the promised bad weather had begun.

'Think we need to mask up,' Luke said, and for the second time that day he pulled a surgical mask over his nose and mouth and swivelled his baseball cap around one-eighty degrees so the peak faced backwards.

Charlie did the same.

Then the shop door opened and a girl in her late teens stepped out.

'That's the daughter,' Luke said.

She had a small rucksack slung loosely over her right shoulder.

'And she's carrying the money,' he added as he slammed the car into gear, flashed his headlights at the Nissan parked further down the road in which Johnny and Jake were sitting, waiting. They flashed back. Luke jabbed his foot on to the accelerator and the vehicle lurched forwards at the same time as the Nissan.

They screeched in on the girl just as she reached the car she would be using, which was parked in one of the customer bays in front of the store.

The two vehicles stopped at sharp angles and all four men leapt out. Jake and Johnny were wearing clothing, masks and hats identical to those of the brothers, but they were brandishing baseball bats, whereas Charlie had the shotgun held across his stomach, parallel to the ground, and Luke's hands were free. He was the snatch man.

The girl twisted, her face horror-struck as she immediately realized what was happening. She screamed for her father and started to run back to the safety of the shop, but did not move fast enough. Luke ran up to her and smashed his fist into her face, instantly breaking her cheek bone and felling her, her brain imploding and her knees giving way. As she dropped, Luke took a step back and kicked her in the side of the head, as hard as if he was kicking a soccer ball from the penalty spot. Luke grinned; his toecap felt the distinct break of bone – it could have been her jaw – as the kick lifted her and sent her slim body sprawling across the ground.

As he was doing this, the other three fanned out in a semicircle to defend him.

Luke bent over and grabbed the rucksack, having to prise it off her shoulders.

Incredibly, and more by instinct than anything, though almost unconscious, she held blindly on to the bag.

Luke tore it from her and flat-footed her in the chest.

Then the shop door opened and a man ran furiously out – the girl's father and shop owner – screaming loudly. He was also armed with a baseball bat, which was raised high above his head as he hurtled towards Luke.

Charlie spun at a crouch, bringing the shotgun around at waist level.

Without hesitation he pulled back both triggers.

The sound of the blast was deafening and the force of the discharge when it hit the man stopped him in his tracks as if he had crashed into an invisible wall – which he bounced off – and threw him backwards off his feet. The shot from the cartridges inflicted a terrible wound in his chest, causing him to spin back and drop face down, releasing the bat as he fell. It clattered on the ground and rolled away.

Luke screamed, 'Come on.'

All four jumped back into their cars and were gone.

And the rain began to pound down.

'How much did you say?' Charlie demanded. 'Fifteen grand?' He picked up the handful of bank notes and waved them angrily in front of Luke's face. 'You said fifteen,' he snarled, his rage building. 'If there's two here I'll show my arse in Burton's window.' He hurled the cash down with disgust.

They were back at Johnny's sister's house on Wallbank estate.

The clothing they had worn for the robbery and the vehicles used had been disposed of, all items set on fire and incinerated. They had changed back into their own stuff which could not be forensically linked to the robbery.

Charlie shook his head, trying to contain his growing rage. 'I told you I needed good money to pay Hassan tonight.'

Luke blinked, thinking, but not daring to say, Actually you didn't.

They were in the dining room at the rear of the house, gathered around the table on which the stolen money had now been dumped into an untidy pile. Not an excessively big pile.

Charlie had watched whilst Jake had slowly counted and stacked the money, disbelief growing on his face as he realized the amount was nowhere near what he needed as a down payment for Hassan.

There was £1,850 exactly.

He needed £15,000 for Hassan tonight – and that had been the point at which he'd snatched up the money, then thrown it back down.

'I don't believe it . . . freakin' imbeciles, you lot . . . couldn't organize a . . .' He found himself lost for words.

'We'll do another job,' Luke said reasonably. 'We've others in mind.'

'I'll just have to hope this is enough for Hassan for the time being,' Charlie said, as if he hadn't heard Luke.

Jake frowned as his eyes scanned the scattered cash. 'Do you mean all this?'

Charlie leaned forward and stuck his face an inch away from Jake's. 'Yes, I mean all this.'

'What about our cut?' he mumbled. Jake was a fairly simple lad from an abused background on a tough Rochdale council estate, not too sharp, and all he wanted from life was a bit of excitement and some extra money on top of his state handouts so he could get bladdered every so

often. Much like the others, he lacked the motiv-
ation or initiative to act independently and the
last two years had been hard for him, living off
the dole and shoplifting to survive, without
Charlie's guidance. He'd wanted Charlie back,
and getting all the stuff Charlie wanted done by
today sorted out with Johnny had breathed a bit
of life back into him.

'You don't get a cut,' Charlie said.

Jake's face screwed up. 'Eh? Wha—?'

'I think you'd better explain it, Chas,' Johnny
cut in. 'We're in the dark here. Who the fuck's
Hassan, why do you need all the money . . .
y'know, what's going on? Me 'n' Jake fixed up
all the transport for today, and the gun, but we
don't know why. Just tell us,' he pleaded.

Johnny was a tough, good-looking young man,
physically stronger than Charlie; if he'd had the
courage, he might have taken him on and won.
But it was Charlie who had the charisma and
leadership skills – and the propensity for
violence, as he had so effectively demonstrated
twice that day already, although neither Jake
nor Johnny knew yet what had happened in
Preston. Charlie was the scary psycho and
Johnny knew he was taking a bit of a chance
by demanding any explanation from him. Charlie
answered to no one.

Charlie looked hard at him, then the others, all
silent, scared. Not even a two-grand job, possibly
a dead man involved, possibly a badly assaulted
female, and not getting a share of it.

'Right . . . right, OK,' Charlie relented. 'Things

42

are going to change around here, with us.' He made a circle with his finger to indicate the gang.

'Think you need to tell us, man,' Johnny said.

'Really? Do I?' Charlie walked around the table and squared up to Johnny.

'Hey, guys,' Luke said. 'No need for this.'

Charlie's nostrils dilated as he glared at Johnny, who had never been his favourite person. Their personalities had never quite gelled.

But he stepped away – and the prospect of a physical encounter diminished, much to everyone's relief.

Charlie glanced at Luke. 'Have we got the party stuff up at the farm?'

'Everything's up there – food, booze, Xbox, dope.'

'In that case, let's go and get rat-arsed,' Charlie decreed. 'Let's celebrate my release and a future of money and women—' he shot a look at Johnny – 'and all will be revealed.'

They jumped into two cars outside the house, an old Range Rover and the battered Chevette, and drove off the estate. They were headed for an old farm on the moors that had belonged to Charlie and Luke's grandparents way back, had been inherited by their father who had run it down and wasted all the assets before dying of a drug overdose and leaving it to the brothers, who lived in it from time to time when it suited. The twenty-year-old Range Rover had come with the inheritance.

They drove on to a road leading up to the moors, but were stunned by the sight of a police checkpoint ahead of them.

43

Charlie, at the wheel of the Range Rover, swore disbelief.

Luke, next to him, seemed to shrivel up in his seat.

'Can't be on to us, surely,' Charlie said. He knew if he did something ridiculous in the tight road, slammed on and reversed away, he would draw unnecessary attention to himself, besides which Jake and Johnny were right up behind them in the Chevette. They had to brazen it out and if necessary take out the rain-sodden, miserable looking cop who stood round-shouldered at the police cordon tape strung across the road.

Charlie was aware that the shotgun he had used on the robbery was in the back of the car, behind his seat, hidden under a plastic bag but just within reach. A shimmer of anticipation skittered through him. The prospect of murdering a cop was quite exciting.

He drew to a halt and the cop came to his window, which he opened a crack.

'I'm sorry,' the officer said, rain dripping off his nose like a snotty kid, 'but there's an ongoing incident at a farm just ahead and we can't let anyone through until it's safe to do so.'

'Right,' Charlie said, his insides seeming to be very, very empty, 'but I – we – live up there.'

'I'm sorry sir, it's a very dangerous situation.' The officer nodded conspiratorially. 'Firearms involved.'

Luke leaned across. 'At old Kirkman's place?'

'Not at liberty to say,' the officer said, suddenly becoming discreet. 'But I'm afraid I have to insist that you turn around. Is there another way up to your home?'

'Yes, there is,' Charlie said. 'We can go another way.'

The cop pointed to the Chevette. 'Is that car with you?'

Luke cut in to answer. 'Yes – I'll tell him to back off.' He jumped out and ran back to the others, hunched against the rain.

Moments later the Chevette began to reverse slowly, followed by the Range Rover, a confrontation with the police avoided.

Victor Toleman's days in prison stuck rigidly to the regime. He wasn't out to upset anyone, just to lead his life, get fed, watch TV, go to various educational classes (he sat there, stared blankly and didn't cause problems like some of the other inmates), get fed again, smoke a few roll-ups. Prison was his life now. As soon as he was released he would go to the bail hostel or probation hostel or whatever short-term accommodation the judicial authorities had lined up for him. He would then spend whatever money he had on whiskey and cider, get paralytic, probably steal something as ridiculous as a charity box, get drunk again, allow the unpleasant side of his personality to emerge and then get rearrested for breaking a shop window or beating up another of the city centre drunks. Then he would be back in the system, which was his life. A repeat offender, relatively harmless, who depended on the security of living behind bars, like many other middle-aged alcoholics who could be found in prison cells right across the UK.

Almost as soon as his cell-sharer Charlie Wilder had been released that morning, he had been replaced by another inmate in a cell shuffle. This one ('unpleasant fucker', as Victor described him) demanded that Victor vacate the top bunk immediately or he would kill him.

Victor didn't care where he slept and acceded to the order without rancour. All he wanted was a bed, didn't mind if it was top or bottom bunk or a camp bed.

After breakfast that morning, Victor shuffled around the prison, passing his time pleasantly enough watching daytime TV and playing chess with a fellow drunk who always cheated, but Victor didn't care. It amused him.

It was just before lunch when Victor noticed one or two unusual things occurring. A couple of prison officers dashing quickly upstairs, some having huddled discussions. Lots of shocked, serious faces, intense conversations.

Something had happened, clearly, but it was impossible to say what.

Victor watched the activity for a while, then lost interest. Whatever was going on didn't seem to be having any effect on prison life.

A little later, he presumed the news – or whatever it was – had spread to the inmates and there was a mirror image of conversations between groups of them, but with one major difference.

Whereas the officers' conversations had been deadly serious, the prisoners were laughing and jubilant. Some even danced and punched the sky.

Still, Victor could not quite work out what was going on. No one told him and he wasn't motivated to ask. Knowing stuff often led to problems.

It was whilst he was having a mid-afternoon mug of tea that he found out. He was sitting in the TV room, sipping a heavily sugared brew, when one of his 'friends' settled in alongside him. The term 'friend' was used advisedly. Victor didn't really have friends, just a few prisoners he talked to more than others. This was a man called Tony the Prick, an alcoholic from Blackburn who led a very similar life to Victor, relying on the state to provide him with bed and board because he could not survive outside. His nickname came about because he had realized that one of the quickest routes to prison was to expose himself to young girls outside schools although he strenuously denied the 'pervert' tag.

'You heard?' Tony asked.

Victor finished his sip of tea and squinted at Tony. 'Heard what?'

'About that screw. That Dawson fucker?'

'Tony Dawson?'

'Yeah, that un.'

'No?' Victor said, a question in the word. 'What about him?' Victor's brow was knitted together, thinking he hadn't seen PO Dawson since mid-morning.

'Been murdered.'

These two words stunned Victor. Not because

47

he had any sort of feelings for Dawson. He hated the bastard of a bully that he was and avoided him at all costs. It was just the thought of someone he knew being killed. It felt odd and unsettling.

'Murdered? What happened?'

'Well,' Tony the Prick leaned in close, 'apparently some guy in a big truck chased him down a street, Fishergate I hear, and ran him over, splat!' On the last word, Tony's hands and arms suddenly imitated an explosion, making Victor jump and spill his tea. 'Then . . . then,' Tony went on enthusiastically, 'guy reversed back over him and squashed his head like a, like a . . . dunno, something horrible . . . pavement were covered like someone'd jumped on a bag of tomatoes and fish paste. Had his arm ripped off, too.'

Victor looked horrified. 'Who told you this?'

'Smelly Man. He hears everything,' Tony said, referring to another inmate who actually did not smell. That nickname came about due to his ability to sniff out information. For the moment, Smelly Man was very much the eyes and ears of the inmates – until his release.

'Smelly Man.' Victor pouted, impressed. He wasn't usually wrong, though he did have a tendency to exaggerate news.

'Just thought I'd let you know,' Tony said, and gave a wink before rising from his seat, leaving Victor shocked and staring unfocused at the TV.

From that moment on, Victor felt uncomfortable. He would've liked to have said that being mown down in the street couldn't have happened to a nicer man but, other than under the influence of alcohol, Victor was a placid man who wished no harm or hurt to anyone. Even Tony Dawson, maybe one of the worst, most bombastic men he had ever met.

The news did spread through the whole of the prison after that and although the exact details of Dawson's demise were not known, it did seem he had been deliberately run down and killed.

Something which preyed heavily on Victor's mind.

In the middle of that afternoon he found he needed to speak to someone and approached a prison officer on one of the landings.

'Sir, can I talk to you for a moment?'

The officer nodded. 'Sure, Victor.'

'Er,' he started doubtfully, 'is it true about PO Dawson?'

'What have you heard?'

'Run over and killed.'

'It's true – why?'

Victor's face became a mass of twitches and nervous tics.

Four

Henry Christie's face twitched as, once again, the image of a horrific death flashed through his mind's eye and he thought about how fate had brought him to witness such a brutal end to a man's life.

Obviously as a detective superintendent and senior investigating officer – SIO – on the Force Major Investigation Team, he accepted that death was his business, but mostly Henry attended scenes where people were already dead. It was less common for him to be there 'at the death', and when he was, it shook him to the core.

At least this time it had done.

His proximity to the act, its spectacular but ghastly end and its amazing speed had made a deep impact on him.

Although it had been quick, and the weather had been dark and appalling and visibility poor, each frame of this particular death was imprinted on his brain cells and could be slowed right down, almost frozen in time to the exact moment the man's head had been blown off his shoulders.

Henry's right eye twitched this time and a terrible judder scythed through his soul. He lifted the single Jack Daniel's, no ice, to his mouth, sniffed the smoky aroma, then downed it in one and brought the heavy-based glass back on to the bar top with a crack, turning peoples' heads.

But none of them could see into his dark, brooding, pain-filled soul.

He looked at the landlord and pointed to the empty glass. 'One more for the road,' he said, then wiped his lips with the back of his hand. 'Fate, eh?'

The 'fate' that Henry was ruminating over was this.

If Abel Kirkman had not shot his dog, Shep, and then turned the shotgun on his wife, Ingrid, and killed her too – and then barricaded himself in his farmhouse and started blasting all comers on that Friday afternoon, Henry Christie would not have had to turn out to that neck of the woods, the most far-flung reaches of Lancashire Constabulary. He would have been at home, socializing in a bar, having a wonderful meal and eventually retiring to bed with his amazing wife-to-be: sheer bliss.

But even when Henry was drinking that glass of JD and thinking that life had dealt him a shitty hand, he did not know that the dealer was already stacking the deck and things were about to get even worse than they had been for him up to that point. He did not know that he was going to end up in a fight for his life which really had nothing to do with Abel Kirkman. Abel Kirkman was just an innocent cog in all that transpired.

But that was what fate did. It tore you up, put you through the wringer, spat you out.

Henry came to be at Abel Kirkman's farm on that rain-drenched Friday because of a situation at work which (though he was at first blissfully unaware of this) was fairly unusual.

He discovered that between two p.m. and six p.m. – four tiny, inconsequential hours – he was the most senior officer on duty in the whole of Lancashire Constabulary. He was the highest ranking cop available, with the exception of the chief constable – but Robert Fanshaw-Bayley didn't count because he wasn't deemed to be operational, whereas Henry was.

It was a situation Henry only discovered when he reluctantly picked up his desk phone and took a call at four minutes past two. In fact, at the moment of the call, Henry was doing something he rarely did at his desk. He was clock watching and daydreaming.

He was supposed to be on duty until six p.m. and after that time one of his colleagues, another detective superintendent, would automatically be 'on call' and Henry could then chill and head home for the weekend. He was now bang up to date with paperwork, having finally completed a very complex file for an upcoming inquest into the double murder of a local jeweller and his girlfriend, basically bringing an end to a far-reaching investigation that had lasted four months. It had taken Henry from the Canary Islands to Florida, involved the FBI, Spanish police and ex-cops. He was happy all the loose ends had been tied tight and the job would not be going to criminal court because the offender – the hit man who had murdered the unlucky pair – was also dead, drowned off Gran Canaria.

The file was stacked and bound neatly on his desk. Done, dusted. He now planned to have the weekend off with his fiancée at the pub she owned way out in the north Lancashire country-side. It was long overdue lovey-dovey time and Henry was looking forward to being a bartender (unofficially, of course: police regulations did not allow cops to serve and sell alcohol, or even live on licensed premises), drinking too much and generally having a good old knees-up with a few friends.

He had glanced out of the window, seen the weather was still dreadful. All across the country it had rained heavily for weeks on end and huge swathes of southern England were flooded, though it wasn't so bad in Henry's part of the world. He was thankful for that but still wished the rain would ease and the dark clouds lift. He was convinced he was suffering from seasonal affective disorder, or maybe he was simply sad.

Then his eyes darted to the digital wall clock: *14.03 hrs*.

Just four hours to go.

He could almost taste that first pint of Stella Artois on his tongue, then on its way down his throat, its icy spread into his chest. Could feel the heat from the open fire in the main bar. He almost groaned with pleasure at the prospect.

The phone rang as the clock flipped: *14.04 hrs*.

He leaned forwards and checked the caller display. It was the Force Incident Manager on the line. Henry scowled with annoyance and emitted a petulant gasp like a spotty teenager might.

Invariably a call from the FIM, the officer in charge of the main control room at force headquarters, situated less than two hundred metres from where Henry was sitting at that moment, meant a call-out.

For the first time in his career as an SIO he

considered ignoring the phone, as a sinking feeling pervaded him, warning that fate was about to piss on his plans. But he knew that ignoring the call would, ultimately, be a useless tactic because the next number the FIM would call would be his mobile and if he failed to answer that, questions would be asked 'in the house', as they say.

He scooped up the phone dramatically, already planning to drop whatever job it was on to some other poor sucker's shoulders. He said his name.

'Boss. Chief Inspector Taylor, control room. We've got a situation . . .'

Even as the FIM was outlining the situation, Henry was trying to work out how to bluster and bluff his way out of it. When he learned that there was literally no one else in the force of equivalent rank until after six p.m., Henry's shoulders drooped, a quiet sigh rose and fell in his chest and he admitted defeat. Someone of his rank was needed on the plot as soon as possible – and he was the only one.

He swore inwardly after he had quizzed the FIM as to the whereabouts of the other supers and chief supers, and although Henry accepted that owing to cutbacks and natural wastage, officers of these ranks were pretty thin on the ground, it annoyed him to discover that two were on leave, one was on a course down south, another was sick . . . and so it went until that big forefinger pointed right down at him in his cosy little office.

He jotted down the bare essentials, ended the call a bit rudely, grabbed his personal radio and coat, and scurried out through the now torrential rain to his car, muttering, 'If only the public knew . . .'

Then he was on his way, not needing to be given directions. Thirty-plus years as a cop in Lancashire had given him an intimate geographic knowledge of the county and he could easily find his way from one side of it to the other without help.

Despite the persistent downpour slowing down the afternoon traffic, Henry made good progress and covered the thirty or so miles in less than forty minutes, speeding down the M65, then up on to the A56, rising high above Accrington – although the remnants of that town's dark satanic mills were hardly visible in the low cloud – towards the Rossendale Valley, a place where he had served as a young cop and revisited on many occasions since, usually to look at dead bodies.

In the course of this journey he made the important call to Alison, his fiancée, using the hands-free set. He told her he was likely to be considerably late and instantly got the message that she was unimpressed by the news. Not from what she said, exactly, but from the way she said it, with those almost imperceptible pauses before the 'OK' and the muted 'Whatever'. She did melt ever so slightly when he told her how much he loved her and wanted to spend the rest of his life with her.

'Oh, by the way,' she said. 'Steve's here.'

Henry frowned. 'Steve who?'

'Flynn.'

Henry's guts did a flip. 'What's he doing there?' he asked. It was his turn to be unimpressed.

'He's here for the inquest next week, as you know. He came early to see his son, but he just popped over this afternoon to say hello.'

'Really.' Definitely unimpressed.

'He's staying with a friend in Lancaster, but I've offered him a room here for the night, so he'll be here whenever you get home, whatever time that might be. Rik's coming up too, isn't he?'

'Mm . . . he caught a nooky job this morning, so I'm not sure when he'll land. Give Flynn my regards.'

Henry ended the call and exhaled long and hard, but knew he didn't have time to dwell on Steve Flynn.

His next call was to the patrol inspector at the scene of what the FIM had dramatically described as 'carnage' and a 'siege'.

He raced his Audi coupé off the A56 towards Rawtenstall town centre and smirked to himself; he realized he had truly reached the far outpost of civilization when, as he approached the main roundabout – Queen's Square – he saw a herd of sheep grazing on it. They had clearly migrated from the moors, maybe having been driven down by the bad weather, to squat in the town instead. They seemed a fairly happy bunch, oblivious to the passing traffic. Henry shook his head in amusement as he recalled how much time he had spent pursuing stray animals when he was a PC in this town.

He took the road towards Bacup but before reaching that town he bore right towards Whitworth, literally the last outpost in that corner of Lancashire, a small, straggly town sitting thinly in a valley floor, winding south, overshadowed by dark moorland. It was like entering a narrow, winding gorge and as Henry crossed the town boundary, the sky seemed to darken even more and the rain got a whole lot heavier.

Once past the police checkpoint manned by a miserable looking and very wet PC, Henry parked his Audi at the bottom of the narrow track leading up to Abel Kirkman's farm. He scuttled around to the tiny boot, slid off his jacket, put on his black zip-up anorak with the word 'POLICE' emblazoned across the back and chest in hi-viz letters. On top of this he squeezed on his stab vest, then a black woollen hat with a reflective chequered band, grabbed his torch, opened his mini-umbrella and started to make his way up the rocky track. On either side ran fast flowing streams of rainwater, channelled down from the moors.

Ahead he could see the track was blocked by police vehicles of varying descriptions.

His first rendezvous was with the patrol inspector, whom he met at the inner cordon tape about a hundred metres from Kirkman's farmhouse. At the farm, Henry could see officers huddled behind walls and fences, some armed, all trying to keep as dry as possible.

The rain pounded on his umbrella, making it hard to hear properly.

The inspector was a man called Rankin and Henry vaguely knew him.

It was immediately apparent that conducting any meaningful conversation in the downpour was going to be difficult, so Rankin beckoned Henry to follow and led him into a long, low farm building with a corrugated iron roof that was in fact a pigsty with probably over fifty of the beasts in stalls inside, snuffling away contentedly in what Henry could only describe as shit. The reek was terrible, but at least it was warm and dry.

'Where are we up to?' Henry asked. He was already thinking he wanted an early resolution to this, not least because he was parched and hungry.

'Abel Kirkman, local farmer, pretty well known – mainly for all the wrong reasons. Got drunk, blasted his dog and wife, then started taking pot shots at two walkers strolling past. Fortunately missed them, but they called us. The first uniformed officer on the scene was also fired at. Abel missed him, too, then ran inside and as best we can tell he's barricaded himself inside. He's smashed a window and fires at anything that moves.'

Henry listened to this. 'Wife's body?'

'Outside the front door, next to the dog. He won't let us recover her, or it.'

'He's speaking to people, then?'

'Shouting at them. Won't answer the house

phone or his mobile. He had a bit of dialogue with the local bobby, who knows him because he's locked him up a time or two for drunkenness,' Rankin explained.

Henry took this in as he glanced at the pigs in their pens.

'So Abel's a bit of a hothead?'

'Yes – he's not a nice man.'

'Yet he still owns a shotgun? I'm assuming it's licensed.'

'It is,' the inspector confirmed. 'It's hard to prevent a farmer getting a firearm – vermin, you know?'

Henry nodded. Despite all the hoops, acquiring a shotgun was still quite easy. 'Anyone else in the house?'

'We don't think so, but we can't be certain.'

'And a negotiator is on the way?'

'ETA half an hour,' the inspector said, 'last I heard.' He touched his PR. 'Doesn't help that radio reception's crap this side of the valley – varies from rubbish to useless. Same with the mobiles.'

'Well,' Henry said, 'anything can happen in the next half hour. Let's just hope it doesn't.'

The traffic department had managed to illuminate the front of Kirkman's farmhouse with a mobile rig and generator, positioning the powerful light just out of range of his shotgun, although he had loosed off a few ineffective rounds at it. The farmhouse itself was in darkness, all the interior lights off. From a position behind a low stone wall about forty metres from the house, Henry could just about make out the double barrels of Kirkman's shotgun poking out through the broken window pane just to the left side of the very sturdy looking front door.

Henry was crouching next to the local bobby, Roy Philips, who had a loudhailer in his hand. Inspector Rankin was squatting behind them and two very drenched firearms officers were huddled by a barn wall with two other uniformed cops. Two more unarmed officers were covering the rear of the farmhouse from a safe vantage point.

Peering over the low wall, Henry could see the body of Kirkman's wife, sprawled in death about ten feet from the front door. The dog lay beside her. In the progressive darkness as the afternoon drew in, and despite the mobile lighting, Henry could not make out any of the features of either body.

He ducked back down.

'It's about fifteen minutes since he last spoke to me,' Roy Philips said, tipping his flat cap back at an angle, causing a rush of rainwater to run off it. Henry knew Philips had been a beat bobby in Whitworth for many years. He was a bit of a legend, sometimes a loose cannon, but completely dedicated to his work and the community, most of whom he knew by their first names.

'What did he say?'

'"Fuck off." I quote.'

Amongst Philips's traits was a healthy disrespect for high-ranking officers. Henry liked that.

'You have any idea what all this is about?'

Philips shook his head. 'I've been to quite a few domestics here recently, but it's always been quiet on arrival, though he can be a handful. His wife is – was – a lot younger than him, maybe twenty years. Rumours circulating the village . . .' he concluded mysteriously, referring to Whitworth as a village.

'Infidelity?'

'Either that, or she's out shagging some other blokes,' Philips said straight-faced. 'Maybe he'd reached the end of his tether.'

Henry grinned and shuffled around on his haunches, feeling his knees straining. He asked Rankin, 'How well equipped are we for a forced entry if needs be?'

'We're not,' he answered truthfully. He indicated the sodden firearms officers. 'These are the only two authorized firearms officers on duty in the division until eight tonight; after then it's a possibility. The rest are unarmed. We've got that traffic cop back down the lane, and the local DC has been, gone and is coming back. The DI is on his way; he's been at crown court today.' Rankin looked up and got a face full of rain.

'I know,' Henry said, seeing Rankin's expression of hopelessness. Having a ton of staff on duty was a thing of the past, but it was something that everyone had to deal with and it looked as if Henry's desire for an early resolution was going to bite the dust. He was already thinking that the best way forward was to keep Kirkman holed up, try to establish a meaningful dialogue and wear the bastard down, probably until morning when, if all else failed, he might be able to muster enough troops to storm the house. But he did need a few more cops on the ground now, just for safety reasons. He didn't want any more unnecessary bloodshed, which was always a possibility when there were not enough cops around.

He turned back to PC Philips. 'Not that I can do any better than you, Roy, but let's see if Abel will talk to me.'

Philips handed the megaphone over with a smirk.

Although he knew he was reasonably safe at this distance, Henry still rose cautiously from the cover of the wall, holding the speaker in his left hand and bringing it up to his mouth. After a screech of ear-splitting feedback, Henry called, 'Abel Kirkman, I'm Detective Superintendent Christie. I'm the police officer in charge now and I wonder if we could—'

Henry did not get a chance to explain what he was wondering; he saw the barrels of the shotgun come up, aiming at him. He saw Abel's hand on the barrel and a flash of his face in the darkened room beyond. Then there was the simultaneous blast and flash of the shotgun and its recoil as Abel yanked back the triggers and fired at him.

Even as he saw the shotgun come up, Henry had started to drop instinctively, leaving the loud-hailer on top of the wall. He heard a shot from the cartridge clatter into it like ball bearings in a bagatelle.

'Fuck – I thought we were out of range,' he

growled at Rankin, who gave a worried shrug as he removed his hands from his head.

'Me too.'

The firearms officers had drawn their handguns and taken up firing positions at the corner of the barn, one above the other, aiming at the farmhouse.

'Put your guns away,' Henry ordered them. He reached for the loudhailer, drew it down off the wall and inspected it inside the cone. It was splattered by buckshot and looked as if it had chicken pox. He blasphemed and felt himself quiver inside. It might not have done much damage, might not have killed, but it would have hurt.

'Maybe he's changed his load,' Rankin suggested. 'More powerful.'

'Whatever,' Henry said through tight lips.

'Sorry, boss,' Rankin said sheepishly.

Henry nodded acceptance of the apology. He tapped the loudhailer and blew into it. Incredibly it was still functioning. He angled the speaker on the top edge of the wall and spoke to Kirkman again without revealing any portion of himself as a target. 'Abel? Detective Superintendent Christie again. That was a very dangerous thing to do—'

Henry heard the response from the farmhouse. 'Fuck you, fuck her, fuck you all.' This outburst was followed by another blast of the shotgun, splattering the low wall protecting Henry and the others with shot, making it sound as if it was being pebble-dashed.

All the cops ducked.

'Maybe a retreat is on the cards.'

Nothing happened for the next half hour, other than the weather worsening. Abel remained cooped up and uncooperative in the farmhouse, where it was believed he was plying himself with much booze. A force negotiator arrived on the scene and attempted to 'open a line of communication' with him, but Abel was clearly in no mood for dialogue and frequently loosed off rounds from the shotgun to keep the cops at bay.

Other reinforcements arrived in the guise of a fully kitted-out firearms team from headquarters and an Operational Support Unit serial. Hot drinks and pies arrived, together with a dozen umbrellas, but where they came from, no one knew.

The cold and wet was getting to Henry, drilling through to his bones despite the coffee and meat pie he consumed.

He was having a tactical discussion in the pigsty, talking to the negotiator, the patrol inspector, the local DI and the divisional Chief Inspector (who had been dragged out of his warm office at DHQ at Henry's insistence). They were also talking things through with the chief constable who, it transpired, was actually and unusually on call that weekend. They were talking to him via mobile phones, but the signal was dicey and unpredictable at best here in Whitworth. The high hills and descending cloud were having a rotten effect on communications.

'I don't mind digging in for the night,' Henry

was saying. 'That's probably the way it'll go . . . no doubt Abel will fall asleep at some point. Then we'll look at going in. That said, I'm not remotely happy leaving his wife's body out all night, nor even the dog's. That, to me, is unacceptable. At the very least we should insist on him letting us cover them up, give them a bit of dignity in death.' This was something Henry felt strongly about. Murder victims lost all dignity, the way their lives ended, and Henry felt that part of his job as an SIO was to restore some of it, somehow.

'I agree,' Rankin said.

The force negotiator, an inspector from headquarters, nodded her head sagely. 'If nothing else, if he concedes on that point, it starts to give us a psychological advantage over him. So far, Abel's called all the shots, literally. If we can get him to allow us to cover the bodies, his house of cards may start to tumble.'

Henry blinked at her and said, 'Yeah, er, sure . . . I'm all for psychological advantage.'

They all looked at each other, waiting for a smidgen of inspiration. Nothing came, so Henry said, 'I'm going to make that happen.'

Henry's black woolly hat with the chequered band was drenched, as was the rest of him, as he rose from behind the cover of the low wall, loudhailer in hand.

'Abel,' he called, 'this is Henry Christie again.'

Henry saw movement at the broken window. The shotgun barrel moved and now, despite having swapped his stab vest for a bulletproof vest from the firearms team, Henry's guts still did a backflip.

'What you want?' Abel hollered, slurring his words and sounding very drunk.

Henry glanced at the firearms officers by the barn wall. They were ready, guns drawn. He would have liked to have a sniper with a bead drawn on Abel's forehead in the form of a red dot, but there was no such officer available.

'Abel? I want you to trust me here, OK?'

Abel snorted at that.

'I want to come over and cover the body of your wife with a blanket – just me, unarmed, unaccompanied. Just let me cover her and the dog up, to keep the rain off them, that's all I'm asking. Oh, and if you want, I've got some hot pies here if you're feeling hungry.'

Henry dropped his hands, stood in the rain.

'You can stuff your pie,' Abel shouted.

'Fair enough,' Henry said through the loud-hailer. 'But can I cover up your wife, please? Nothing silly, I promise. Just let me do that and then I'll back off.'

'I might shoot you.'

'You might; it's a chance I'll have to take, isn't it? But you won't, will you?'

'Well done, sir,' the negotiator hiss-whispered at Henry. 'This is more than he's said all day.'

'It's a natural talent,' Henry said through the side of his mouth, not telling her that he had once been a trained negotiator, but the qualification had lapsed through lack of use and, to a degree, patience. He bent down and picked up an aluminium foil blanket similar to the ones used by athletes to keep body warmth at the end of a long race. It was his intention to cover the woman's body with it and secure it down with some stones. He raised it in his hand and called out to Abel, 'Are we on?'

No response.

Henry waited, his shoulders drooping.

'OK then,' Abel shouted. 'Just you, and no fucking tricks.'

'Promise,' Henry said. He placed the loudhailer down.

'Talk to him whilst you're there,' the negotiator instructed Henry. 'Establish a rapport.'

'I will,' Henry said and started to walk slowly towards the farmhouse, resisting the temptation to say to the firearms officers, 'If he kills me, kill him.'

It felt like a very long way, suddenly exposed and vulnerable and under no illusions about the protection offered by the ballistic vest. A blast from a shotgun might not blow a hole in his chest but could just as easily blow his head off. The drumming of the rain on his head was replaced by the pounding of the pulse in his temples as he took slow, deliberate steps so as not to increase the tension, although it clearly did. What he didn't want to do was spook Abel, who no doubt had his finger coiled around the trigger of the shotgun.

The two bodies, woman and dog, were lying about ten feet away from the window where Abel was positioned.

Henry got to them and for the first time saw the dreadful damage inflicted.

Abel's wife, Ingrid, had been blasted from close range and her face was no longer recognizable, looking as if she had been smashed repeatedly with a sledgehammer. The dog had a huge, jagged hole in the side of its chest.

Henry took a steadying breath and looked through the broken window. The farmer's wide face seemed to have no expression on it.

'We need to talk, Abel.'

Abel jerked the gun at Henry, who winced instinctively, expecting to be fired at. But Abel said, 'Just get on with it.'

Henry nodded and started to unravel the blanket over Ingrid.

'Thanks for letting me do this,' he said, bending over her and seeing the real detail of her horrendous wounds, which made him gasp. His limbs seemed to tighten up and his breathing became short. 'Bloody hell,' he whispered as he drew the blanket up and over her chest.

'Stop!'

Henry stopped instantly, still bent over the woman. He angled his head to look at Abel, truly believing he was now going to meet the same fate, but Abel withdrew the shotgun from the window, then disappeared. Henry came slowly upright, glanced back at the officers behind the low wall and the firearms officers by the edge of the barn. All he could see were several pairs of worried eyes.

He heard bolts being drawn back. A key turn in a lock.

Then a creak as the farmhouse door opened

and Abel Kirkman stepped out, his shotgun held diagonally across his body. He staggered slightly – drunk, Henry assumed – then moved forwards.

Henry's mouth dried up, his whole body tense and ready to do something, dive one way or the other, launch himself into Abel's abdomen or – his personal favourite – run.

'Hello, Abel,' he managed to say.

Abel nodded, walked to the body of his wife and looked down at her, then the dog, both still only half-covered.

'Oh God,' he said.

'Do you want to give me the shotgun, Abel?' Henry suggested softly, reaching out, his palms face up.

Abel looked Henry straight in the eye and said, 'No,' before he swung the weapon around.

The landlord placed the second JD down in front of Henry's sagging face. Henry looked at him, said thanks and wrapped the fingers of his right hand around the square, genuine Jack Daniel's tumbler to stop them trembling. He gripped the edge of the bar with his left.

So it wasn't altogether true.

If a person was desperate, desolate, determined and drunk enough to want to kill themselves with a shotgun, and if their arms were long enough, their thumbs big enough, there was no need to go to any great, intricate lengths to pull the trigger with a big toe, or rig up a piece of string and slam a door. If the arms were long enough, all that person needed to do was position the muzzle

69

under the cleft of the chin, angle the barrels at, say, forty-five degrees, then jam that big thumb on to the triggers and push.

Abel Kirkman had done just that.

For a nanosecond, Henry had thought that Abel was going to blast him, but he had been mistaken.

His dexterity unaffected by the copious amount of alcohol he had imbibed since shooting his wife and dog, one moment he held the gun across his chest, the next he had spun it around and forced the barrel into his neck.

Henry had lurched forward at that point, but Abel's eyes stared defiantly at him.

He forced back the triggers with his thumb and Henry stopped moving mid-streak as both barrels were fired upwards and at just the correct angle to go through the 'V' of the underside of his flaccid jaw, up through the back of his mouth, into the rear half of his brain and then take most of his skull off in a spectacular burst that, in a strange, parallel thought, reminded Henry of a party popper being pulled.

Henry's eyes rose and met those of the pub landlord, who said, 'You seen a ghost, mate?'

Henry's mouth twitched. 'No, no ghost.' He raised the JD and said, 'Rather than one for the road, I'll raise this one to the hand of fate.'

He was about to throw it down his gullet when the pub door burst open and a young woman hurtled in, fell to her knees, screaming, 'Help me, help me, please . . .'

Henry's glass stopped an inch away from his

bottom lip and his head swivelled around to see what the commotion was.

The blood on the woman's hands and smeared across her face made him groan inwardly.

Five

The actions of Abel Kirkman had transfixed Henry and for what seemed an eternity he stood there with the foil blanket scrunched in his hands, next to Abel's wife and dog, staring unblinkingly, open-mouthed, at what remained of Abel himself, the dead man's legs twitching in a macabre jig.

He found himself in some kind of horror world, immobile in the heavy rain, completely drenched, stunned by the terrible suicide. The moments felt like an aeon, but he knew it was really only a matter of seconds before other officers joined him, as shocked as he was.

'Boss, you OK?' Inspector Rankin asked.

Henry had to shake himself physically out of the reverie and said, 'Yeah, yeah,' knowing that he wasn't remotely OK. 'I couldn't stop him . . . it was like I froze.'

'You couldn't have stopped him, boss,' Rankin assured him. 'He'd obviously decided to top himself. Literally.'

Henry now started to blink the rainwater off his eyelids and looked at Rankin, who was also staring in shock at Abel's now motionless body.

'Fuck me, what a way to go,' Rankin said. 'Why? Just why?'

Henry shrugged, unable to think why, but said, 'We won't know now.' He glanced around. One of the firearms officers was looking at Abel, too. Suddenly the PC retched. Henry saw it coming.

'Over there,' he shouted, pointing.

The PC lurched over to the house wall and was copiously sick over some pansies in a stone tub.

'Let's get the crime scene tent over this,' Henry said decisively, postponing his own emotional reactions until later, in private. 'Get a CSI team in, a pathologist – you know the score, and let's do it quickly.'

Rankin nodded and moved away. Henry went to the front of the house and took some cover from the eaves, then fished out his mobile phone: nothing. The signal was still intermittent and weak, sometimes non-existent.

'Boss?' he said, when he managed to get a connection by walking back into the rain in the middle of the farmyard. He was on the line to the chief constable, Robert Fanshaw-Bayley, or 'FB', as he was known to friends and enemies alike. Over the years, Henry had been both his friend and enemy. 'It's Henry. This, er, situation has been resolved . . .'

After a brief, broken discussion, Henry tuned in to autopilot, put the exploding head of Abel Kirkman out of his mind, started to work in the here and now and get the practical side of the job done at a scene that was both a murder and a suicide.

A lot of decisions were made in the dry and warmth of the pigsty, not least of which was the short-term plan for Abel's farm. He reared pigs, kept a lot of sheep up on the moors above the farm and had a barn full of battery hens that all needed feeding, watering and generally caring for. Roy Philips, the local bobby, said he knew another local farmer who could take care of that. He also volunteered to see if he could find a suitable relative to pass the news on to, although he wasn't hopeful that any of Abel's relations would be even half-interested in his death – other than his legacy. He then set off, after Henry arranged for him to be back on duty at six a.m. next day to continue with the incident.

Three hours later, the scene had been dealt with as far as was possible in the horrendous weather. A Home Office pathologist had made a flying visit to the scene and, after everything had been recorded and photographed and seized for evidence, Henry had called in an undertaker to move the bodies to the public mortuary. Previously the nearest mortuary had been at Rawtenstall, not too far away, but with cutbacks and centralization of resources, Burnley General Hospital was now used which, from Whitworth, was a long and very inconvenient trek – one Henry could not be bothered making. He therefore delegated the task of following the two hearses to the local DC so that a basic chain of evidence could be maintained.

By then it was getting into the evening.

PC Philips had arranged for a neighbouring farmer to look after Abel's livestock, but hadn't had much luck in finding any relatives of Abel or his wife. Henry told him to start that search in the morning. He didn't really like leaving the relatives thing, but he was sagging physically and, if he was honest, he'd had enough for the day. With regards to the scene, he ensured that Abel's farmhouse was secure – and found the keys to his shotgun cabinet, which contained a further four twelve-bore shotguns. Henry locked this up, locked up the house, took down the forensic tent and dismissed everyone, pocketing the keys himself.

It would all resume first thing, by which time Henry would have had some sleep, he hoped, but not the evening he had originally planned.

He was the last one to leave the scene, trudging back down the track to his car, completely saturated; even his mini-umbrella had given up the ghost. It drooped uselessly, not even water-resistant any more. But one thing kept him going – something he had resisted doing all afternoon and into the evening. Like any half-decent detective, he always carried a change of clothing with him in the boot of the car. Socks, underpants, trainers, jeans, a T-shirt and a zip-up windjammer. At least he knew the journey home would be comfortable; he would not be driving forty miles in wet clothing. And he had a towel in there, too, which he laid carefully on the driving seat of the Audi, then got in and started up.

Then he aimed for the nearest pub, which he

knew from days gone by was called the Cock and Magpie; this was where he intended to get changed.

It was only as he parked on the narrow road outside that the thought of having a drink entered his head.

Just the one.

A bit of quiet reflection over a JD, maybe.

Think about life and death.

Think about retirement.

His change of clothing was in a holdall, which he pulled out. He walked across to the pub and went straight to the gents', where he stripped and re-dressed. He stuffed his wet gear in the bag and entered the bar for a warming drink before commencing the long journey home. He did make a quick call to Alison using a payphone in the toilet corridor and told her he'd be about another hour. It was an awfully long way from Whitworth to Kendleton.

He couldn't resist asking her, cynically, if Steve Flynn had made himself comfortable. Just as cynically, Alison said yes, he'd got his feet under the table, bringing a snarl to Henry's lips.

It was only then that he had the first drink and, staring into it, relived Abel's suicide, and considered the implications of fate. He was only vaguely aware of what was going on in the pub, a place where, many years before, he had been to a few retirement '*dos*'. But he hadn't been here for a long time, though when he did glance around it seemed not much had changed. It was still homely and welcoming, like a decent local should be.

He glanced around only once.

A few local residents were in, but the two young girls huddled together in an alcove, eagerly inspecting their iPhones and giggling, seemed slightly out of kilter for the pub. They were dressed provocatively in short skirts, tights and cut-off blouses showing their stomachs. But Henry didn't spend too much time trying to work them out. Probably just local girls taking a rest-stop here before heading into Rochdale for the night. So, really, when he put that spin on it, there was nothing out of the ordinary and his assumptions seemed to be confirmed when a young man popped his head through the door. The lad's eyes sought out and alighted on the girls, who were obviously waiting for him. He beckoned them – a sharp gesture and an angry face. Clearly though, he was their lift or boyfriend and they collected their coats and hurried out of the pub.

Henry didn't watch them go.

Instead his eyes had returned to inspect the honey-coloured liquor in his glass, and his mind to his bleak thoughts, and just as a judder cut through his soul he downed the JD in one.

It was when, just about to send the second JD in the direction of the first, he was working out the practicalities of blowing one's own head off with a shotgun, that the young woman came flying through the pub door and fate took a turn. Although he wasn't to know it at that moment, it was probably just as well that he didn't get the chance to neck that second whiskey.

She came in hard through the door, panicked, terrified, desperately pleading for help.

The landlord rushed from behind the bar and swooped down next to her.

The other customers did little to help, just milled around and watched in the detached but amused way in which (mainly) men holding pints of beer tend to when something interesting kicks off that isn't their business.

Henry held back also. Despite his annoyance at the interruption, he placed his drink down and although his inbuilt urge was to go and help, he hesitated. Maybe this would be something that would pan out without the necessity of his involvement and his declaration of being a cop.

He knew he was kidding himself.

Ultimately, he could never just be an observer when someone needed help. Wasn't in his blood to look the other way.

But for a moment, he watched.

The landlord helped the woman up on to a chair and knelt in front of her.

She was deeply upset, inhaling/exhaling immense gagging chokes. The blood – and there seemed to be lots of it – didn't seem to be all hers, though her hands and face were smeared with it.

'First off, love, are you hurt?' the landlord asked.

'N–no.' She shook her head. 'Yes, no.'

'So what's up? Whose is the blood?'

'My boyfriend's . . . he's hurt, really hurt.'

'Has he had an accident?'

'No, no, he's been assaulted. Oh, God,' she cried.

The landlord stood up. 'Bad?'

'Yeah, yeah, I think so,' she gasped. 'I don't know . . . he's hurt.'

She held up her blood-smeared hands, at which point Henry gave a last longing look at his JD, then pushed himself away from the bar. He walked over and showed his warrant card, but didn't actually introduce himself.

'Have you called an ambulance?' he asked her.

Open-mouthed, she looked up at him, shook her head.

'Does he need an ambulance?'

'Yes, yes.'

Henry looked at the landlord and arched his eyebrows. The man got the message instantly and scuttled to the bar, grabbing the phone.

'So you're not hurt?' Henry confirmed.

'No . . . not really.'

'What's happened? There's a lot of blood.'

'Oh, I don't know . . . it all got out of hand. I dunno . . .'

'You must have some idea.'

'Somebody hit him with something.'

'Where is he now?'

'Up at . . . up . . . look . . .' Suddenly she became wary, as if talking to a cop wasn't such a good idea. 'It's all right . . . no need for an ambulance . . . I don't think it's that bad . . . really.'

Henry could see she was coming down from a point of virtual hysteria and was now thinking things through. He had no doubt that his unexpected, untimely appearance was now influencing her thought process. A flashed police ID could sometimes do that – make people think twice.

'I'm on to the ambulance service now,' the landlord called from the bar. 'Need some names and locations.'

Henry looked at the girl – he estimated she probably wasn't much over twenty, so to him she was a girl. She looked as if she had been dragged backwards through the proverbial hedge, her hair a mess. Her clothing was wet, bedraggled and dirty. Her running make-up and mascara reminded him of a badger.

'Well?' he said. 'Does he need the hospital or not? But let me tell you this,' he said, like a parent to an uncooperative child, 'even if you say no, you're going to take me to the scene of this assault. I don't believe he doesn't need treatment, because of all this blood. It's no-win for you, lass.'

She now looked like a cornered badger.

'Where is he?' Henry demanded.

'Britannia Top Farm,' she admitted.

'Where's that?'

She pointed half-heartedly in a vague direction.

Henry turned to the landlord. 'Britannia Top Farm,' he said. The landlord nodded. Henry turned back to the girl.

'I don't want the police,' she mumbled, afraid.

'You got 'em,' Henry informed her.

Her head dropped into her hands and she began

sobbing again, gut-wrenchingly so, her stomach tightening.

'I'm dead . . . I'm dead,' she said.

Henry squatted in front of her, smelled the booze on her breath. 'What happened?'

She shook her head dismissively. 'Oh, nowt, nowt. Just a fallout – friends, you know . . . party . . . release day,' she blabbered slightly incoherently.

'What has your boyfriend been hit with?'

'A pickaxe.'

'What?'

'A pickaxe – right up his arse.'

'Shit.' Henry rose to his full height and stepped over to the bar. The landlord had just finished talking to the ambulance service. 'Will you call the police at Burnley and let them know I'm going to attend this incident?' He flicked his business card on to the bar. 'That's me.' Then he had a thought. 'No, scotch that, I've got a radio in my car. I'll use it to tell them directly, if I can get a signal.' He gave his JD on the counter another look – a longing glance – then went back to the girl, who was just in the process of running out of the pub.

He shook his head, gave a sigh and followed.

She hadn't got far, just to the middle of the narrow road outside the pub – Back Cowm Lane – where she twizzled around, desperately trying to make up her mind which way to flee.

Henry, who had started running, stopped and watched her indecision with a contemptuous twist on his lips.

She saw him and stopped her twirling, defeated. Her shoulders fell and the rain flashed down her sorry frame.

The downpour seemed to have increased in intensity since Henry had been in the pub and was so powerful and noisy that it was only at the very last moment Henry heard a car approaching from the direction of the moors. His head cricked to the left, but although he could now hear the scream of the engine, getting louder and closer, the rain blanketed his view and made it hard to see the car because its headlights were off.

The car was careering towards her.

His head flicked back to the girl's forlorn figure in the middle of the road – then back at the car. He realized she was going to get mown down if she stood there in her indecisive daze. He didn't know if it would be intentional or accidental; he just knew it was going to happen.

Henry's instincts kicked in instantaneously and everything slowed down for him, even though the reality was it was all happening at breakneck speed, and his mind and body reacted in a series of simultaneous thoughts and movements.

All at the same time he started to run towards the girl and his mouth opened to scream a warning. His brain computed the what-if image of her being smashed by the car, being flicked over the bonnet like a fragile gazelle. And also the thought that if he mistimed this, he would be the one ending up as a broken bundle under the front wheels of the car.

He launched himself at her, propelling himself off his right foot.

The car, dark, scary, a screaming menace, was almost on them. Only feet away, engine ear-splittingly revving. Only a nanosecond away. He saw the girl's face now. Her mouth open in horror and confusion – and also realization. But she was riveted to her spot and Henry powered into her with a scream of his own and smashed into her just below her waistline.

He sensed the car almost on them.

He felt the girl fold over his shoulder, heard the horrible gasp of air as he drove it out of her lungs; also felt the lightness of her as he picked her up in mid-flight and they both went through the air in a tangle of limbs. And the car shrieked as it sped past, throwing up rainwater from the road. Henry felt the rush of air, heard the engine right there – and then it was gone and he and the girl were a bundle in the gutter.

She gasped and sobbed as they disengaged.

Henry picked himself up slowly, wondering what he had hurt.

He had landed on his right knee and elbow, but he seemed to be OK, even if his change of clothing was now looking decidedly dodgy. He lifted her to her feet and she swayed unsteadily.

'Are you hurt?'

'I . . . don't think so.' She leaned against a parked car. 'Oh, God . . . mess.'

'Understatement,' Henry said. 'Was that a friend of yours?' he asked about the car as he tried to visualize the make. It had all happened so quickly he couldn't say what it was, which annoyed him because he knew his cars pretty well. He exhaled in a Zen kind of way to try and reduce his palpitations.

She shrugged.

'You're not a lot of help in any department, are you?'

'No,' she admitted.

'Right, come on. Get into my car, let's go up to this farm.'

'I don't want to.'

'Nor do I particularly, but your boyfriend's up there with a pickaxe up his bum, he's bleeding and you came to ask for help. Let's do what we have to do.' He moved over to her, placed a hand on her shoulder and ushered her to his car. She acquiesced sullenly but without complaint. Henry moved the towel that was on the driver's seat over to the passenger seat, sat in and reached across to open the door for her. She slumped in like a sack of bones.

'What's going on?' he asked, starting the Audi.

'What do you mean?'

'Up on the farm.'

She stayed tight-lipped, and Henry groaned crossly.

Henry's PR was in the driver's door shelf. He picked it up, switched it on and called up Burnley comms, thinking again how ridiculous it was that it was so far away.

The radio operator already knew of the reported assault, having been given details by ambulance control. Henry asked if another local officer could be sent too but was told that the nearest uniformed PC was in Rawtenstall and was too busy to attend.

'Charming,' Henry said, recognizing another result of cost-cutting – a very big lack of cops on the streets. So he wasn't surprised by the response and also understood that because it was a Friday evening, most police resources in Rossendale would be concentrated in the larger towns – which, of course, was no reassurance to the good citizens of Whitworth.

'Where's the farm?' Henry asked the girl.

'Back up the road, then when you get to the reservoir, bear right.'

'Up past Abel Kirkman's place?'

She shrugged.

'Is it drivable all the way?'

She nodded. Henry swung the Audi out and around, then set off past the Cock and Magpie up towards the hills. He knew there were huge quarries up on the moor tops and had once been to a murder at one of them, maybe fifteen years earlier, when he had been a detective sergeant on what was then the Regional Crime Squad.

'What's your name?'

'Annabel . . . Annabel Larch.'

'How old are you?'

'Twenty-two.'

'Where do you live?'

'Rochdale.'

'And why are you over here?'

'With my boyfriend, I suppose.'

'Who is?'

'Johnny Asian.'

Henry logged the unusual name.

He drove carefully up the road, which was smoothly tarmacked at first. Despite the continued downpour he could still make out the smooth triangular blackness that was the surface of Cowm Reservoir down to the left. He recalled vaguely that years ago there was a story going around that the water in the lake had been polluted in such a way it could never be used domestically, but didn't know if that was a myth or not. He did know that the reservoir was currently a popular location for water sports activities.

'Here – go right here,' Annabel directed him, and he did turn on to the track that led to Kirkman's farm. This was Back Lane, a narrow track with dry stone walls on either side. He was already regretting coming back up. It had been a bumpy ride earlier in the gloom and rain of the afternoon, but now, as evening started to turn to real night time, and the rain continued unabated, he knew this was not a route for an Audi coupé. His sump scraped over a large rock and made him wince.

This was Land Rover territory.

After a couple of hundred metres there was a sharp bend and, as Henry negotiated this, he came face to face with a Range Rover blocking the track, its headlights on full beam and several figures silhouetted in the beams.

Two men were all Henry could make out at first.

Then he saw a third man lying between them on the lane. The two standing up were savagely beating him with either pickaxe handles, baseball bats or thick sticks. The appearance of Henry's vehicle did not seem to deter the attack.

Annabel screamed.

Henry braked, grabbed his radio and leapt out of the Audi, marching towards the scene.

'Oi! Police,' he shouted. The words stopped the men, who turned to face him, and for the first time he saw they were wearing baseball caps backwards. Even though they were bathed in light he couldn't see their faces clearly, as his eyes were squinting against the headlights of the Range Rover. 'Drop the sticks,' he ordered them.

'Up yours, pal,' one said.

Henry saw the quick exchange of looks between them, then they came at him, wielding the bats.

Henry was not a great fighter. He mostly relied on sweet-talking people into submission, or if that failed, overpowering them as opposed to beating them up. The fast approach of these two guys, sticks raised, made him realize that the talking stage had already been passed, that he was unlikely to overpower them and that, against his better judgement, the best thing he could do now was attack rather than defend.

They loped menacingly towards him.

Dark shapes, silhouettes, unrecognizable.

Henry ducked, and ran at the one on his right, dropping his shoulder low, trying to bend under the fast swinging stick that was arcing around to his head. He felt the whoosh of fresh air just above the back of his skull as he tucked in and drove his shoulder hard into the man's sternum like a rugby player (which he had once been), almost lifting the man off his feet because he was much lighter than Henry had expected. He lifted and drove him back against the front grille of the Range Rover – Henry's second rugby tackle of the evening.

The bat flew out of the man's grasp as his spine arched painfully backwards over the bonnet of the four by four.

The man fought hard, trying to clatter Henry around the head, but Henry kept hunched low into him, punched him on the lower belly, whilst at the same time trying to keep some sort of tab on the other guy. But he had moved out of Henry's line of sight – a worry. That knowledge made Henry haul the man he had tackled to one side, turn and face number two, wherever he was.

But though Henry had moved quickly, he really wasn't quick enough.

The second guy's bat was already coming around at Henry's head.

Henry dropped, raised his right shoulder and angled his body just enough to protect himself from a head blow, but with tremendous force the bat still connected with Henry's upper left arm, just below the shoulder joint.

He emitted a squeal as pain coursed through him.

The man struck again, knocking him sideways across the front of the Range Rover. Henry's whole body jerked with the blow. He raised his hands protectively, but the man managed to smash the next blow into his rib cage, creasing him agonizingly. He slumped down to his hands and knees.

Somewhere he heard the girl scream something.

The first man now came back at him, delivering a flying kick into his side, sending him rolling on the hard, stony ground.

He curled up, expecting more, but heard a, 'Let's get the fuck out of here.'

Annabel screamed again. Henry saw one of the men grab and drag her across to the Range Rover, then heard a door slam, the engine rev, a gear crunch into place. The car lurched backwards, swerving side to side along the constricted lane, not quite hitting the walls.

Henry rose to one knee, hugging himself as he watched the car go, the headlights jumping. Then he got to his feet and stumbled over to the figure who had been the victim of the attackers. He lay there unmoving but conscious, the rain pelting into his face.

Henry stood upright and only then realized why the men had run away: the flashing blue lights snaking up towards them from further down the lane.

They had probably mistaken them for the approach of a police car, but Henry knew otherwise.

He had never been so glad to see an ambulance.

Six

Henry Christie was thankful that the baseball bat wielded by the attacker – because he was now sure that was what it had been, not a stick or a pickaxe handle – had only connected with the biceps of his left arm and the left side of his rib cage. A few years before he had been winged by a shotgun blast in his left shoulder, an injury that could have been serious but had only resulted in flesh and muscle wounds around the joint. After an operation to pick out the pellets the shoulder had healed well.

After that he had taken a bullet in his right shoulder – just to balance things up – when a very irate woman who had just murdered her father and uncle had shot him at almost point-blank range. That had been a much more serious injury than the shotgun wound and, though it was technically healed, it still caused him a lot of pain and discomfort and, to a degree, a loss of movement in that joint.

He was therefore very protective of his right shoulder, the left slightly less so.

If he had been whacked on the right, he knew he would have been in triple the agony. As it was, he was in agony, but manageably so.

He raised himself tentatively on the hospital bed and looked at the nurse, giving her his signature lopsided grin, the look he'd once believed could melt the heart and willpower of any pretty female in his sights. Now it was just a lazy expression that meant he couldn't be bothered to smile properly. In fact, he hardly noticed just how pretty she was.

'The X-rays have come back – nothing broken,' she announced.

'Good to hear.' He shifted painfully.

'That said, the doctor suggests you might want to put that arm in a sling for a few days, and you shouldn't drive.'

'Maybe just some painkillers,' he suggested. 'Unfortunately, still got work to do.'

She nodded. 'I'll get you some analgesics.'

'Thanks.'

He started to put his T-shirt back on over his head. 'How's the other patient?'

'Better than you'd think: cuts, bruises, and a very deep hole in his bottom – from a pickaxe, I believe.'

'So he has a matching pair?' Henry guffawed at his own toilet humour.

The nurse was stone-faced. 'It could have been very serious. As it is, the point went into his gluteus maximus – his buttocks, in other words – and he's only got muscle damage, so it's just a case of cleaning, disinfecting, stitching and giving him a tetanus injection.'

'Then he'll be fit to go?' Henry asked hopefully, knowing that the only place the lad would be going was straight into a police cell, injured or otherwise.

'I would imagine . . . but the doctor will decide that, not me.'

She helped him to finish putting his T-shirt back on. It was wet and dirty, as were his jeans and windjammer from the few moments of rolling around outside the pub with Annabel after pushing her out of the path of the car, then his time on the ground in the track. He didn't have another set of clothes.

He slid off the bed on to his feet and pulled back the curtain which divided off his cubicle in the Accident and Emergency department at Rochdale Infirmary. When the ambulance had arrived on the farm track the paramedics had put the injured young man into the back of it. Henry had also climbed in after identifying himself. He watched them do a quick inspection of the victim, but had been ushered out when they saw that his jeans were soaked in blood – obviously from the wound in the buttocks – and they needed to remove them.

In the rain, one of the paramedics gave Henry a quick once-over in front of the ambulance head-lights, then Henry had to drive himself in his Audi ahead of the ambulance because it would have been impossible for either of the vehicles to have turned around or reversed. Fortunately Henry found he could branch off on to another track that ran almost parallel and brought him back on to a proper road near to the Cock and Magpie.

Pulling in to allow the ambulance to pass him, he then followed it as it blue-lighted its way to

Rochdale Infirmary, feeling the pain in his arm and side, doing his best to drive with just his right arm.

On arrival, the assault victim was stretchered quickly into the A&E treatment area whilst Henry, even though he was also an assault victim, had to queue up and wait to see a triage nurse.

Fortunately the unit was not too busy – it was still early – and he was soon being examined by a consultant, then sent to X-ray.

As Henry's feet touched the tiled floor, the minute jarring of the manoeuvre sent a jolt of pain from his shoulder to his ribs and he stopped moving very quickly.

The nurse looked concerned.

'You sure nothing's broken?' he asked weakly. 'I feel like everything's moving where things shouldn't be moving.' He gave her another of his smiles, accompanied by puppy-dog eyes, which probably looked more like a grimace and made her frown with confusion. His facial expressions seemed to have lost all meaning. She grimaced worriedly, then scuttled away to find some pills for him.

Henry rolled his left shoulder to keep the blood flowing and rotated his torso slowly, to try and ward off stiffening up.

There was still work to do.

By following the screams of agony through the A&E department, he soon found the cubicle he was after. He opened the curtain and saw that the young man really had been pickaxed in the bottom or, more precisely, the right buttock.

As Henry shoved his head through the gap in the curtain, the consultant treating the lad had just taken a step back in order to get a helicopter view of the wound.

The patient was lying on his left side, facing away from Henry. He was now wearing a surgical gown, his lower clothing having been removed and dumped in one corner. The gown was pulled up, exposing his thin bottom, his knees drawn up, giving Henry an unexpected view of his bum in all its gory glory.

The point of the pickaxe had entered the lower part of his right cheek, an inch or so right of his crack, and made a ragged, almost star-shaped hole about two inches across, possibly an inch and a half deep, Henry could not exactly say. It looked a dirty, bloody mess and very painful indeed.

Henry winced empathetically, especially when the doctor moved back and gently inserted a surgically gloved forefinger into the wound, most of which disappeared and must have touched an exposed nerve. As though he'd been jabbed by a cattle prod, the young man screamed horribly and his whole body convulsed in a spasm of agony.

The doctor removed his finger and said, 'Sorry, son, but I need to know how deep the hole is and that was the most effective way of finding out.'

The lad sobbed pitifully.

Henry thought that someone had meant to do

this young guy a great deal of harm, and the subsequent baseball bat attack only confirmed this. Henry wondered what would have happened if he hadn't turned up when he did and guessed there would have been a body in the lane waiting to be discovered next morning. Henry might just have saved his life – and got battered himself in the process.

A nurse in the cubicle looked up and noticed Henry's face in the crack of the curtain.

He gave her the lopsided smile.

Clearly unimpressed, she said sternly, 'Excuse me, but what do you think you're doing?'

The doctor turned and recognized Henry, whom he had briefly examined after the triage nurse.

'It's OK, nurse,' he said and indicated that Henry should step back. Henry retreated and the doctor came out of the cubicle, peeling off his blood-covered surgical gloves, jerking his head for Henry to follow him to a position out of earshot. 'How are you feeling? I saw the X-rays, nothing broken.'

'Old and sore and a bit cross . . . a wicked combination. How is he?'

'Well battered, but only superficially, really. The wound in his bottom is quite bad, but it's in the muscle and hasn't ruptured or touched anything serious. It needs to be cleaned, packed, stitched and dressed and time will heal it, ultimately.'

'Can I have him soon, then?'

'I would say so. I'm going to get a nurse to clean the wound, then I'll be back to do the rest.'

'Thanks . . . and he'll be fit to spend the night in a cell?'

'Yes.'

Another nurse hurried up to the doctor, spoke urgently. 'Ambulance en route with a serious casualty from a car accident,' she informed him. 'Head and neck injuries.'

The doctor nodded. 'Be with you in a moment.' He turned back to Henry. 'And so Friday night begins. I may have to delay treating our friend in there . . . let me see what's coming in.'

Henry shrugged philosophically. Such was the nature of A&E units.

'Can I have a word with him anyway, just to start getting details?'

'Be my guest.' The doctor binned his soiled gloves and hurried after the nurse.

Henry exhaled tiredly, filtering everything through his slightly addled brain, wondering how best to handle the 'Axe-man', as he had unofficially named him.

Because Rochdale was part of Greater Manchester Police's area, if Henry arrested the wounded man – which he fully intended to do, no matter what – he should first be conveyed to Rochdale nick, then booked in and transferred back over the border into Lancashire. At least that was the theoretical procedure, but Henry did not want to be bogged down by that. It was bad enough that he had to take a prisoner all the way to Burnley, but going via Rochdale would make time drag even more, and what Henry wanted to do was stick the Axe-man in a cell, have some sharp words with him, then find Britannia Top Farm, wherever it might be, and knock on the door. Or preferably, kick it down.

He had stumbled on to something he wanted to sort out and the best way to do it was to get all concerned locked up, after which he would sort the mess out at his own pace.

Tired and hurting though he was, he felt quite excited by it.

This was one of those bread-and-butter jobs he always liked dealing with when he was a uniformed cop.

It would, he thought, make a nice change from murder.

First, though, he needed to make a few calls.

The rain was still heavy. Henry found a spot in the entrance foyer of the A&E unit and fished out his mobile phone. He called the comms room at Burnley to bring them up to speed with his current situation.

'I'm going to need transport for one prisoner, Rochdale Infirmary to Burnley,' he explained to the call-taker.

'I'll have to get back to you on that one, sir.'

'OK. I know we're a bit thin on the ground, but I need it to happen.'

'Understood. I'll call you back.'

Henry ended the call and watched the rain, mesmerized by it for a while, then feeling very uncomfortable in his sodden clothing, and shaking his head for not having had the foresight to bring two spare sets of clothes with him instead of just the one. He made the next call to Alison, wondering how he would explain to her why he wasn't home by now.

'And so it goes on,' he thought cynically to himself as he found her number. 'Once more I'm putting the job first – and at my age.'

She answered. He could hear the sounds of pub-related activity behind her, some raised but happy voices, glasses chinking.

'Henry,' she said suspiciously. 'Why are you not here?'

'Hey, sorry love,' he began, very annoyed at himself.

'What's happened?'

'I . . . er . . . got involved in something . . . got a bit of a kicking . . .'

'For fuck's sake, Henry.'

'Oh I know, I know.' He tried to remind himself that he found it cute when Alison reverted to gutter language when she became annoyed – one of the many charming traits he adored about her.

'Where are you now?'

'Rochdale Infirmary.'

'*What*? Are you all right?'

'Yeah, yeah, but you know . . . I'm sorry, I kind of need to see this thing through. People who have thumped me need arresting, so I don't see myself being home any time soon.'

She uttered an exasperated gasp.

'Sorry,' he said.

'So long as you're all right,' she said, relenting slightly. Her voice broke.

'Is Flynn still there?'

'Yes. Like I said, I've sorted out one of the guest rooms for him.'

'I hope he's paying full whack.'

She chuckled wickedly. 'Special rate for a special guest,' she teased, knowing what Henry thought of Flynn.

'Mm.' He gave a low, warning growl like a lion seeing a rival circling the pride.

'And Rik and Lisa have turned up too – better late than never,' she said, rubbing it in, referring to DCI Rik Dean and Lisa, Henry's once-wild child sister. They were now a couple with marriage looming.

'Are they on a special rate, too?'

'Yes.'

'It's more like a doss house than a business,' Henry said. 'That won't be happening when I'm running it properly with you after I retire.'

'You still plan on that?'

'Course.' He was going to spend his autumn days working with Alison in the Tawny Owl – at least that was the idea. 'Look, I'll be as quick as possible here. A lad's been badly assaulted, I've been thumped and I don't want to let it go cold, that's all,' he said, then added, 'I love you.'

'Same here.'

In the hubbub behind her he heard someone order a pint and wished it was him.

'Just get home, OK?' she said.

'I will – and you keep that Flynn at arm's-length. I know what he's like; he'll be all over you like a rash, given the chance.'

'I will,' she promised, but just before she hung up he heard her say, 'Steve, darling . . . just hand me back my panties, will you?' Then the line went dead and Henry had to laugh at her naughtiness. It went well with the gutter language.

His phone rang almost immediately: the comms room at Burnley.

'Sir,' the operator said, 'got a vehicle on its way to you, just setting off from Rossendale Police Station; just one officer on board, though.'

'That's OK, I can work with that.'

'In a Land Rover.'

'Even better,' Henry said, visualizing the prisoner cage in the back.

'And – it's the chief constable driving it . . .'

Henry didn't even bother to ask. Instead he took himself back into A&E and found a coffee machine, knowing he needed a shot of 'fully leaded' – caffeinated – in order to keep him going, no matter how poor the quality might be. He had the correct change in his pocket, which he sorted from amongst the two sets of keys also in there – his car keys and the keys to Abel Kirkman's place. He selected a black coffee from a dispenser that still dropped a thin plastic cup down into a holder and filled it with a very muddy brew. It seemed a long time since he had bought a drink from such a machine and he was vaguely surprised they still existed.

The coffee didn't taste too bad and the first few sips of the boiling hot, bitter liquid hit the spot.

He lounged at that location for a few moments to assess how he was feeling and also to plan what was going to happen over the next few hours.

First, tackling the girl, Annabel, to get her out of the path of the speeding car had caused him to land heavily on his right knee, although the adrenalin surge then and shortly after ensured he didn't realize he had hurt that part of his anatomy until later. The subsequent beating was more directly painful and he knew he would be very sore and stiff in the morning. The pain killers given to him were actually having some numbing effect, which was good.

Then he worked through things.

Arresting the lad with the pickaxe hole in his bottom was next on the agenda, but that could wait until the Land Rover arrived. He didn't want to spook him until necessary, though he did want to speak to him to start to pull the story together. What had happened up at Britannia Top Farm? Who was up there? Why had a fairly serious assault taken place? Which of the bastards had attacked him and where was Annabel likely to be? Was she safe or in harm's way?

After dropping him off in a cell it was Henry's intention to find the farm and get tough.

He started to walk back to the casualty department, his mind shuffling through the logistics of it all.

He was on a corridor leading to A&E. At the far end was the emergency entrance door through which paramedics wheeled stretchered patients straight into the unit from the back of an ambulance. On his right, twenty metres ahead, was a double door that also led into the unit and directly opposite was a double door to the reception and waiting area.

Henry saw a flurry of activity at the far end of the corridor.

There was the reflection of rotating blue lights from an ambulance outside. Some shouting, then a door burst open and a stretcher pushed by a paramedic crashed through, a patient on it. Another paramedic held up a clear drip channelled into the patient's arm. The doctor Henry had been dealing with and two nurses were alongside the stretcher, being briefed by the paramedics.

Henry guessed this was the road accident victim who had been mentioned a few minutes before.

Then the stretcher was inside the unit, the double doors clattering shut.

This meant there would be a delay in dealing with Henry's proposed prisoner, unless the bottom stitch-up could be delegated to a nurse or there was another consultant on the ward, though Henry hadn't yet seen one, which didn't surprise him. A&E units were often skeleton staffed, then slammed for not hitting the stupid targets set by out-of-touch authorities.

'Skeleton staff,' he murmured to himself, chuckling at his own medical humour.

He had now paused by a chocolate dispensing machine and was considering buying a Mars bar to accompany the caffeine hit and keep up his flagging energy levels.

He was still about twenty metres away from

the two sets of double doors that were directly opposite each other – the one on the right into the unit, the one directly across the corridor leading to the waiting area. He wasn't paying particular heed to people going across from one door to the other because he was deciding whether a Mars bar was the correct option. Maybe it should be a Snickers, he thought, wrestling with himself. Then his chain of thought latched on to the fact that Snickers used to be called Marathon; why did the manufacturers have to change the name? The name changed, of course, before actual marathons became as popular as they now were. He wondered if the makers now regretted the change.

Though his mind was churning with this uncon-nected mush, he did see a movement out of the corner of his eye and glancing up he saw two men clatter through the doors from the waiting room and cross quickly to enter the A&E department.

They were dressed in jeans, trainers and zip-up jackets and both of them, Henry guessed, were in their early twenties, but he could not be completely certain of that because they were wearing back-to-front baseball caps on their heads and what looked like surgical masks over the lower portion of their faces.

In their right hands, hanging loosely, almost discreetly and casually, down the sides of their legs, were baseball bats – and in that moment, Henry knew that he had been right to conclude that those were what he had been assaulted with, not pickaxe handles or just plain sticks.

It took them maybe a second to cross the corridor, with no sideways looks or checks. They just went straight through, as if on a mission.

It was just a glimpse for Henry at the exact moment his Snickers bar dropped into the collection tray.

He dropped his quarter-drunk coffee into a waste bin, shot down the corridor and spun into the A&E unit.

There was a corridor straight ahead of him, wards and cubicles branching off either side.

Henry knew exactly where the two men were going.

He ran to the second ward on the left and skidded into it just as a nurse screamed from the cubicle where Henry's prisoner-to-be was lying waiting for his buttock to be sewn up.

He sprinted as the nurse staggered out backwards, having been shoved roughly, crashing against a trolley which she caught as she lost her balance and flipped on to herself, spilling all the contents – bed pans, plasters, bandages and syringes.

As Henry got to her, he heard the first cry of, 'No!' followed by the hollow thud of a baseball bat connecting with something, then a scream of pain.

Another thud – wood on bone – and another shriek.

Henry skidded into the cubicle and took it all in.

The two masked men were raining down blows on the injured lad, who was curled up defensively

103

on the bed, his hands covering his head and face, though this only helped partially; as Henry came in, he saw one of the bats crash down on to the side of the lad's head with a sickening echoing clunk.

With a roar, Henry pitched himself at the nearest attacker who saw him coming and swung his weapon wildly at Henry, who ducked, but tripped sideways against the cubicle wall.

This time, however, Henry was determined not to go down.

He hit the wall and, using the reverse energy from the collision, threw himself back up at the man who was already slicing his bat back down at Henry's head like an executioner with a huge sword.

Henry dinked sideways, deflected the blow with his left forearm, and although he felt the hard wood crack the apex of his elbow – which hurt – he fought through that and took advantage of the fact that, for just a moment, the attacker was wide open and vulnerable.

For once in his life, he was going to pack a great punch.

He knew his attackers were violent and ruthless and the only way to deal with them was to hit harder than them.

So in that very tiny window of opportunity, Henry went for it.

He threw himself off the cubicle wall, drew back his right arm, bunched his hand into a fist and, as he came back like a boxer off the ropes, he powered that fist through the air and slammed it as hard as he could right into the centre of the man's face, on the point of the nose.

For the first instant of impact it was like hitting a brick wall.

Then – a euphoric moment for Henry – the man's nose seemed to crumble like a cake and imploded. His head jerked back, then he sank to his knees, dropping the bat, his hands going to his face as blood gushed and filled the mask.

It was only a fleeting, satisfying moment for Henry, tempered by the fact that his right hand and wrist now hurt terribly and what he wanted to do was hold them and rub them better, while standing over the man to gloat over his victory. But that was only a parallel thought to the reality of what was happening.

The second bat-wielding individual had run from the opposite side of the bed to help his stricken mate and was coming at Henry, who scooped up the discarded bat and launched himself back at this man, swinging it around and aiming it at the side of his head.

Clearly accustomed to assaulting with and being assaulted by long chunks of wood, the man bobbed skilfully sideways out of the arc and Henry swished fresh air, pivoting right around with the momentum and slamming the bat into the wall, leaving himself defenceless.

Holding his stick double-handed, the man swung it around mid-height towards Henry's already bruised rib cage. However, with the agility of a very overweight ballet dancer, Henry managed to complete a full three hundred and sixty degree turn and brought his bat into contact with the attacker's left shoulder. Just a glancing blow, but enough to send him off sideways and into the unfortunate nurse who had just about managed to get back on to her feet.

The man clung to her, then flung her away, by which time Henry had managed to step out of the cubicle, completely regain his equilibrium, take a proper double-handed hold of the baseball bat and drop into an aggressive combat stance, twirling the stick in his hands whilst putting a look of pure menace on his face.

'Right, come on lads,' he growled with much more ferocity and confidence than he actually felt. 'Let's get this done . . . payback time.'

The one he had punched in the face had pulled himself upright on the bed, swaying unsteadily, disoriented by the blow, blood soaking the mask and running down his neck and upper chest.

The other one faced Henry but his body language revealed his uncertainty as he looked back and forth from his mate to Henry.

'You put that down,' Henry said. 'I'm a police officer and you are both under arrest.'

'No fucking way,' the still-armed one said.

'OK, let's go for it then,' Henry offered. Inside he was now feeling a surge of anger which was drowning out his trepidation. He had rattled these two bucks and now he had to press home the advantage. 'I'll bet I've got at least thirty years on you, but I'm still gonna put you down.'

He brandished the stick threateningly.

Suddenly the one with the bat charged him.

Henry stepped back, twisted and weaved out of the man's way, cracking him on the shoulder blades as he stumbled past.

The other one turned and ran.

'Shit,' Henry said.

The one with the bat had managed to stay upright and he came back at Henry with a scream, the bat swishing wildly. Henry brought his up and the bats connected like *Star Wars* light sabres, cracking resoundingly, shaft to shaft, sending shock waves up Henry's arms, which jarred both shoulders.

Then the man heaved Henry out of the way, pushing him against the bed in the cubicle, and raced away after his partner in crime.

Henry went after them.

Armed with the bat he charged down the ward and followed them through the double doors, across the width of the outer corridor, through the next doors and into the waiting area which was now packed with amazed people.

Henry halted, the bat slung diagonally across his chest, catching his breath, having lost sight of them.

A waiting patient – a man holding a blood-soaked handkerchief over one of his hands – pointed to Henry's right.

A quick nod of thanks, then Henry ran to the main exit.

He emerged into the ambulance-only parking area just in time to see the men scramble into a Range Rover which set off towards the car park exit.

Henry raced after it, pulling on his energy reserves, not altogether certain of what he hoped to achieve. His red mist visor had come down and he charged after the vehicle – which he recognized as being the same one he'd come face to face with on the farm track earlier.

Quickly scanning the layout of the car park, Henry saw that to get to the exit, the vehicle would have to turn sharp left. This spurred Henry on and he worked out that if he did a diagonal sprint it might be possible to get close enough to the vehicle at least to get the registered number, which he had failed to do last time.

As he ran past his own parked car, he had a sudden change of tactics.

He swerved sideways, pulled out his remote lock for the Audi, pointed, clicked, slid into the car, fired it up and put it in gear, then went after the Range Rover which had turned right out of the car park, heading towards the main road, the A671.

When Henry reached the junction with that road, he had lost sight of it. Turning right would have taken him to Rochdale, left back towards Whitworth.

He chose left, back in the direction he had come from, and floored the accelerator, pleasurably feeling the power surge of his well-tuned motor.

There was little traffic on the road, even though it was Friday evening.

Within a couple of minutes he was almost back

at the boundary with Lancashire where the main road did a ninety degree turn into the county. This was the point where Henry caught up with the Range Rover because it had been held back by more slowly moving traffic.

Henry saw a face pressed up to the back window and knew he had been spotted.

The Range Rover swerved dangerously across the road, crossing double white lines in order to pass a car and also causing a car coming in the opposite direction to brake and veer up on to the pavement. The Range Rover then deliberately crashed sideways into the car it was overtaking, forcing it off the road and not stopping.

Henry was torn by the old cop conscience thing, wondering if he should stop and check whether anyone had been hurt. Quick sideways glances either way seemed to confirm that the occupants of both cars were OK, so he continued to pursue.

As the Range Rover reached the sharp bend, the brake lights suddenly went on and the car lurched left, almost seeming to overbalance on its springy suspension, then turned off the main road and plunged on to the steep side road that dropped into the Healey Dell Nature Reserve, a place that itself held some horrific memories for Henry: years before, he had been held in a warehouse there and savagely assaulted. That was something now tightly compartmentalized in his brain and he didn't even give it a passing thought as he slammed on and followed the Range Rover down the hill.

It was a tight, twisting descent, dropping under the quietly spectacular viaduct that once carried the rail line from Bacup to Rochdale, then into a steep wooded glade and eventually flattening out on the valley floor of the River Spodden, which was called Dell Road.

Here were the remnants of old industrial heritage, with former mills on either side of the road in various states of repair.

The Range Rover bounced recklessly down the incline, Henry not far behind.

But it was on the valley floor, where the deserted road widened, that Henry realized that his pursuit of this vehicle might be a touch fool-hardy and end badly. For him.

A hundred metres ahead, the Range Rover's brake lights came on again and the vehicle slewed to a stop slantways across Henry's path.

He too slammed on and stopped, his windscreen wipers swishing away the heavy rain.

Nothing happened.

Henry wondered if this was what the term 'Mexican stand-off' meant.

The wipers cleared the screen.

Henry sat still, gripped his steering wheel.

He licked his lips nervously.

A bad feeling skittered through his innards. He was pretty much alone here on a road rarely used by any other traffic except for visitors to the nature reserve. At this time of day it was deserted.

His left hand rested on the T-shaped gear stick of the automatic box.

He could see the shapes of three people in the Range Rover.

He exhaled, feeling and hearing his heart beating.

His engine ticked over, almost in sync with his heart.

They were waiting. He was waiting.

Then the doors opened and all three occupants emerged in the rain, formed a line and began to walk decisively towards him.

They had baseball bats in their hands.

Henry's fingers curled around the gear lever.

It was hard to see properly through the windscreen.

They walked towards him.

He peered through the rain and saw that two of them definitely had bats in their hands, but the third one, the man in the centre . . . what he carried looked somehow different. Shorter, stubbier.

A sawn-off shotgun.

Ten yards away they halted in a line.

Henry slid the Audi into reverse, his right foot still on the brake.

Then they came at him, jogging in a line, the baseball bats raised, the man in the middle aiming what Henry was now certain was a shotgun. It was the signal he needed to retreat.

Henry J-turned the Audi, feeling it smash into something hard and low at the rear.

The two men flanking the shooter ran at him, bats raised.

Henry rammed the gear lever back into drive

but fumbled momentarily in his rush and the bat holders were on him, raining down blow after blow on the front wing and soft top, both screaming hysterically at him.

He couldn't see their faces behind their surgical masks.

Then there was a shout from the shotgun holder and the two men split away.

Henry looked and saw the shotgun was raised and pointed at him.

He floored the accelerator, pulled the wheel down and sped away from the scene; his last view of the men in his rear-view mirror was of all three dancing a victory jig in the torrential rain.

Seven

Easing himself out of his car on dithery legs, Henry took a few moments to check the damage to a vehicle which, not many minutes before, had been his pristine pride and joy.

Even in the pouring rain he could see the dents on the front wing, and the expression on his face was one of disgust and anger verging upon rage. He had to control his breathing now as these feelings grew inside him at the sight of his lovely car and the realization that he had put himself in extreme danger, something he was getting far too old for. But on top of that, he had also run away. Although he knew this had been the sensible option, it did not sit easily with him. He might joke about running away from things, but it wasn't something he did lightly. As a cop, he didn't really have that choice.

If it hadn't occurred to him before, it did now. He was clearly dealing with a group of very dangerous people who had no compunction in causing serious injury or death to those who crossed their path, either deliberately or accidentally. He wanted to know who they were.

He stood by his car, shoulders slouched, drenched, outside the A&E unit at Rochdale Infirmary.

Glancing up, he saw the headlights of another vehicle enter the car park and move towards him.

It was the police Land Rover from Rawtenstall and at the wheel was the portly figure of Lancashire Constabulary's chief constable, Robert Fanshaw-Bayley, or FB.

The Land Rover pulled up alongside him and FB opened the driver's window a crack, not wishing to get himself wet, and through the gap he shouted, 'You look like a drowned rat.'

Through the rain, Henry eyed his ultimate boss malevolently and said, 'Thanks for that.'

FB closed the window and manoeuvred into a parking spot and when he had put the vehicle in a position that suited him – parked jauntily across two bays – he still did not get out, but beckoned Henry over.

Blinking rainwater off his eyelids, Henry reluctantly walked over and climbed into the passenger side.

The heater was on full blast but not working well. The wipers ploughed diligently through the rain.

'So what's happening here, Henry? I thought you'd turned out to a mad man with a gun.'

'That was just the start of a great day.'

'And what's happened since?'

'Oh, let me see . . . not a lot, really,' he said sullenly. 'Been almost mown down, been battered by thugs with baseball bats, saved the bacon of two quite ungrateful sods, prevented a serious assault here and, icing on the cake, had my car trashed. Not bad to say I should be half-cut now in front of a roaring fire.'

Pretending to be impressed, FB said, 'Wow.'

'And, boss,' he said pointedly, 'if we had any staff on, none of this would have happened to me.' He folded his arms with their drenched sleeves and turned his head very slowly towards his chief constable, a man he had known for thirty-odd years and whose career had intertwined or, more accurately, repeatedly car crashed with his own for that length of time. Their personal relationship was the only reason Henry could generally speak his mind to FB without too much fear of rank-related reprisals.

FB pouted and shrugged. 'Good job I'm here, then – to rescue your arse.'

Let me just consider that, Henry thought. *A fat bloke in a ten-year-old Land Rover – I don't think so*, he wanted to scream. But he held back. His familiarity with FB could only be pushed so far.

114

But he did say, 'Yeah, saved my bacon again.'

FB smiled, taking it as a compliment.

'So how come you're here?' Henry asked, running a hand through his soaking hair. 'On the edge of the civilized world as we know it?'

'I'm on call; same situation as you in some ways. Not enough Indians, as it were, so occasionally I have to cover. I usually try to wriggle out of it . . . I'm not really operational, as you know, but there was no one else. The Dep's at a do, and the three ACCs are doing something, not sure what. Because you got involved in that domestic, I just gravitated over to Rossendale – our old stamping ground, eh?'

Henry looked blandly at him. A long way back, Henry had been a PC in uniform in the valley when FB had been the detective inspector, ruling the roost with an iron fist. That had been the inauspicious birth of their relationship.

'You could say that.'

'I just happened to be in Rossendale Police Station when Burnley comms phoned in a tizzy, needing to get someone out to you to help convey a prisoner. Well, Rawtenstall and Bacup are kicking off despite the weather, no one's available and the cheeky fucking patrol sergeant looked at *me*, the fucker. This heap—' FB indicated the Land Rover with a sweep of his hands – 'was the only vehicle left. I almost had to climb through cobwebs to get into it and here I am, having left my Jag in the back yard. It's like driving a tank. I don't think anyone's used it for a year.'

'You really are a trooper,' Henry said.

115

FB gave him a sharp look, good enough to act as a warning. 'What's the plan?'

'Take the lad in there back to a cell, have a chat, circulate the Range Rover with the three rednecks on board, then come back and kick a door in.'

'Fair dos,' FB said. 'Might just tag along for all that.'

'Amazingly he hasn't been hurt any further,' the nurse informed Henry. This was the lady who had been thrown violently out of the way by the two attackers.

'What about you?' Henry asked, concerned. He had seen her crash into a trolley and tip it over. 'You hurt?'

'I'm fine,' she assured him. 'Just another Friday night in A&E.'

'I'll get them,' he told her, meaning the men who had assaulted her. She nodded, but her expression did not seem to hold out much hope of that. They were standing at the end of the treatment cubicle where the injured young man lay. 'What about his backside?'

'Stitched, packed and dressed.'

'So he's ready to go?'

'He's all yours,' she said. 'As you can see he's all dressed again, even if his clothes are a mess.'

Henry turned to the man and smiled savagely. 'Did you hear that? You're mine, all mine.'

'What's that supposed to mean?' He was lying on his side, scowling at Henry.

Henry came up alongside the bed and extracted his warrant card.

'All we've been through and we haven't even been introduced to each other. My name is Henry Christie—' he pushed the ID right up to his nose – 'and I'm a detective superintendent from Lancashire Constabulary. This gent—' he thumbed at FB – 'is the chief constable, which means you've got the best of the best looking after you . . . and you are?'

'Johnny Asian.'

'Ahh, the well-known Johnny Asian. Is that your real name?'

'It's what I'm called.'

'Not what I asked.'

'It'll do. It's what I get called because my skin's a bit dark. Anyway, what is this? I'm the injured party here. I thought I'd be going on to a ward for the night, for observations, like.'

'No such comfort for you, laddie. You've been discharged and now you've been arrested.'

'For what? I'm the one who's been beaten up.'

'Be that as it may, Johnny Asian, or whatever your name is, I'm arresting you for affray . . . there's a lot of questions need answering here.'

'No chance.' Johnny sat up quickly, realized too late he had put weight on to his wound, screamed and leapt off the bed as if he'd been electrocuted. Henry grabbed him and yanked him around. He was thin and weightless like so many youngsters Henry came across but that didn't stop him snarling like a cougar and struggling to get free. Henry rammed him up against the wall, pinning him there with his right arm across the lad's chest.

'You're locked up and you're going nowhere but into a cell until I've sorted this shite out. You do not have to say anything, but it may harm your defence if you do not mention when questioned something which you later rely on in court. Anything you do say may be given in evidence,' Henry cautioned him through gritted teeth.

FB stepped up behind Henry and held out a set of handcuffs as Henry growled into Johnny's face, 'I've been battered and bruised by your mates, Johnny. My car's a wreck and I'm in no mood to arse about, so stick your wrists out in front of you and let me cuff you. Make no mistake, you're under arrest, so don't make me kick your bottom, lad, because it'll hurt.'

Henry looked around at FB, who was swinging the cuffs on his finger. Henry noticed they were the old-fashioned chain link type as opposed to the rigid ones that were now standard issue to operational officers. He looked up at FB. 'Where did you get them from, the Bow Street Runners?'

'Funny, ha-ha.'

The journey back from Rochdale all the way through Whitworth, then Bacup, then over the Deerplay Moors to Burnley seemed interminable, particularly for Henry who, in his Audi, followed FB in the Land Rover. FB drove slowly and carefully at a speed which grated on Henry.

So, apart from mulling over what had happened from the moment the young lady, Annabel, had burst in through the pub door and interrupted his

JD, Henry was also feeling annoyed about how Lancashire Constabulary, so constrained by budget cuts imposed by successive governments, was expected to operate with anything like efficiency.

He hated harping back to the good old days, but the fact was when he had joined the police there had been a cell or cells in each police station in each town in Rossendale. Now there was only one actual police station, which had cost a hefty three mill and which was not even equipped to deal with prisoners, other than 'in-and-outs', that is, prisoners who could be processed quickly. All other prisoners – and that meant the majority of them – had to be conveyed over the hills and far away to Burnley nick.

It was bad enough having to haul a prisoner from Rawtenstall, which was only just over the hill from Burnley. Having to convey someone from the far reaches of Whitworth was verging on ludicrous. Henry also knew that Burnley's days as a custody office were numbered, too. Soon, all prisoners from Rossendale (and all the far-flung towns east of Burnley) would have to be taken to Blackburn.

Inconvenient to say the least and a terrible waste of a cop's time. Henry knew this situation often left streets un-policed for hours on end, which he thought was an abysmal disservice to the public.

It was therefore a good thing that the chief constable was on the prowl tonight. He could experience first-hand just how hard the cuts were chewing away at policing the streets.

Not that FB was too concerned.

He was the one who had driven the cuts as dictated by the Home Office but now he was due to retire, not least because he did not get along with the newly elected Police and Crime Commissioner, with whom he'd had two very public differences of opinion about the cutbacks and how the new post of PCC seemed to guzzle money without conscience.

Henry decided he would have a dig at FB later about the cuts, just to wind him up. Just for some sport.

As the two vehicles crossed the road at the top of the moors, the rain seemed to intensify and visibility dropped considerably on the poorly lit roads. Even the efficient headlights of the Audi struggled to pierce the darkness. Henry jumped when he felt water drip on to his neck and he groaned angrily as he twisted to see that the convertible roof had started to leak from being struck and damaged during the baseball bat attack.

He swore as he thought about the future repair cost and the hassle of dealing with insurance claims.

Just as the vehicles began the long, winding descent off the moors to Burnley, the Land Rover signalled and pulled into a lay-by close to a derelict brick mill. Henry shook his head irritably and drew in behind. Although he was getting wet he was reluctant to get out of the Audi.

'What the . . .?' he muttered.

The driver's door of the Land Rover opened

and FB rolled out and scurried back to Henry, who made him wait in the rain for just a fraction longer than necessary before opening the window.

'What's happening, boss?'

'Lad keeps banging and shouting on the cab window.'

Henry blinked. 'OK.'

'Says he feels sick, woozy and wants a piss.'

'We'll be there in less than five minutes, now,' Henry said. 'He'll have to wait.'

'I don't want him messing up the back of the Land Rover.'

'What do you want to do?' Henry asked, hoping he was masking his rising irritation at the chief. He didn't want to lose it, but this was just being a bit silly and wasting time.

Both officers looked at the back window of the Land Rover, on which the spare wheel was fixed. The prisoner's face was pressed up against the inner grille.

'Let him be sick and have a pee?'

'You sure?' Henry asked.

'Henry, I am not mopping out the back of a Land Rover covered in urine and vomit.'

'He can do it,' Henry said. As far as he was concerned, this was a non-discussion.

'No, I'm going to let him do it out of the back,' FB said. 'He's still cuffed. I'm not taking them off.'

'Boss?' Henry started to say, but FB had already turned away and was walking back to the vehicle. Henry watched him, aghast, as he unlocked the door, at which moment Henry realized what a big mistake that was.

121

As soon as the door was unlocked and FB had lifted the handle, Johnny Asian booted the door with the flat of his foot and with all his strength. This caught FB unawares and the heavy door, made heavier by the spare wheel, slammed into him and forced him off balance. He tripped and fell splat on his backside into a deep, muddy puddle.

Henry moved as Johnny leapt from the back of the Land Rover like a greyhound out of a trap, weaved sideways – and here Henry saw that he had somehow managed to squeeze his right hand out of the cuffs – and sprinted away. Before Henry had even got completely out of the Audi, the last sighting he had of Johnny was of him flashing across the road and vaulting the low wall into the dark valley beyond and into blackness.

Eight

Johnny had actually been dreading Charlie Wilder's return home from prison. He would have been much happier for him to have rotted in a cell for the rest of his life.

Johnny had a very big, increasingly fat reason for not wanting Charlie back on the scene, one which that night had become much more serious.

Johnny had known Charlie and Luke Wilder for most of his life.

With Jake, the lads had spent their early years

growing up together in very poor, high-rise council flats in Rochdale. They had attended the same primary and secondary schools, though the verb 'attended' could only loosely be applied to the four of them as far as educational establishments were concerned.

They formed a loose-knit gang and spent years running free and uncontrolled through the streets, gradually becoming more feral and dangerous as they grew into teenagers. All four got a lot of pleasure from beating up other kids and some adults – such as teachers – over whom they swarmed like a pack of hyenas bringing down injured prey – and they hurt their victims, often badly.

Crime was part of their upbringing.

Petty crime at first. Shoplifting in Rochdale town centre, stealing from individuals, then robbery – using force to take money or goods, often from defenceless, unsuspecting older people they targeted on pension day. As they grew older they gravitated to armed robbery and gleefully 'took down' countless small convenience stores across the Greater Manchester area. Their offences became increasingly violent and aggressive, and although the police hunted for them, they managed to avoid their clutches.

It helped that Charlie's father inherited his father's farm in Whitworth when the old man died. Charlie's dad – a rogue and drug addict – moved him and Luke up to Whitworth, which, of course, was over the border in Lancashire, not in Manchester. This meant that the gang committed their crimes in one county, but lived in another, making it much harder for the police to capture them.

They would plan the robberies, commit them, then hurtle back across the border and go to ground in the farm as though they were the Hole in the Wall Gang. They took great pains never to rob anywhere in Lancashire because, as Charlie drummed into them, 'You never, ever shit on your own doorstep – golden rule.'

All four eventually ended up living in Whitworth, with Johnny and Jake living mostly with Johnny's elder sister on the Wallbank council estate.

Life was fairly good for them, the combination of state benefits and money from crime keeping them all reasonably happy.

On the whole, the relationship between the four young bucks was never really dented by the appearance of girls on the scene. Females were generally treated badly, screwed and dumped, sometimes shared, but they never became a source of conflict or jealousy.

That was until Annabel Larch crashed into them and Charlie started going out with her. It was more than his usual casual relationship, though the macho Charlie was often at pains to describe Annabel to the rest of the gang as 'just another fuck', but the others could tell they were hollow words.

He had pretty much fallen for her; otherwise, as Luke once commented drily, 'Why would he put up with her shit?'

The biggest problem with Annabel was that,

after the first flush of hot lust, it transpired that all she wanted was a steady home and a peaceful life. She had been as wayward as anybody in her teens, but as she crept into her twenties, thoughts of motherhood started to overpower her and she became desperate to settle down and have kids.

For his part, Charlie tried his best to impregnate her just to stop her from moaning, but despite his best efforts, his issue did not appear to have enough 'whumph' to pierce its way into Annabel's very fertile eggs.

It was for this very reason that Charlie ended up in jail.

After six months of trying and no success, an argument ensued between the couple as she intimated that their relationship might be doomed if he couldn't get her 'up the spout', as she so colourfully described the beauty and mystery of motherhood.

This point of the argument was reached after a lot of alcohol in a pub in Whitworth and their loud exchange, which verged on violence, resulted in Charlie being asked to leave the pub by the landlord. When he refused, the landlord ejected him forcibly with the help of the police.

Charlie staggered drunkenly through the streets of Whitworth, simmering with rage and embarrassment. He then had an encounter with an entirely innocent middle-aged man out walking his dog, whom he had never met or seen before. For no good reason, this man made the error of inadvertently glancing at Charlie and became a victim.

Charlie attacked him ferociously, then set about kicking the life out of the unfortunate dog, which was pounded to death by the flat of Charlie's shoe. The man was left unconscious with a fractured skull and just for good measure Charlie rifled through his pockets and stole his wallet.

Had Charlie left it at that, he might have got away with it, but he reeled into an off-licence and bought some more booze with the injured man's cash. Unknown to him, as he fumbled with the man's wallet he dropped a credit card, which was left behind as Charlie left the shop bearing his six-pack.

The shop owner knew Charlie, so when he picked up the card and saw the name on it wasn't 'Charlie Wilder', he called the police.

From that point on it was fairly easy for the local cops to join up the dots and an arrest swiftly followed.

After two months in custody on remand, Charlie found himself standing in front of a grim-faced Crown Court judge and jury where his guilt was easily established. His defence counsel argued well for him and despite the judge calling him an 'evil, violent man', he was fortunate not to get more than the four-year jail term handed down to him. He came out two years later under licence and wearing a tag.

The man he assaulted recovered slowly from his injuries – but was never the same again. The dog, sadly, was buried.

Charlie never once thought about his victim or the dog he'd stomped to death.

On one of her frequent visits to him in custody, Annabel professed her deep and undying love for him and promised to be there on his release, when they would try again for a kid.

She did try her hardest to remain faithful.

Luke, Johnny and Jake visited Charlie as often as possible initially, but travelling over to Preston each week was a tedious, expensive journey and as time passed the visits became fewer and fewer and the three remaining lads, having lost Charlie's vigorous impetus, became more lazy and dissolute.

It was about twelve months into Charlie's sentence when Johnny bumped into Annabel in the Dog and Partridge pub in Whitworth. She said she was going to visit her banged-up boyfriend next day but was struggling for a lift. Johnny said he could use his sister's car, an old banger, and would be willing to take her if she wanted.

She said yes, thanked him and gave him a peck on the cheek, the imprint of which stayed with him all that night.

Johnny drove her to Preston next morning and she went in to visit Charlie. Johnny didn't show his face and asked Annabel not to mention he had given her a lift. Even though Charlie was in prison, Johnny was wary of him.

On the way home, Johnny took the scenic route, driving back through Blackburn and over the high moors across into Rossendale. As the car chugged over Grane Road, snaking over the moor, Annabel unexpectedly leaned over and planted a sloppy kiss on Johnny's cheek. He almost swerved off the road.

'Thanks,' she cooed.

After bringing the steering wheel back to its central position, Johnny said, 'No problem.' He felt a flush up the neck and a rush down into his groin.

'Always liked you, Johnny. Always thought you were the decent guy in the gang,' she said, watching his profile and his colouring up with a smirk on her face, knowing full well the effect she was having on him.

'Ta, but I'm just as stupid as the others.'

'No, no you're not.'

She leaned over, but this time slid her right hand on to his left thigh, tucking it intimately down between his legs where his balls rested.

He jumped. 'What you doing?'

'D'you fancy me?' she whispered seductively in his ear.

What was there not to fancy, Johnny thought, in his simplistic head. She was fit, slim, had lovely tits and he had always harboured a fantasy about screwing her behind Charlie's back. But he had never let this show. Charlie was far too dangerous an individual for Johnny to make a move on his girl.

Annabel tucked back a wisp of her hair behind her ear and leaned even closer.

She moved her hand, twisted her wrist and cupped his balls over his jeans.

Johnny emitted a gasp as the blood flooded into his penis. 'You're Charlie's lass,' he said, but at

128

the same time he did not want her to take her hand away.

'And Charlie is in a friggin' cell . . . and I haven't had a cock in my hand for a year and it's driving me crazy.'

She started to unzip him.

He swerved around the next bend as she peeled down his underpants and revealed a very rampant member.

'Oh God,' he groaned.

'Shine a light,' she said appreciatively as she took hold of him. This time the swerve across the road almost caused a collision with an oncoming car. Johnny only just managed to correct the car in time.

'I'm pullin' in here,' he hissed urgently. He slammed on and drove on to a car park for the Clough Head Visitor Centre off the Grane Road. There was a small café here and it was a popular start and end point for hillside ramblers. Johnny veered across the car park and skidded to a grit flinging halt and before he knew it Annabel had lowered her head and had taken him into her hot, wet mouth. His left hand snaked down the back of her skirt, into her pants, and cupped her pussy, which was as hot as a blast furnace.

And that was the beginning of their relationship.

They kept it under wraps. Johnny did suspect that Luke had sussed what was going on, though he said nothing, even if his looks and the odd comment betrayed his knowledge. Jake, the least intelligent member of the gang, did not have a clue.

As Charlie's release date approached, things became tense between the two young lovers who had become smitten with each other.

Johnny did not really have a lot of time to consider things, because from his prison cell, Charlie began calling the shots again. Luke returned from his visits to Preston with instructions and promises from Charlie, and he expected Johnny and Jake to do what they were told. The gang was getting its act together and prosperity loomed over the horizon.

Luke and Jake were excited.

Johnny wasn't, but he was sucked in and realized he could not pull out of it.

There were jobs to suss out and other things to do.

Charlie wanted to carry out a robbery on the day he was released. It had to be an afternoon job and have a substantial amount of cash. Luke found an Asian-run convenience store in the Spotland area of Rochdale that seemed ideal. The gang watched it for a few weeks and followed the daughter of the owner to the bank a few times. Jake claimed he watched her deposit fifteen grand, but that later turned out to be rubbish. There was also the mysterious property Charlie wanted Luke to find for him. Somewhere in Rochdale, some run-down shop or something. Luke never told Johnny and Jake what Charlie was thinking, but it eventually became clear to Johnny that Luke hadn't got a clue either. He was just following instructions.

There also had to be several vehicles sourced, which was Johnny's speciality.

Johnny stole a big four-wheel drive Toyota Land Cruiser from Manchester and changed the plates, then left this vehicle in Preston for Charlie and Luke to use for the 'bit of personal business' Charlie needed to complete on the morning of his release. Johnny also arranged for another car for Charlie and Luke to swap to after this mysterious business so they could travel back home after the Toyota had been dumped and torched. Whilst this was all going on in Preston, Johnny and Jake would be driving back to Whitworth in the Chevette (another car acquired, but not stolen, by Johnny) carrying Charlie's electronic ankle tag.

Johnny also had to arrange for two vehicles to be used in the robbery itself, as well as sourcing a sawn-off shotgun and ammunition for Charlie to carry.

Johnny knew he was good at getting all these cars and stuff and although he didn't exactly know what was going on in terms of Charlie's big plans, he had to admit he was actually quite enjoying pulling all these bits together.

However, the question of him and Annabel still hung in the air.

Johnny tried hard when Charlie arrived home and found it exciting to go on the robbery, but even he was shocked by the high level of pent-up violence in Charlie and the image of the shop-keeper being blasted by the shotgun lingered vividly in his mind, as did Luke's unnecessary beating up of the shopkeeper's daughter – but Johnny guessed that was just bravado on Luke's part, sucking up to his brother, trying to prove himself.

Late that afternoon, they got together at the farmhouse up on the moors – after having the shit-scare of the police roadblock on the lane, which turned out to be nothing at all to do with them, but something happening at Abel Kirkman's place. That had been an anxious couple of minutes as the cop talked to Charlie and Luke, who were driving the old Range Rover, followed by Johnny and Jake in the Chevette. Johnny had half-expected to see the officer's head get blasted off.

They made it unscathed to the farmhouse where, waiting for Charlie's triumphant return home, were stacks of booze, food, some weed, DVDs and an Xbox linked up to the TV with lots of games to play.

And Annabel.

Charlie made a very public display of slobbering kisses all over her and touching her up in front of everyone, and although she made occasional eye contact with Johnny, she made a good job of welcoming home the returning hero and lover, who, on the way, had murdered two men and was not even thinking about it.

After Charlie had fondled Annabel's bottom and made a few remarks about it having grown somewhat, he turned his attention to the booze and tossed a four-pack to each gang member before dragging Annabel across to the settee, plonking her on his lap and expertly flipping the tab on his beer with the thumb of one hand, whilst wriggling his other hand up her short skirt.

Then he looked around, beaming, raised the can and said, 'I'm fucking home, lads.'

They all raised their cans in response, but maybe Johnny's did not go up quite as high or as enthusiastically as the others'.

His girl was on the lap and in the arms of another man, whose hand was up her skirt – and it hurt badly.

The great plans that Charlie had for the future were unveiled expansively and authoritatively as the drinking, eating and smoking began.

Johnny sipped his beers slowly, listened quietly, but Charlie's overfamiliarity with Annabel was getting him more agitated and he had to fight hard to control himself, especially when she managed to give him a hopeless look of despair. He also did not like the fact that Charlie's plans were a done deal; the thought of essentially being a pimp did not sit well with him.

Sometime in the early evening a car drew up in the farmyard outside. Charlie heaved Annabel off him, saying, 'You've become a heavy bitch,' and went to the door as someone knocked.

A few moments later he re-entered the living room followed by Hassan.

'Guys, guys,' Charlie said. 'I want to introduce you to Mr Hassan. Mr Hassan, this is Johnny.' Johnny raised his beer can. 'And this is Jake. You already know Luke, my brother.' Hassan smiled warmly, clasped his hands together and bowed graciously. 'Mr Hassan is our new business partner.'

An announcement Johnny found somewhat ironic, bearing in mind Charlie's recent gunning down – with glee – of an Asian man, as though killing an Asian person conferred a special status . . . and now he was working with one.

Johnny almost guffawed into his beer.

Charlie and Hassan stepped back into the entrance hall, closed the door behind them. Their muted voices could be heard through the door and at one point the decibel level rose into an argument, then subsided again. The front door opened and a couple of minutes later Charlie stepped back into the living room ahead of Hassan, who roughly pushed two young girls in ahead of him. Luke immediately recognized them as the ones he and Charlie had had sex with earlier at the brothel in Preston.

Johnny sat upright, frowning.

Jake did the same, but his eyes lit up. If the gang had been a litter, Jake would have been the runt. He appreciated anything he could get, was happy to chase scraps and be Charlie's gofer.

But Johnny was instantly uncomfortable and did not like the look of these girls. Even a fool could see they were drugged up to the eyeballs, which were wide and dopey looking. Their whole demeanour was slow and not 'with it'.

'This is what it's all going to be about,' Charlie declared. 'And these two ladies are just some tasters for you guys to nibble on.' He laughed dirtily.

'Magic,' Jake said enthusiastically, rubbing his hands together.

'Thought you'd like it,' Charlie said. But he eyed Johnny and his lack of eagerness with suspicion. The girls stood on thin, unsteady legs, swaying slightly. 'Go on, lads, one each for you guys.' He indicated Johnny and Jake. 'Screw 'em till your heart's content.'

'What about me?' Luke whined.

'Didn't you have your fill this morning?'

'Yeah – but I want it again.'

'Sloppy seconds, then.' Charlie pushed one of the girls towards Jake, who stood up and had to catch her before she fell over. 'Upstairs, back bedroom.'

With an expression of dumb happiness etched across his face, Jake waltzed the girl out of the living room.

Charlie put his hand on the lower back of the other girl and forced her towards Johnny.

She was extremely beautiful, Johnny had to admit. Dark skin, lovely green eyes shaped like almonds, slightly oriental in her looks, with a slender neck and body.

He took her to a smaller room upstairs, just a single bed in it. As if she was on autopilot she pushed him down on to the edge of it, gyrated her slim hips sensuously in front of his face and began to remove her clothes. This was not a particularly complex manoeuvre as all she wore was a pair of three-quarter length cargo pants and a baggy T-shirt. Under these garments she had on a grubby bra, and a gold thong ran through her shaved pubic area. She took off these last items and continued the rhythmic dance, squeezing and rolling her nipples and sliding her middle finger into her vagina.

Johnny watched, wincing, petrified and full of distaste. Not at her – she was the victim in all this – but at what Charlie wanted to get them into. He would rather rob supermarkets or steal cars, thank you. That seemed a far more honest way to make a living than using other human beings.

She sank to her knees in front of him, between his legs, and unzipped him.

Before she could take anything further, Johnny gently took hold of her round, pretty face and looked into her dead eyes.

It was almost as if she was seeing nothing.

'No,' he said.

'Those guys'll thank me . . . I brought them a coming home present,' Charlie boasted, leading Annabel up the stairs to the front bedroom of the farmhouse after waving Hassan goodbye. He would be back sometime later to collect his goods. He led her by the hand and almost swung her through the door, then flung her on to the double bed. 'I've been waiting for this,' he said, and pushed up her skirt, pulled down her panties and flicked them aside, burying his face between her legs.

Annabel grimaced at the ceiling, a tear rolling from her right eye, as she tried to accommodate and understand Charlie's pent-up lust. But she was tight inside, wound up, and although she emitted the right noises she felt nothing as he licked and probed her with his tongue and fingers, without finesse.

Then he rose above her, having discarded his jeans and underwear.

'Babe – you've got a tub,' he remarked, drawing his hand across her lower belly. 'Put on a bit of weight since I went away . . . kinda like it,' he said, and slid his hands underneath her backside to raise her so he could slam brutishly into her.

'No, no, no,' she screamed and wriggled away from underneath him, rolling off the bed on to her knees, where she covered her face with her hands and sobbed uncontrollably.

'What the hell?' he demanded. 'I'm home, I want a shag – is that too much to ask? Get your lardy arse back on to this bed and suck me off,' he ordered her.

'I can't,' she cried, 'I don't want to.'

Rage surged through him as he leapt off the bed and hauled her roughly to her feet, shaking her, the two facing each other with the lower portion of their clothing missing.

'You can't? What d'you mean, you can't? You're my girl and we do what I want,' he growled, jerking her close by gripping both her elbows. His mouth was close to her ear. 'Get that? I'm outta stir and I need something that you have,' he whispered as his hardness brushed against her. 'So you lie down on that bed, open up and we will shag until the cows come home, yeah? Until you hurt, because that's how I'm feeling.'

He stood back, his lips ripped into a snarl, his booze-ridden breath overpowering her, making her feel sick. She tried to push him away, then sagged on to her knees and retched on the floor.

'Jesus,' he said contemptuously, 'what have you been eating?'

Annabel wiped the spittle away from her mouth with the back of her hand, then she rose unsteadily and stood bravely before him. She thrust out her belly. 'You said I was fat? Big arse, big gut.' She placed her hands above and below her stomach, tenderly cupping it.

'Yeah, you got fat.'

'No . . . no I didn't, I got pregnant.'

Charlie's face screwed into a ball of disorientation. 'What do you mean?'

'You know what pregnant is? Up the duff? Well, I'm up the duff. I'm going to have a baby and I'm glad about it.'

Suddenly the bedroom door crashed open and Johnny came in.

Charlie and Annabel's eyes shot towards the intruder.

'I'm pregnant and Johnny's the dad.'

Charlie had got over his incomprehension and abruptly understood each word. He spun savagely to her and punched her hard in the stomach, as hard as he could. She doubled over and sagged down to her knees, clutching herself.

Johnny leapt across the room with a roar, arms extended.

Charlie twisted, brought up his forearms and

knocked Johnny sideways, deflecting the attack. Then he laid into him.

In pure physical terms, Charlie should have been no match for Johnny, who outweighed and outreached him. What made the difference was Charlie's mindset of merciless, no-conscience aggression – and that would always reign victorious.

He fell on to Johnny in a frenzy, using his fists to beat him into submission.

'So this is it, eh?' Charlie paced the floor. 'I get banged up and then I get cheated on by my girl-friend and one of my best friends. One of my gang. I thought you were my family,' he screamed.

He stopped pacing and stood directly in front of Johnny.

They were all back in the living room, fully dressed.

Johnny and Annabel had been thrown across the settee.

Luke and Jake stood by the door, both terrified by the events.

The two prostitutes had been herded down the cellar steps, the door closed and locked behind them.

Johnny and Annabel watched Charlie.

'This,' his hand swept around the room, 'is the thanks I get.'

He was bouncing with rage, shaking with it.

'Bastards!' he hissed. 'Bunch of bastards.' He spun ferociously to Luke. 'Did you know? Did you know they were shagging?'

Luke swallowed, shook his head in a lie. He knew all right.

'I feel like I've been shafted, well shafted.'

'We're in love,' Annabel cried.

Charlie glowered hard at her, the strength of his stare forcing her to cower. 'Love my arse. I've been taken advantage of. I'm in the friggin' slammer for two years and you know what I'm doing? No? I'm plannin' our future, getting us out of the robbing business into something easier, more lucrative . . . real money.'

'What?' Johnny sneered through his cut and swollen mouth. 'Keeping girls prisoner while blokes come and fuck them?'

'If you want to see it like that, yeah. But they're just business, that's all. And anyway, that's not the point. Point is, while I've been banged up, working out our future – our future,' he stressed, 'you two fuckers have been having it off behind my back, taking me for a complete nob.'

'I don't want your future,' Johnny said. 'At least there's a dignity, a bravery in robbery . . . not keeping girls as slaves.'

'Fuck you and fuck what you think.' Charlie leaned into him, then he stood upright, turned to the silent, awestruck Luke and Jake. 'You two with me?'

They nodded.

'OK – drag this bastard out to the stable and chain him in one of the loose boxes. We're going to beat him to death.'

Annabel tried to hold on to Johnny, covering herself with his blood, but they dragged him free and out through the front door. Annabel raced to the window to watch and screamed with horror when, halfway across the yard, Charlie scooped up a pickaxe that was just lying on the ground and whammed one of its points into Johnny's backside, causing him to scream and fall and roll in agony.

He was in total blackness. A dirty hessian sack had been pulled over his head and tightened with a drawstring around his neck.

His hands were bound in front of him with thick parcel string, then a loop of rope had been threaded around the string between his wrists and he had been tied to a metal ring in a loose box in the stable block, which had not seen a horse or any other type of livestock in it for twenty years. The place was in virtual decay, but the fixtures and fittings were still there, if rotting and rusting.

He stood, straining to hear.

He knew Charlie and Luke were circling him silently, like leopards. He could sense them.

Then he heard a dull slapping noise.

He knew what it was.

Baseball bats being smacked into the palms of hands.

Sounded like dull applause.

Johnny's breathing became tight as he tensed himself for the first blow, already knowing how this would go because he had once seen Charlie attack someone with a bat. That time he had relished a laid-back approach and had not started with the head because that would have ended it all far too quickly. Charlie had gone for the limbs first. The muscles in the arms and legs, softening them up, causing them to spasm in pain. Then the joints. Knees, elbows, shoulders, causing excruciating pain. Then the stomach, back and ribs, until finally, at the point where the victim had thought he had felt all the pain that could be dished out, Charlie went for the head.

Charlie would begin that section with a bit of playful prodding and tapping of the skull. Then the force of the blows would increase in power, gradually building until there was a crescendo of contacts, after which point the victim would be unconscious and would not know if he had lived or died.

The slapping stopped.

Johnny tensed.

The first strike was on the back of his lower right leg, the calf muscle. Charlie hit him hard. Johnny gasped and sank to his knees, only to be heaved back on to his feet as the pain from the blow radiated up and down his legs, making him want to vomit.

'Pussy,' Charlie sneered.

'You gonna hurt me, just get it over with,' Johnny hissed through his clenched teeth.

'I'm going to have too much fun to get it over with quickly,' Charlie said, his mouth close to the side of Johnny's head. He rammed the end of the bat into Johnny's ribs and pushed him sideways.

Johnny heard the swish of air, braced himself, not knowing where this one would land.

Whack! The other calf muscle.

Johnny dropped to his knees, his head drooping.

He heard Charlie laugh harshly. 'This is the cost of betrayal.'

Through the hessian, Johnny heard running footsteps and breathlessness.

'She's gone, done a runner,' he heard Jake's voice say urgently.

'You what?' Charlie demanded.

'She's gone, must have legged it.'

'And how did that happen?'

'Dunno.'

'All I wanted you to do was keep an eye on her while I sorted this scum-bucket out, you useless sack of—'

'I know, Charlie. I just went for a piss and when I got back, she'd gone . . . sorry, sorry,' he said piteously.

'We need to get her,' Luke said.

'Come on,' Charlie said. 'This one can wait . . . you take the Chevette, Jake, see if you can spot her on the lanes, me and Luke will take the Range Rover – hey, and if you see her, run the bitch down. You have my permission.'

Johnny heard their feet as they ran out, then the vehicles starting up and driving away, leaving him. He immediately started to pull the sack off his head and then, bracing himself against the wall, tried to rip himself free from the ring.

Without any idea of what had befallen Annabel, but knowing she had managed to escape, Johnny eventually broke free and began to run away from the farm into the night, stumbling through the heavy rain, limping badly from the wound in his backside, along stone-strewn paths, trying to keep his balance, jogging, falling, tripping, but putting distance between himself and the farmhouse.

But then, vehicle lights appeared behind him.

He sank down to his knees in their beam, recognizing the sound of the Range Rover engine. He was exhausted, drenched and in a praying position, fully expecting to be killed this time.

Nine

The irony of a situation was rarely missed by Henry Christie, or any associated cringing embarrassment.

The last time he had lost a prisoner who had been in his custody – one who had simply managed to slip out of his cuffs and do a runner, as opposed to one who had been broken free by a gang – was in 1982.

Over thirty years ago, when he had been a uniformed constable.

Even now, all those years later, Henry still winced at the memory. He had driven all the way to Dover to pick up a young man who had been circulated as wanted for burglary in Lancashire and had been picked up by Kent Police at the port. On the journey back, whilst the car Henry was driving was stuck in traffic on the M6, the prisoner had managed to squeeze his hands out of his cuffs, unlock the door of the car and leg it across the motorway. Even the fact that he later successfully rearrested him didn't soften the shame of it all.

In the bollocking that followed, Henry's feet hardly touched the ground.

And that, of course, was the irony. He and the young policewoman who had been accompanying him on the prisoner escort had been obliged to parade on at Rawtenstall Police Station and have their dressing down delivered by the detective inspector.

That man had been a self-centred, controlling monster, who had ruled the roost with a rod of cold, hard steel.

His name had been Robert Fanshaw-Bayley.

The man who, at that very moment, was slumped mournfully in the patrol inspector's chair in Rossendale Police Station in Waterfoot, which had now replaced all of the old police stations in the valley, including Rawtenstall.

The man who had gone on to become Lancashire Constabulary's chief constable.

FB.

He was drenched, dishevelled, and looked as though he had been thrown from a coal scuttle into the chair.

He raised his eyes piteously at Henry, who stepped into the office and gently closed the door.

'Fuck me, Henry,' FB said despondently; but then, in his true, inimitable style, he reapportioned the blame for the escape. 'What a pair of silly old twats we must look.'

145

Henry blinked, took it on the chin. FB was the chief, after all.

'Those young 'uns out there must be wetting themselves,' FB said.

'Those young 'uns out there are too busy running around like blue-arsed flies, trying to keep a lid on the town, to be chortling over it. Despite the rain, Rawtenstall and Bacup have both kicked off, big style.'

'And hardly anyone on duty – which I already know.'

Henry shrugged. He had just been talking to the patrol inspector, who had filled him in on staff numbers.

'Covering the whole of the valley tonight,' Henry said, 'are eight constables, two sergeants, two PCSOs and four special constables . . . and there's a dog handler out there somewhere.'

'That's plenty.'

'Between five towns,' Henry stated.

'Shit,' FB said, slumping back. 'Is that all?'

Henry nodded. 'Yep – so there won't be anyone searching for our lost boy. He's the least of anybody's worries. Best thing we can do is circulate him and leave it at that. He'll turn up. They always do.'

'What do we do then?'

'Well, I don't know about you, boss, but once I get my ducks in a row, I'm going to go knocking on a door or two.'

Henry left FB stewing in the inspector's office, reasonably sure that he hadn't even considered any of the historic irony that Henry had seen. He probably didn't even remember humiliating Henry and the poor policewoman and Henry wasn't about to remind him.

He made his way to the canteen, did a search through the cupboards to see if he could find materials to make a brew. He discovered some hidden tea bags, some milk in the fridge, and was able to put a brew together in two mugs. He took one down to FB, then went into the sergeant's office, which was deserted.

He had one or two calls to make.

Johnny had raced away from the back door of the police Land Rover leaving the tubby cop in a puddle of dirty water, sprinted across the road and sprung over the low wall, not knowing what he was jumping into, other than a completely black void.

From the road, the dry stone wall was about three feet high. On the other side, the drop was about twice that and Johnny fell through the darkness for what seemed like a disorientating aeon before hitting the ground, which fortunately was soft, wet, deep grass. It was also a steep slope and Johnny began to half-cartwheel down the incline before coming to a stop at what was the bottom of a tight valley with a narrow stream running through it.

The breath was smashed out of his body and he lay there in desperate pain from both his injuries and the bone-jarring halt, staring up into the sky, the rain pounding into his face.

He remained still, but twisted his head slightly

to look back up the slope and could just make out the figures of the two cops peering stupidly over the wall, trying to see him.

He did not move, got his breath back, his eyes fixed on the cops who walked up and down, gesticulating angrily, then giving up. They were not coming after him and he heard the engines of their vehicles start up and drive away.

Slowly he got into a kneeling position, feeling the pull of the sutures which had closed the wound on his buttock.

He knew he had to get going, but spent the next ten minutes painfully easing his left hand out of the handcuffs. It didn't come out as easily as the right one had done – because he had the ability to self-dislocate his thumb and little finger on the right, which enabled him to minimize the circumference of that hand – painfully, it had to be said – and draw it out of the cuff ring. The left hand wasn't as simple, but with some very tough manipulation and scraping of skin, he eventually squeezed it free, then tossed the cuffs into the stream.

He slithered and slid his way back up the slope to the road, reaching the wall and looking cautiously over it. The cops had definitely gone, so he clambered over and began to jog-trot back towards Bacup.

His mind was on Annabel – and a baby he hadn't known about until he'd burst into Charlie's bedroom with the intention of dragging Annabel out of the situation and declaring everything to Charlie. He had come through the door just as she had revealed her pregnancy to Charlie and the news had stunned both men.

Johnny ran on in the rain, limping badly from his wounds and beatings, but with only one thing on his mind – to get back to Annabel, rescue her from Charlie's dangerous clutches, and maybe kill Charlie if he had to.

The inner chant he kept repeating to himself spurred him on.

'Gonna be a dad, gonna be a dad, gonna be a dad . . .'

'Have you any idea what time of day – or night – it is?'

Henry did not respond to the voice at the other end of the phone line. He had expected this type of rejoinder and waited patiently for the tirade to subside, even though the person he was talking to was of a much lower rank. A lowly detective constable, to be exact.

The reason why Henry allowed this person to be such a cantankerous and insubordinate jerk was that Jerry Tope was a little bit of a whizz where computers were concerned. Tope had very 'well-honed on-line investigative skills' – as he liked to call them – with an uncanny ability to drill down for information. In other words he could hack into other people's computer systems anywhere in the world and, if he so chose, leave no trace of his visit. He had once been caught foraging through an FBI database and was pursued around the world by FBI computer geeks, who pinpointed him to his actual computer in his office at Lancashire Constabulary HQ. They were so impressed by him that he had been almost headhunted by the FBI and he had never made the same mistake again. His job was as an intelligence analyst in the Intelligence Unit of the force, and he was much valued and sought after by many people, including Henry, who allowed his obnoxiousness up to a point – especially at this time of day.

'I know exactly what time of day it is,' Henry said. He checked his watch and raised his eyebrows, not realizing it was that late. He had called Tope at home and disturbed him from his bed, but sometimes that was how it was and Henry did not feel apologetic. Nor did he want Tope to hack into any computer he wasn't allowed to; tonight he just wanted him to do his job.

'And yet you disturb me.'

'Yes. I want you to do some background and body checks for me,' Henry said. He was impatient now, just wanted to get on with things.

'Now? Won't a PNC operator do?' Tope moaned. 'I'm in my jim-jams.'

'No; I want you to dig behind the headlines,' Henry said. All a PNC operator would do was check a name or car registration number, not necessarily delve beyond that. 'Got a pen?'

'Wait . . . don't want to wake Marina,' Tope said, referring to his wife. Henry heard shuffling, footsteps, doors closing, then a big sigh. 'Go on then.'

'Annabel Larch, early twenties, born Rochdale at a guess. Johnny Asian, ditto. Both from

150

Rochdale or Whitworth, but I don't think Asian is his real name.'

'Dates of birth would be helpful.'

'Nope . . . see what you can dig up.'

'For the morning?' Tope said hopefully. 'You know I was at work until nine this evening with Rik Dean's case, the murder of that prison officer.'

'No, I didn't know, Jerry, and no again, not the morning, now.'

'But I'm sat in my living room in my jim-jams,' he reiterated.

'And I know you have a computer from which you can access the force mainframe and any other mainframes you bleeding well want to.'

'Not officially.'

'No, not officially, but do it, eh?'

'Why so important?'

'Because I think I'm about to go into the lion's den.'

'How very fucking dramatic.'

'That's me, Jerry, a real drama queen. Oh, there is one more thing . . .'

Jerry Tope hung up and shook his head crossly, but not too crossly. He had worked regularly for Henry for the past few years and, whilst it would be wrong to say he had enjoyed every moment, Henry was a good boss and had saved him a couple of times from major downfall. Henry looked after his people and in turn expected them to jump when he yelled.

Tope yawned and stretched, then went back upstairs to the spare bedroom he used as a study.

Though he was a computer nerd and it might have been expected that he would have a bank of screens and monitors and stacks all lined up, there were actually only two laptops in the study. Most of the space was crammed with home-brewing equipment, with various beers and wines fermenting away in the room.

His love of computers themselves was minimal. He saw them only as a means to an end, because what really drove Tope was his inquiring mind, his thirst to search, to get into places he wasn't allowed to be and discover hidden gems. In some ways he saw himself as the Indiana Jones of the cyber world and sometimes he enjoyed being discovered and chased, likening it to being pursued by a huge boulder that he always escaped from when it hit an opening only he could fit through.

At least that was the metaphor he had in his mind to explain and make interesting what he did.

He sat at his desk, shook his mouse and brought one of the laptops to life.

He hadn't closed down the work he had been doing for DCI Dean and the Preston murder, although there was precious little at the moment. A couple of witness statements had already been inputted on to the HOLMES system, which was the computer system used by all forces in England and Wales to record and cross-check information generated by large investigations.

Tope had been looking through the statements to see if there was any information he could extract that would be useful in helping to nail the offenders, but there was very little in a statement from a window cleaner or one from the woman who had been having an affair with the dead prison officer. Statements would start to flood in later; then he would be really busy.

His eyes glanced briefly through the two statements, then he shut them down and diverted his energies to Henry Christie's requests.

Annabel Larch knew she would eventually have to face Charlie and she was dreading the moment, but the way she envisioned it working out was nothing like the horrific reality that transpired.

She had well and truly fallen for Charlie four years earlier when she was eighteen and coming under the spell of a guy like him was no surprise to her. From the age of twelve when she had lost her virginity in a backyard shed on a Rochdale council estate to a lad very much like Charlie, she had gone for the bad boys.

Loved them, ran with them, was there for them whatever.

She went through a series of low-level drug dealers, drunks, fighters and loud-mouthed oafs who treated her badly because she let them, but they also gave her a good time in return for lots of sex and excitement.

It was a period in which she drank heavily, snorted coke, smoked cannabis and generally had a ball, with a few minor convictions chucked in there for good measure.

Then she met Charlie in a pub in Rochdale and hooked up with him, realizing he was a very big step up from the other lads she had been seeing.

He took his violence to another level.

At first, this excited her.

Over a four-week period, once, she witnessed him seriously assault six people, not one of whom deserved it. But that didn't matter. It made the violence more compelling, watching the victims' incomprehension as Charlie jumped on their arms and heads, hearing them sometimes plead, 'Why?'

The fact that Charlie also headed a small gang of criminals also sent a shiver of anticipation through Annabel. He was on welfare benefits, but made some real money carrying out armed robberies at corner shops and convenience stores around Manchester. The gang was even nick-named 'The Surgeons' because of the modus operandi of always using a surgical face mask and back-to-front baseball caps to hide their iden-tities, and, of course, they were never caught. This was, Charlie boasted, because he led them well – plus they always ran back over the border into Lancashire to lie low after a job.

Strangely, Annabel thought it was evidence of Charlie's love and devotion to her when once, after a robbery, when he was buzzing on adrenalin and she had given him a blow job to bring him down, he had grabbed her by the hair, twisted her face up to his and warned her, 'You know you're mine, don't you?'

She swallowed. 'Yeah, yeah.'

'And if you ever – ever – go with anyone else, I'll fuckin' kill you and him. You know that, don't you?'

'Yeah, Charlie, I won't ever do that. I'm your forever girl . . . I love you.'

That was before she wanted a baby.

That in itself had been a very odd, unsettling sensation, one she never ever thought she would feel. It was probably not helped by the fact that most of her girlfriends were now pushing kids around in prams, meeting up in cafes and pubs, and having a completely different social life to hers. She was being left behind and, also, when she looked at a tiny baby, something inside her melted like soft toffee, but she couldn't quite understand what she was feeling. She just knew she had to have a rug-rat, as Charlie so colourfully called them.

She had broached the subject during one night of sex with Charlie when, as he rammed himself into her, she stopped him gently and looked into his lust-tinged eyes.

'Charlie, Charlie, stop,' she'd cooed.

'Why? I'm nearly there,' he gasped.

'I know, I know, I know . . .' She kept her eyes locked into his. 'Charlie, d'you love me?'

'Yuh, now can I—?'

'I want us to have a kid – your kid,' she informed him.

'What?'

'I want to be a mummy, I want you to be a daddy.'

He was excruciatingly close to his orgasm, although he was encased in a condom. 'OK, so what are you saying?'

'Take it off.'

He did, and the intercourse was over seconds later.

Almost six months later she still wasn't pregnant and the tension was growing between them, arguments, disagreements bubbling constantly, until the night in the pub in Whitworth when Charlie's anger spilled on to the streets and he made the mistake of attacking a man walking a dog.

Even when he was jailed for four years, Annabel had every intention of remaining true to him, but then she began the ill-fated fling with Johnny Asian, fell in love, got pregnant easily.

The scenario she ran through her mind was that on his release, she and Charlie would have a civilized discussion, a quiet understanding, maybe one last kiss goodbye. Sort of romantic, in a way. Painful, maybe . . . not a horrible night of torrential rain and Johnny being led away to be executed like a Taliban prisoner. Two years without daily contact with Charlie had dulled Annabel's knowledge of just how bad a man he really was and when she saw Charlie swing the pickaxe into Johnny's leg as he was taken across to the stable, she realized that things had got as bad as they could.

Escaping from Jake had been the easy part – in spite of the horrendous pain in her stomach following Charlie's punch. Jake was the dim one in the gang and she convinced him that if he needed to go to the toilet, as he complained he had to, she would stay where she was.

He went and she had done a runner into the cold, wet night.

Grabbed her coat, ran into the dark fields, heading down towards Whitworth, eventually bursting into the Cock and Magpie, then found herself being driven back up to the farm by the detective, who had proved to be completely useless as Charlie had embroiled her back into the nightmare.

And now she was back with Charlie whose anger had not lessened. It had continued to grow with violent intensity.

After Charlie had grabbed her back into his custody on the track, he had driven her up to the farm, dragged her upstairs and thrown her into the main bedroom, then locked the door.

After this he had gone on the hunt for Johnny to the hospital and sent Luke and Jake into A&E to deal with him while he stayed at the wheel of the Range Rover.

Once more, that same cop had intervened and had had the effrontery actually to chase them back to Whitworth, but Charlie had returned victorious and, from what Annabel could hear with an ear pressed to the bedroom door, they had somehow ambushed the cop and driven him away with his tail between his legs.

She heard footsteps on the stairs.

She drew away from the door, sat on the edge of the bed, listened to the lock turning, watched the handle go down, the door creak open.

Charlie looked terrifying, standing at the door.

Annabel's whole being contracted, everything in her going to protect the unborn child.

He stepped in, closed the door softly.

Said one word. 'Betrayed.'

'Charlie—' she began pleadingly.

He raised a hand, palm out, for silence.

Her mouth clamped tight shut.

He stood in front of her, looking down at her through dead eyes.

'Charlie, I don't feel well,' she whispered. 'My stomach. It hurts so much.'

He wriggled his fingers, inviting her to take his hands. Tentatively she reached out and he raised her gently to her feet. She trembled from head to toe, could hardly keep upright because of the terror that blanketed her. She stood in front of him, swallowing, looking into his eyes.

'Betrayal,' he whispered.

'I know. I'm sorry. It wasn't planned.'

'Clearly.'

She could hardly breathe now.

'You know I'm going to kill him, don't you?'

She nodded.

Then without warning he punched her hard and deep in her stomach with his fist, driving it in with all his power.

She doubled over as the pain shot through her and all the air rushed out of her body.

Charlie took a step back and smashed the back of his hand across her head, sending her sprawling across the bed. Then he leapt on to her, straddled her chest and slowly, very deliberately, placed his hands around her slim neck and began to squeeze, softly at first, then ferociously.

Ten

FB was still sitting despondently in the inspector's office when Henry returned. His face hung long, his embarrassment still deep. He looked through tired eyes at Henry as though he had surrendered everything.

Henry frowned for a moment as he looked at the man who had pretty much ruled most of his career as a detective.

FB had also been a career detective, up to being a detective chief superintendent, but things changed at and above that rank when cops simply became managers and little else.

'I feel very fucking old,' FB said. 'Too old for this, anyway.'

Henry settled himself on a chair and said, 'Operational policing is a young person's game.'

'Yeah – and they can keep it,' FB said. He shook his head miserably. 'I can't believe I fell for that,' he said absently. 'I just can't.'

'Happens to the best of us,' Henry assured him.

FB grunted, unimpressed. 'How are your ducks swimming?'

'Just waiting on a call back from Jerry Tope.'

'Ahh, computer geek guy. Is he still on duty?'

'From the moment he stupidly answered my call.'

FB chuckled, his mood lightening a little. 'So you're going to go and knock on a door?'

'Kick it down if I have to. It's what I do.'

'It's what I used to do – a bit, anyway. Always liked to send in the expendables ahead first if at all possible.'

'No expendables available tonight,' Henry said. 'Just the unemployables – me and you. The patrol inspector said, and I quote, "they're fighting in lumps out there". All expendables run ragged.'

'And you think you need to go and pay this farm a visit tonight?'

'I'd say so.'

FB thought about it and made a decision. 'I'm coming,' he declared.

'Could I send you in first?' Henry asked irreverently. 'You could be my expendable.'

They both laughed . . . but they were words that would come back to haunt Henry.

Whilst the distance from the point where Johnny had escaped from the police Land Rover, back over the moor road and down into the tiny village called Weir that straddled either side of the main road, was not so great, pushing against the wind and rain, and suffering from his injuries, it seemed to take him a long time to get to a place where cars were parked up.

Johnny needed to get a ride and the only way he knew how, other than thumbing a lift, was by stealing a car – something he was good at.

In Weir, rows of terraced houses lined either side of the main road, with cars parked both ways along the road outside the houses.

Johnny had two rows to go at.

160

He walked slowly through the village in the direction of Bacup, keeping to shadows whilst slyly trying door handles, because he knew the easiest way to steal one was first to get into a car that was already open. It saved having either to force the lock somehow or simply smash a window, which was always a danger point.

Frustratingly he did not find one that was unlocked. His spirits lifted when he came to the Weir Hotel and saw four cars on the unlit car park, all of which looked old; older meant easier and better for a car thief without tools.

Keeping to the shadows, he sneaked into the car park.

The pub was all in darkness, the houses across the road too.

He looked at the cars, weighing them up.

The one he chose was an old Peugeot 205, a two-door hatchback. He crouched and crossed over to it and to his absolute joy found it was unlocked.

He was in it quickly, dismantling the box under the steering column, exposing the ignition wiring. He did it all by touch, expertly running his fingers along wires, knowing from instinct and experience which were the relevant ones that needed ripping out and touching together to fire up the car.

It started first time.

He drove it quietly off the car park and didn't switch on the lights until he was a hundred metres away from the pub, heading towards Bacup.

His mobile rang. 'Henry Christie.'

'Me, Jerry.'

'You got something for me?'

'Yeah, yeah,' Tope said indifferently. 'What you asked for, I think.'

'OK, fire away.' Henry raised his eyebrows at FB, still occupying the inspector's chair. Henry reached for a pen and paper.

'First off, Johnny Asian: like you said, that's not his real surname. He is actually Jonathan Richard Goode, born 1992 in Rochdale. Johnny Asian is his nickname because—'

'He's quite dark-skinned?' Henry guessed.

'I was going to say I assume that. I have a not too recent photo of him and he looks slightly Asian, but I don't think he is at all.'

'And?' Henry urged him.

'Got a couple of convictions from his early teen years for car theft in Rochdale, not on us. Last known address is Rochdale, but that doesn't mean anything.'

'Associates?'

'Not listed on what I'm looking at; I'll probably have to delve into GMP's intel database for that.'

'Do it,' Henry said. 'What about Annabel Larch?'

'Bit of form. Shoplifting cautions as a juvie, one minor public order conviction when she was eighteen. Also from Rochdale, last known address there, too.'

'Associates? Boyfriends?'

'Nothing more than that so far.'

'Keep digging.'

'But it's my bedtime.'

'Mine too, yet here I am, turning out – with the chief constable, of all people – possibly to make some arrests to show shiny-arsed bastards like you how it's done.'

'Thanks for that,' Tope said.

'If the cap fits.'

Tope pressed the disconnect button on his own mobile phone, sat back and closed his eyes. Before long his head dropped forwards, chin on to chest, and he drooled disgustingly before jerking awake. Then he glared at the computer screen and was suddenly a little annoyed with himself. The information he had found out for Henry, whilst valid, had not been very much. In fact, a PNC operator could have found it without much effort and Jerry Tope considered himself a rung or two above PNC operators, valuable though they were. He was cross with himself because he hadn't tried very hard and was uncomfortable with it.

However, he was having problems concentrating.

He knew the remedy for that, so he shuffled quietly down to the kitchen and filtered a strong coffee, laced it with sugar and milk, then carried it back up to his study, plonked himself down again and shook his mouse.

'Right.' He geed himself into action. 'Let's see what I can find.'

The chief constable had long since given up travelling with much police equipment, other than his personal radio and old-style handcuffs, so Henry decided that he needed to be kitted out as if he was actually serious about doing a ride-along with him. That meant finding him some gear.

Fortunately the patrol inspector was still racing around the police station and Henry collared him to explain his requirements.

'I need a stab vest for the boss, plus a utility belt with CS, handcuffs, a baton and a torch, and if there's a hi-viz jacket knocking about, it might be useful.' The last item was the short waterproof jacket worn by most officers when out on patrol. If he and FB were going knocking on doors in the rain and the darkness, Henry thought it would be prudent to be wearing clothing that easily identified them as cops. Henry already had one, but the chief, it transpired, had not.

Another irony, Henry thought. The chief would gladly bawl anyone else out for not having equipment; it was that well-worn rule of management, 'Do as I say, not as I do.'

'Follow me.' The inspector beckoned. He took Henry to a storage room on the first floor in which a lot of things had been discarded. He found a tattered hi-viz jacket that looked roomy enough to encompass the chief's body mass, plus an old utility belt which, he explained, belonged to an officer who had recently been sacked. The guy, in a fit of pique, had unceremoniously dumped all his gear at the front door of the nick and it had all subsequently been put into storage with a view, eventually, to sending it back to clothing stores. He then led Henry back to the sergeant's

164

office where he unlocked the CS store. Henry and FB each signed out a canister. He also managed to find each of them a small Maglite torch (but made no promises about the battery life) and an extendable baton.

Henry got his own gear from the boot of his Audi, cringing, almost crying again at the sight of the damage to the car caused by the baseball bat attack.

Back in the sergeant's office, FB put on the stab vest, then the hi-viz jacket, then wrapped the thick leather utility belt around his wide circumference, rather like wrapping a saddle strap around an elephant. He inserted the CS gas canister into its slot, then the baton into its loop and the torch into its pouch.

Henry was doing the same, experiencing a bit of a thrill of excitement at this prep work.

When both men were fully kitted out, they appraised each other.

'Lookin' good, boss,' Henry said.

'And you, officer.'

FB checked himself in the full-length mirror. It was the closest he had ever been to actually putting on a uniform for operational reasons in about thirty years. He occasionally wore one for ceremonial or other duties which required him to be in blue, but otherwise he avoided it like the plague. 'I'm not sure what I look like,' he said disconsolately.

'A cop what means business,' Henry said, trying to big him up a bit. Losing the prisoner seemed to have had a very big negative effect on him.

'Yeah, yeah,' he said, turning as if he was trying out a new suit, looking at how it fitted around his rump, 'I'll have that. Mean and nasty.'

Henry found the patrol inspector again and asked him if there was a large-scale map of Whitworth. There was. Henry, FB and the inspector unrolled it and laid it flat on a desk, pinning it down with radios and, inexplicably, a battery-powered salt grinder.

They tried to pinpoint Britannia Top Farm. Although it was quite a detailed map, they couldn't see it, even as Henry circled his forefinger on the area where he supposed it might be, following the route he had taken with Annabel, past Abel Kirkman's place, up to the point where he had stumbled on the assault on the farm track.

'Doesn't seem to be there,' he mused, frowning. 'There's Abel's place, then Red Pits Farm – but I assume we drove past that one . . .'

'Maybe you misheard?' the inspector suggested politely.

'Always possible, I suppose,' Henry conceded, his eyes roving the map. 'There's Britannia Quarries, which we know of old.' He glanced at FB, who blinked. 'We went to a murder there many moons ago.'

'Yeah, I recall . . . long time ago,' FB fibbed.

'So,' Henry mulled, 'how do we find it?'

'Knock on doors?' FB suggested. 'Isn't that what cops do?'

The inspector ducked out of the room and came back a moment later having snaffled a Thomson

Local directory which he was flipping through under the farm listings. 'Not in here.'

'Might not be a real farm, y'know, could just be a converted farmhouse or barn or something,' Henry said.

'In that case, let's knock on some doors, shall we?' FB said, now impatient.

Henry nodded. He liked knocking on doors.

'I mean, if you are worried about this girl Annabel, and these guys did attack you with bats,' FB said, 'let's get going, show these young buckos how you do it.'

'Yeah, I am actually quite worried about her,' Henry said. 'I do wonder why they grabbed her . . . can't quite work that one out. So, yeah, I'm concerned about her but I also want to catch the little gits who assaulted me and battered my car.'

'Hiya babe.'

Henry stood under the protection of the front awning of the police station, the rain still falling heavily. Despite the waning charge on his mobile phone battery, he had decided to make one last call home before setting off to Whitworth. Alison had picked up the phone at the Tawny Owl quickly.

'Hello.' She sounded cool and clinical.

Henry gulped. This evening was not going well in so many ways. 'You OK?'

'I am.' Pause, then, 'Where are you Henry? M6 northbound?'

'Still stuck in Rossendale.'

Her impatient intake of breath was very audible.

'Sorry, but things've kinda got complicated . . . need to go and rattle some cages.'

She tutted and said, 'Henry,' with frustration.

'I know. Got to be done, though, love.'

'Well, take care. How are your injuries, by the way?'

'Sore. Car's not very happy now, either.'

'What?'

Henry explained and she said, 'Jesus, you're a walking disaster.'

'I know. Is Rik there?'

'I'll put him on.'

There was rustling on the line, an unidentifiable whisper, then Rik Dean's voice came on. 'Henry, what the heck's happening in the land of the lost?'

'Just got caught up in some shenanigans,' Henry said, explained a little and concluded, 'just have to see it through.'

'But you're OK?'

'I'm with FB, how could I be anything other?'

'Yeah, course.'

'How is the prison officer murder going?'

'Not sure yet, but there will be a full team on it tomorrow, incident room at Preston is sorted, eight a.m. kick-off.'

'Good. Put Ali back on, will you?'

She came back on the line. 'Henry?'

'I'll be back as soon as I can, love,' he promised.

'Good,' she said firmly, then, 'Henry?'

'What, sweetie?'

'Can this be the last time? I . . . well, you know

what I feel . . . I want you back here, not galli-vanting all over the place at stupid o'clock, getting battered.'

'I'll do my best.'

She had softened now and they exchanged a few lovey-dovey words and hung up. As he did so he noticed that his screen was warning of a low battery. He stood there for a few moments, watching the rain tipple.

He could empathize with Alison's point of view. She had previously been married to a soldier who had been serving in Afghanistan. She too had been a soldier, a medic. One day her husband had gone out on a routine patrol with his unit and never returned. He and his colleagues had been ambushed in a tiny village and stoned to death. As much as she had moved on from the horrors of those days, they still haunted her occa-sionally and, whilst Henry was unlikely to encounter situations nearly as dangerous as those her husband had faced, she was understandably wary when Henry was late coming home. She was desperate for stability and safety and for Henry to retire so they could live and work together full time – and get married.

In his turn, that was also what he ultimately wanted.

Somehow he could not quite let go of being a cop. He knew he was being weak and stupid – but.

FB came out and stood beside him. He grunted a greeting and pulled out a packet of cigarettes, lit one up. Henry didn't even know FB smoked.

It came as a bit of a shock, but he made no comment.

FB blew a lungful of smoke into the atmosphere.

'E.T.?' FB asked.

'Eh?'

'Phoning home?'

'Ahh.' Henry nodded, getting the cinematic reference.

'Still shacked up with that landlady?'

'Very much so.'

'Nice.'

FB inhaled more smoke, hissed it out through his nostrils and stared at the rain in the fluorescent glow of the street lights. 'You phone home a lot?'

'Not as much as I should,' Henry admitted. 'Big mistake not to.'

'Yeah,' FB said pensively.

'I thought I'd be different, y'know, with this one.'

'What do you mean?'

'Made too many mistakes with Kate, then left it too late to put right. I tried, but she was gone before—' Henry stopped, wondering why he had begun to say all this here and now. In all the years he had known FB, the two of them had hardly spoken a personal word with each other.

'I know what you mean,' FB said, surprising Henry.

'You do?'

'Oh ay.' FB took another drag. 'I made mistakes like that. I mean, don't get me wrong, my wives didn't die—'

'Your wives? You've had more than one?'

'On my third now. First two couldn't hack it, both pissed off and we got divorced quietly. I'm not proud of it, but I only realized too late that the important thing is family, not work . . . though you can never repeat that,' he warned Henry.

Henry shook his head, realizing he knew so very little about that side of FB.

'Going to make it right,' Henry said determinedly.

'Good for you,' FB said. He took a final drag on the cigarette and flicked it out on to the foot-path where it sizzled in a puddle. 'We going to bust some bollocks, then?'

Henry nodded.

Tooled up, Henry and FB set off from the police station towards Bacup, then bearing off to Whitworth. Henry was driving a type of vehicle he had not used for many years, and remembering just how uncomfortable a Land Rover could be. Hard seats, terrible suspension, foot pedals that required a ton of power to operate, steering that required lots of biceps muscles and windscreen wipers that were virtually ineffective in clearing rain off the windows. And a heating system that blew only cold air so the windscreen was constantly steamed up.

'Bloody hell,' Henry whined, wiping the steamed-up window with the back of his hand and having to open his door window a crack to get air to circulate, in an effort to keep the screen clear. The pay-off was that rain came through and soaked his shoulder.

171

'Used to drive these all the time,' FB said, 'when I was in uniform.'

Henry didn't respond. Despite the drawbacks, they were actually good vehicles for policing places like Rossendale, dependable and sturdy. They went up and down hills very well.

He drove on, still thinking about Alison and about phoning home and his unreliable history.

He tried not to have regrets or carry any guilt from his past, but he still blenched when he thought about Kate, his now dead wife. In a roundabout way, she had been introduced to him by FB, inasmuch as Kate had been unfortunate enough to discover the body of a missing girl and the then very young Henry had taken a witness statement from her. That was the start of their relationship and subsequent marriage.

Much to Henry's distress, he realized he had given her too many unpleasant times during their marriage but even though they had got divorced at one point, Kate had really stuck to Henry, and following their remarriage he had really tried to be the husband he should have been in the first place. Sadly it had been a relatively short-lived period because of the very aggressive cancer that invaded her body, and she died before Henry could really give her the life she deserved. That was one regret he allowed himself.

His own life had moved on with Alison Marsh, to whom he was now engaged. In Alison he knew he had found a gem, but there were still times when he found himself putting work first again when he didn't need to, especially at this late stage in his career.

And the awful truth was, he really did not need to be making his way to a bleak farmhouse in the middle of nowhere, on a stormy night, to knock on the door of a bunch of toe rags, but here he was. Driven to do it. The knock on the door could have waited until the morning and any sane person would be at home, tucked up in bed, spooning up to a hot-arsed partner.

Which was probably the crux of the matter.

He wasn't completely sure if he was normal and sane.

Eleven

Johnny abandoned the Peugeot at the top of Oak Street in the Facit area of Whitworth. Although he knew he had to move quickly, he realized that driving the car straight up to Charlie's farm, even in the pouring rain, lights off, would be foolhardy. What he needed to do, if he was to have any chance whatsoever of rescuing Annabel and the baby from Charlie's clutches, was get up to the farm by stealth. He had no plan other than that. He had no idea where she would be or even if anything untoward had happened to her. For all he knew, they could have kissed and made up, but he doubted that.

Charlie forgave no one, ever. Especially not a pregnant girlfriend.

Johnny knew the area well, and by ditching the car on Oak Street he could take a short cut via the fields and footpaths on to the moors to sneak up to the farm.

He was soon creeping through the darkness.

After sinking the remaining mouthful of lager, Charlie Wilder screwed up the can and threw it fiercely against the living room wall before releasing a disgustingly powerful belch.

He picked up the sawn-off shotgun and held it diagonally across his chest, then broke it open and pulled out with his fingernails the spent cartridges used during the robbery – the ejector spring did not work – threw them down and slid two new ones in from his pocket, then snapped the weapon shut.

He focused on the gun for a long time before raising his eyes and looking at his brother Luke and friend Jake. His eyes were set deep and dark in his skull now, fearsome in their intensity and hatred.

'Well?' he asked Luke.

'What?' Luke answered with trepidation.

'Is she alive?'

'Yeah, yeah.'

'What happened?'

'I don't know, I don't know,' Luke babbled.

The brothers locked eyes.

'I don't know,' Luke said again, weakly. His nose had started to bleed again and he held several pieces of scrunched-up kitchen roll to it. He was feeling dithery and afraid now. He had been outside the bedroom earlier, listening to what was happening inside as Charlie exacted his revenge for Annabel's unfaithfulness.

Then it had gone silent and a moment later Charlie had appeared at the door, his face strained and terrible, and pushed Luke aside, at the same time ordering him to 'sort the bitch out'.

Swallowing and terrified, Luke had slowly entered and seen Annabel on the floor, curled up into a tight foetal ball, gasping for breath, clutching her stomach and emitting a low, pitiful, moaning sound.

Luke stood watching her, not knowing what he should do, still covering his own face with a blood-soaked kitchen cloth. He wasn't sure if his nose was actually broken, but it was his own fault for letting that cop at the hospital get too close to him.

He watched her while she managed to get on to her hands and knees, her head hanging loosely between her arms, blood dripping thickly from the facial injuries – even worse, there was blood between her legs. But he did not move to assist her as she dragged herself, leaving a smear of red across the carpet, into the en suite bathroom and slammed the door behind her.

'She's still in the toilet, I think,' Luke said. 'Doesn't look good.'

'What are we going to do, Chas?' Jake asked.

Charlie's death stare turned slowly to the other gang member. 'If you'd managed to run her over, we wouldn't be in this mess, would we? You can't do frig-all, you lot.'

'I nearly got her,' Jake said defensively. 'But that cop pushed her out of the way.'

'Whatever . . . take her out to the stable,' he growled in a low, deep voice. 'Tie her up, then we'll have a think.'

Jake remained transfixed, unmoving.

'Like now,' Charlie said. 'Both of you, get her, take her to the stable and tie her up like the fucking animal she is.' He swung up the shotgun. Both ducked. 'Now,' he screamed, making them surge into action.

She was back in the bedroom, perched on the edge of the bed, when Luke and Jake entered.

'Luke, Luke,' she said, speaking through a mouth that had had six teeth either knocked out or loosed. Her eyes were black, swollen, and there were terrible marks on her neck, around her windpipe. 'Help me, please, I think I've miscarried.'

Luke hesitated, a quick weighing up of the pros and cons, then thought better of it. There was no way he could help her. Instead, he steeled himself and strode over to her, grabbed her arm and heaved her to her feet, saying, 'Got what you deserved.' He swirled her across the room to Jake and between them they half-carried her along the landing, down the stairs to the front hallway where Charlie, the shotgun held across his chest, waited.

She was light, easy to manhandle, had no fight in her. Luke and Jake had no trouble dragging her between them on her knees, the ground tearing at her flesh, into the stable where Johnny had previously been held.

They dragged her to the same loose box, then Luke bound her wrists with flex and yanked her across to the wall, ran wire between her wrists and secured her to an animal tethering ring like the one to which Johnny had been tied.

As he worked through the scenario, Luke could see no good end to this. Charlie had gone mad, of that there was no doubt, but to stand up to him could be disastrous.

Luke stood up. 'Done. She'll not get out of this.'

Charlie nodded.

'What we doing about those prossies?' Luke enquired delicately, remembering the two women locked in the cellar.

It was a question Charlie could not answer well. 'Hassan's supposed to be coming for them at some stage, don't know when. They can stay there till then.'

Charlie turned and headed back to the farmhouse.

Luke and Jake exchanged a look, then followed.

'I want to kill him and I want to kill her.'

A long shiver shot through Luke Wilder's whole being at his brother's words, which were spoken quietly, but with the venom of a cobra. He now seemed to be in some kind of demonic stupor.

The three young men were back in the living room.

Jake hovered by the front window overlooking the yard and the stable opposite.

Luke was sitting across from Charlie who was on the settee, trying to control his breathing.

'Bro, bro,' Luke said softly. 'You need to take a step back from this. I know how you're feeling, mate, I know how you must be hurting—'

'No you do not know how I'm feeling,' Charlie said, angling his head towards Luke, his eyes in deep shadow. 'I feel like I've had my guts torn out by Jack the Ripper, that's how I feel.' He exhaled long and hard. There was another can of lager in his hand. He tipped it to his lips. 'And that's how I want him and her to feel. I want to rip their insides out. I want to plunge a carving knife into their guts and disembowel them. I want to hang them both up by their ankles and let them bleed out a horrible, painful death with their innards hanging down in front of their faces. That's what I want.'

Jake's stomach turned at the thought.

Luke said, 'That's not going to happen, Charlie.'

'You challenging me?'

'No, no I'm not, Charlie, but we need to sit back here and think things through.'

'Why? Why should I?'

'Look, man,' Luke said pleadingly. 'You have to back off here . . . this should have been a great day, yeah?'

'Yeah, should have been – and it was until I was betrayed,' he spat.

Luke tried not to let his eyes roll in irritation.

'So . . .' Charlie sat upright, stared at Luke. 'Did you know that Johnny was banging her?'

'No,' Luke lied firmly.

Charlie saw through the untruth, but rotated his head slowly to Jake, who shrank under the gaze.

178

'What about you, Jake boy? Did you know?'

'No, honest, Chas, I didn't,' he insisted, but his body language – the shrugs, the jerks, the tics – indicated otherwise.

'Liars, both of you.' Charlie sat back, disgusted.

'Charlie,' Luke tried again, plaintively. 'We don't need any more shit today. We took out that screw and got away with it. We pulled a job and downed a Paki, and we got away with that, too. Why don't you just cut these two loose? She's just a friggin' girl after all, a nothing. You can have any girl you want. But if you top her and top Johnny, then we'll achieve nothing. Don't you get it? The cops'll be on us like a ton of rocks. And Johnny won't say owt to the cops, because he's too shit-scared of you. Me and Jake'll follow you to the ends of the earth, mate . . . but you have to let this go.'

Luke and Jake stared expectantly at Charlie, who seemed to be taking it all in, seeing sense perhaps.

Then a hint of movement in the yard outside caught the edge of Jake's vision.

Hiding behind the wreck of an old tractor, Johnny had seen his three friends drag Annabel across the yard from the house into the stable. It had taken all his willpower not to rise, shout, confront and intervene. He had remained silent and still, even though a fierce rage churned inside, not foolish enough to show his hand because of the shotgun – that he, Johnny, had supplied, together with lots of ammunition – in Charlie's hands.

The wait for them to reappear from inside the barn was never-ending.

His imagination made him feel faint as he wondered what they could possibly be doing to her. She looked as though she had already suffered greatly under Charlie's fists, but the lighting in the yard was poor and all Johnny could really make out was the fact that Jake and Luke were dragging her across the ground like a carcass.

They came out and ran back to the farmhouse, Charlie storming ahead of them.

Even then, Johnny did not move.

He remained concealed in the shadow thrown by the old farm vehicle, watching the house.

It looked as if they had gone back for the duration.

Johnny started to creep slowly on his hands and knees towards the stable door. He kept to the deep shadow, focusing on moving slowly, deliberately, and getting to Annabel without being spotted.

Eventually he reached the stable door. This was where he became completely still again, now on his haunches. He looked across at the farmhouse, seeing Jake's figure at the window with his back to the yard, the curtains not drawn. Jake's shoulders rose and fell as if he were shrugging.

The three were obviously in deep discussion, probably arguing.

Johnny seized that moment, pulled the stable door open wide enough to ease through the gap.

Once inside he came up on to his feet, feeling the tug of stitches on his buttock. The shot of pain made him jerk, but then it was forgotten as he saw Annabel tied up in the same loose box he had been in.

She wasn't moving.

'Need a fag,' Jake said. 'Going out.'

Charlie and Luke glared at him, said nothing.

Jake fished a crumpled packet of cigarettes from his pocket, and a disposable lighter, and fitted a cigarette between his lips.

After one last, surreptitious check of the brothers, he left the room, walking past the under stairs door that led to the cellar on his way out. The thought of the two prostitutes locked in the blackness down there sent something unpleasant slithering through his veins, but he carried on out and stepped into the open porch that protected the front door.

Here he lit up, inhaled, exhaled, and squinted across at the stable.

Johnny turned her over carefully. She was not moving, didn't seem to be breathing.

'Babe,' he whispered, terrified, and fumbling desperately he started to unfasten the bindings that held her wrists together. 'C'mon, babe.'

She was still, lifeless.

Was she breathing?

Was her heart beating?

He could not tell, could not be certain.

As he turned and lay her gently on her back, her head lolled as if it was on a broken spring.

Johnny knew nothing about first aid, but he pushed two fingertips into the soft flesh of her neck, just under her jaw, feeling for what he thought was a pulse on the jugular. He bent over, trying to concentrate, to feel something.

Possibly.

He removed his fingertips and put his ear to her nose, listening for an intake of breath.

Nothing.

The stable door creaked.

Jake stepped in edgeways.

Johnny looked over, saw who it was and said, 'She's dead.'

It was as though Jake hadn't heard the words. 'You need to get out of here, Johnny. Charlie's going to kill you,' he whispered hoarsely.

'I said, she's dead.'

'I heard . . . and so will you be unless you get lost. You got to run, Johnny. From a mate, you got to run.'

Johnny wiped the back of his hand across his mouth.

'Did he kill her?'

Jake nodded.

'And you didn't try to stop him?'

'I–we . . .'Jake stuttered pathetically. 'We couldn't.'

'I remember times,' Henry Christie said nostalgically, 'when I was on crime patrol way back here in the valley, all those years ago, when me and one partner in particular used to have musically themed evenings.'

FB gave Henry a look of disbelief. 'Musically themed evenings?'

'Yeah, you know? A Beatles night, or a Stones night . . . even country.'

FB shook his head sadly.

'Simpler times,' Henry said wistfully.

'You fancy a sing-song now?' FB asked. 'I'm an opera buff, incidentally. I do a very creditable "Toreador".'

'I only know the rude version of that one,' Henry admitted. Seeing FB's look of puzzlement, he added, 'The one about masturbation.'

They were in Whitworth and Henry had driven the Land Rover up past the Cock and Magpie, heading up the hill, retracing the route from earlier when Annabel had been directing him towards Britannia Top Farm. The Land Rover bounced lumpily over the rough track and in a fleeting thought Henry wondered why he'd been stupid enough to take the Audi on the same route. He could have ripped the sump open.

He bore right at Cowm Reservoir and reached the point where he had stumbled on Johnny Asian being attacked.

He drove on slowly until the farm track split at a staggered T junction. To go right would take him back towards the Cock and Magpie – the route he had taken earlier ahead of the ambulance – so he turned left and stayed on the track past Abel Kirkman's place, ignoring any turn-off, of which there were a couple. He knew the moor was criss-crossed with tracks and paths, some suitable for vehicles like Land Rovers, others only just about suitable for sheep. He only glanced at Kirkman's place, but pointed it out

183

for FB's benefit. The route then really did start to become steep and Henry knew that if he kept on going he would reach the moor top on which were huge sandstone quarries, once the biggest in Europe, hacked into the landscape, leaving scars that would be there until the end of time.

A few hundred metres along they came to the first farm with a sign saying 'Welcome to Red Pits Farm'. The farmhouse was set back and Henry turned through an open gate into a farm-yard. He stopped outside the farmhouse.

The front door opened and a man appeared in typical farming gear: an oilskin coat, flat cap, wellington boots. A sheepdog panted at his heels.

Henry slid back the window.

'Sorry to bother you,' he shouted across the divide. 'I'm looking for Britannia Top Farm.'

'Never 'eard of it,' the man said gruffly.

'Oh.' Henry turned to FB. 'He says he's never heard of it.'

'I might be old, but I'm not deaf,' FB said sarcastically.

Henry poked his face out of the opening. 'Can you tell us what other farms there are up ahead?'

'Yeah, I can.'

Henry hissed quietly, 'Fucking farmers,' then asked, 'What are they called and how do I get to them?'

'Next one up's Lower End Farm, then after that, just before t' old quarry, is Whit'orth Top Farm.'

'But no Britannia Top Farm?'

'Nope,' he said lugubriously.

'And you don't know Britannia Top Farm?'

'Not as such, no.'

'What does that mean, sir?'

'Well, Whit'orth Top Farm used to be called Britannia Top Farm years back an' a lot of folks still call it that. It's interchangeable.'

'Oh, so when you say Whit'orth Top Farm, do you mean Britannia Top Farm?'

'That's what I said, din' I?'

No, Henry thought, you didn't, wondering why the farmer didn't just freakin' tell him. 'Who lives there?' he asked.

'Bunch o' scrotes,' the farmer said colourfully.

Jerry Tope knew he functioned best between the hours of nine a.m. and one p.m., at his headquarters desk, and after eight hours of good, solid sleep. He was nowhere near this peak when hauled out of bed after a long day and given a job to do with a frazzled brain, gritty eyes and not much information to go on.

The main problem with this scenario was his power of recall.

Between nine and one he was as sharp as a knife, could accumulate information both in his head and on the computer, see links, churn intelligence over and make connections based on the most tenuous of reports, sightings and statements.

He was good at his job.

He prided himself on just how good he was.

But not just now with a thick head from tiredness, and it was frustrating the life out of him.

It wasn't as though he had even unearthed very much information for Henry. He ran it through his mind. All he had done so far, since Henry had rudely woken him, was run a name search on two individuals, a male and a female, find out some information and pass it back over to Henry.

Still, there was something missing and his brain could not pinpoint it.

He rose from the laptop in his study and wandered back to the bedroom door, behind which his much-beloved wife Marina was soundly asleep and snoring loudly.

From there he retraced his steps, mentally and physically.

On the phone to Henry . . . downstairs . . . blah, blah . . . taking a few scribbled notes . . . listening to Henry's over-dramatic retelling of the night's events . . . going back to his computer, which had still been logged in to the HOLMES system regarding the suspected murder of a prison officer . . . closing down that link, then starting to search for the names Henry had given him.

It was there, somewhere.

He went back to his laptop, stared blankly at it, willing his scrambled-egg brain to kick into gear.

He took a long drink of his now tepid coffee.

Johnny Asian. Annabel Larch.

Stared at the computer screen for inspiration.

It was here, somewhere.

He swore, one word, continually, trying to drive his brain, tapping his forefinger on his desk with the rhythm of his chant.

Then he had it.

It was in Henry's verbal description as to what had happened at the hospital when the two men had arrived and attacked Johnny Asian, and also in a snippet from a witness who had seen the prison officer get run over and murdered. That was the connection Tope's brain was searching for.

Tope's throat dried up as he re-entered the HOLMES system and retrieved the two witness statements.

'Yes!' he murmured victoriously.

And there was something else, too, an item he had seen earlier on TV, the North West News. There had been the on-scene report of the death of the prison officer in Lancashire, followed by breaking news of an armed robbery in Rochdale in which a shopkeeper had been brutally gunned down and his daughter badly assaulted by a gang.

On the face of it, no link as yet.

A murder in Preston. A robbery/murder in Rochdale.

And Henry Christie's account of an assault at Rochdale Infirmary.

Slowly the pieces slotted together for Jerry Tope.

He snatched up his phone.

Johnny looked past Jake's shoulder and Jake himself spun guiltily.

The stable door had opened and Charlie entered, Luke at his shoulder, the shotgun cradled in his left arm.

'Well, well, well,' Charlie said on seeing the tableau in front of him. Johnny kneeling down by Annabel's unmoving figure, Jake standing close by. 'Looks like a Christmas card,' he sneered. 'Definitely a scene I'll be putting on my Chrissie cards this year.'

Removing his hands from underneath Annabel's head, Johnny rose slowly to his feet.

Jake backed away, his body language distancing himself from the couple.

'Did you know he was here?' Charlie said to Jake.

'No, honest . . . I just saw some movement—'

Charlie chopped his right hand down through the air like an axe falling, cutting off Jake's explanation. He did not want to know anything now as he looked across at Johnny.

'Come back to rescue her?' he asked.

'Actually, yeah – but she's dead.'

'Ah well, such is life. Now you can join her, Johnny.'

'You killed a baby too, by killing her.'

Charlie smiled at that. 'I'd already killed that. I killed it before she died, and I enjoyed it. I made her lose it.'

Johnny's face registered his horror. 'You bastard.'

'Yeah, what about that, eh? How does that feel – to have it all come fucking crashing down around you, EH?' He slapped the shotgun into the palm of his left hand, the forefinger of his right around the triggers.

Johnny raised his hands.

'If I shoot from here, I'll probably just splatter you with buckshot, but you know what I want to do, Johnny? Do you?'

'No.'

'I'll tell you what . . . I want to relive a dream I had. I want to put both barrels of this gun right up against your heart and pull the triggers. I want to blow your heart to shreds because of what you've done to me. In the dream, I couldn't see the face of the man I killed, but now I know it was you . . . I can see into the future.'

Charlie took his right hand off the butt, holding the shotgun with his left. He bunched his fingers into a fist and banged it against his own chest to reinforce his next words with a gesture.

'I—' *bang* – 'have—' *bang* – 'no—' *bang* – 'heart—' *bang*. 'You took it and danced on it.'

'We didn't mean to hurt you,' Johnny pleaded. 'These things happen, it wasn't planned, no way.'

'Did you know that every action has an equal and opposite reaction? I learned that in my GCSE physics class I took when I was in prison. That's when I was in prison being humiliated by you two. Remember that?'

His voice had started to rise uncontrollably up to a shriek. He brought the shotgun up and like an infantry soldier rapidly advancing, he stormed over to Johnny and forced the side-by-side barrels hard up against his sternum, then drove him backwards against the wall of the loose box and pinned him there, so they were eye to eye.

Then he laughed as he pulled both triggers and blew Johnny's chest apart, and because Johnny was pressed so hard against the wall, the recoil and back-blast were incredible and Charlie was splattered with Johnny's blood and shredded organs.

'Sorry to bother you, sir,' Jerry Tope said meekly.

There was a groan at the other end of the line as DCI Rik Dean attempted to wake up. He sat up, then walked naked over to the en suite bathroom, hoping not to disturb Lisa, fast asleep still, but also silently cursing because in the location he was in – a bedroom at the Tawny Owl – it was usually impossible to receive a mobile phone signal.

'It's all right, Jerry,' he slurred. 'I just hope it's good.' He yawned and scratched.

'Me too,' Tope said, still trying to arrange his own thought processes.

'Spit it out; it's been a long day and going to be another long one tomorrow.'

'Tony Dawson, the prison officer? One of the witness statements, the one from the window cleaner?'

'Un-huh.' Rik put the toilet lid down and sat on it.

'He says he got a glimpse of the occupants of the Toyota that did the deed.'

'Yeah.'

'Said he thought they were wearing baseball caps backwards and face masks.'

'Yep.'

'Er, could the masks have been like, y'know, doctors' masks? I know the guy describes them as making their faces look like Voldemort in the Harry Potter films.'

190

'It's possible, I suppose, but he didn't get that good a look. It was more of an impression. Why? Why is this important at this time of day? Couldn't it have waited?'

'Well, I dunno . . .'

'Jerry!'

'Well, I've been speaking to Henry about this job he's got sucked into over in Whitworth. You know what I'm talking about?'

'Yeah.'

'Well, while he was at A&E in Rochdale with an assault victim, two guys in back-to-front baseball caps attacked the guy again – and Henry, who chased them off, but they had another go at him when he caught them.'

'Right. Lots of yobs wear back-to-front baseball caps.'

'And surgical face masks?'

'Seriously?' Rik became interested.

'Something else, too,' Jerry went on. 'Mid-afternoon today, there was an armed robbery in Rochdale when, guess what? Offenders were wearing baseball caps on backwards and surgical masks. They killed a shopkeeper with a shotgun.'

Rik waited. He knew there would be more.

'I did a bit more digging and discovered that a team of robbers who always wore face masks and reversed baseball caps committed a ton of jobs over the Greater Manchester area. They got the nickname "The Surgeons".'

'OK.'

'Then I thought I'd have a look at this guy Charlie Wilder. He was released today from

Preston Prison, as you know. The one his cell mate said had made some threats to the prison officer.'

'Yeah. But I checked him out. It wasn't him,' Rik said.

'Why do you say that?'

'Because he's out on licence and has been tagged. I spoke to GuardSec, the security firm who monitor tagged offenders, and his read-outs show he wasn't even in Preston when my guy was crushed by the four by four.'

'Mm, yeah . . . I checked that out, too, in a roundabout sort of way.'

Rik didn't ask. He knew Jerry's computer hacking skills were legendary and that he'd probably been looking in the security firm's system.

'According to the records, he was nowhere near the armed robbery in Rochdale, either.'

'So – dead end?'

Tope winced. 'Maybe not – but I also did some digging on our intel re the address that Charlie Wilder has offered up as his home address, which is where the tag-tracker has shown him to be all day, since about an hour after his release. It's a council house on Eastgate, on the Wallbank estate in Whitworth.

'Current occupant according to the Burgess List is Monica Lee Goode. Henry was dealing with an assault on a lad he thought was called Johnny Asian, whose real name is Johnny Goode. Monica is his sister.'

Rik sighed. 'Where is all this going, Jerry?'

'It's just dots, I know; but another person Henry

192

was dealing with is called Annabel Larch, and she is Johnny's girlfriend, according to what she told Henry. She has a few minor convictions going back a while and on GMP's intel database, they have her boyfriend down as one Charlie Wilder and she gave evidence of his character at his trial.'

'Head hurts, Jerry. Bum's cold, too.'

'OK, OK. The last time this gang, the Surgeons, hit anywhere was just over two years ago. Charlie Wilder gets out today and, lo and behold, there is a robbery, and a serious one at that. The Surgeons are suddenly back in business. And we both know that Charlie was sent down for a serious assault two years ago . . . huh? Huh?'

'Keep going.'

'When he was arrested for that offence by a Whitworth bobby, his address was Whitworth Top Farm.'

'Fuck! So?'

'Whitworth Top Farm, according to council and Post Office records, was previously known as Britannia Top Farm.'

'And the guy has an electronic tag on his friggin' ankle, Jerry, which tells us he was nowhere near a murder in Preston or a blag in Rochdale at the appropriate times.'

'Um, yuh, bit of a stumbling block that,' Jerry agreed.

The two men fell into a concurrent, silent cogitation.

'Unless—' Rik started to speculate.

193

'He had the tag removed,' Jerry concluded for him.

'Is that possible?' Rik asked.

'Anything is possible.'

'Which now begs the question, why are you telling me all this? It could have waited until the morning briefing and you would have looked almost brainy. And why not tell Henry in the morning, too?'

'What d'you mean,' Tope asked, puzzled, 'tell Henry?'

'Well, he's in bed, isn't he?'

'Uh – no.'

Rik blinked. He had gone to bed quite late, after having spoken briefly to Henry on the phone, then waited up with Alison and Steve Flynn, but as Henry didn't show, Rik had gone to bed with Lisa, knowing he'd need a decent night's sleep to set him up for the next day, which would be long. Sitting there on that cold toilet lid, Rik had just assumed that Henry had landed at some stage and was tucked up with Alison.

'Where is he, then?'

'On his way to Whitworth Top Farm. I've tried to contact him on his mobile without success and spoken to Burnley comms to shout him and tell him to hang back, but neither of us can get through. I just thought that it would be prudent for him to go in mob-handed, as opposed to just him and the chief constable. He could be there now for all I know. I mean, it might all be OK, but—'

'Have Burnley deployed anyone to go and check?'

'No one available.'

'Well, he can look after himself, Jerry, and him and FB are pretty formidable.'

'I know what you're saying, boss, but if these are the guys he's already had run-ins with, they don't mind going for cops. He's already been assaulted by them and if he shows up on their doorstep out of radio and mobile range, it might just get dicey. That's all I'm saying . . . I just wanted your thoughts on it.'

'All right,' Rik said assertively, 'you get back on to Burnley comms and ask them to keep trying Henry and also to deploy a patrol as back-up, even if it means leaving an area without cops. I'm going to turn out unless I hear things are different.'

Charlie wiped the blood splatter from his face, flicking it away with disgust, but also with a grim smile of satisfaction. Luke stood just behind him, staring at Johnny's rag-doll body.

Smoke rose from the barrels of the shotgun.

Jake sank slowly to his knees, horror-struck.

Suddenly Luke's head flicked sideways. 'Hear that?'

'Hear what?' Charlie said.

'A car, a vehicle of some sort . . . on the lane . . . *listen.*'

Charlie tilted his head. It was there, the sound of an engine getting closer, someone approaching.

'Go see,' Charlie said.

Luke ran to the sliding door and pulled it back, then ran to the farm gate from where he had a view of the track leading to the farm.

One vehicle, lights on.

He cursed, then raced back to the stable.

'Cops!' he gasped.

Charlie regarded him cynically. 'Yeah, right, good joke.'

'It's true. A fucking police Land Rover.'

Charlie knocked his brother out of the way and strode out, saw the vehicle and ducked back in.

'You deal with 'em,' he told Luke decisively. 'Me and Jake'll do something with these two.' He indicated the bodies of Johnny and Annabel.

'What?' Luke said helplessly. 'Just what am I supposed to do or say?'

'Wing it, bullshit 'em. And if the worst comes to the worst, we sort 'em, OK brother?'

Twelve

'Guessing this is it.'

Henry drove the Land Rover in between the stone gate posts and pulled up in the yard between the farmhouse and the stable. He allowed the vehicle to idle and stand there in the incessant downpour while he took in the setting. A very decrepit farmhouse which had been allowed to deteriorate and had seen much better days. A lot of old, rusting machinery and tools were strewn around, including the decomposing hulk of a tractor.

There was a light in the farmhouse and Henry saw the shadow of movement.

Charlie and Jake dragged Annabel and Johnny across the stable by their legs and deposited them side by side in a stall in the far corner of the building. They tried to work hurriedly but it had proved more difficult than they imagined hauling dead weights, and the task had been forbidding and unpleasant.

Once in the stall, Charlie found a big square of rotting and brittle tarpaulin that had once been used for covering the contents of open trailers. He dragged it over the bodies to hide them.

That was the point at which Jake had sunk to his knees and vomited copiously on the stable floor.

Charlie watched him contemptuously, then spun away as he heard the police Land Rover drive into the yard and saw the flash of its headlights.

He pulled Jake to his feet, as he wiped spittle and vomit from his mouth. They ran across the stable, then up a ladder which led to a hayloft above, which was in essence a suspended wooden ceiling where winter supplies had once been stored for the horses once stabled there. Now it was empty, except for discarded farm equipment.

Once in the loft, they drew the ladder up behind them, though with its lack of use it had rusted on its runners and they could only pull it just over halfway up before it got stuck.

'Shit. Lie down, keep still.'

Charlie rolled on to his back, broke the shotgun and pulled out the spent cartridges with his fingertips. He fumbled one and dropped it. It rolled towards a gap in the loft floor and before he could catch it, it fell through to the stable floor fifteen feet below where they were lying.

Charlie found two more cartridges in his pocket, slotted them into the barrels and closed the weapon as silently as he could. Then he rolled back on to his stomach, edged to the loft hatch and looked down into the stable and at the big sliding door.

Outside, he could hear the lumpy engine of the Land Rover ticking over.

Henry stayed at the wheel, looking through the windscreen as the wipers continued to drag themselves ineffectually across the glass.

'Someone's in,' he said.

FB nodded, then said, 'Do you ever get the feeling . . .?'

Henry wanted to say something along the lines of, You mean that feeling honed by over thirty years of being a cop and dealing with the shitty end of the social spectrum, always expecting the worst from people but somehow never being pleased when good things happen? You mean that feeling, boss?

Instead, he simply said, 'Yes.'

FB shuddered involuntarily. 'Someone's just walked over my grave.'

The farmhouse door opened and a young man

appeared. He gave the officers a wave of acknowledgement.

'Recognize him?' FB asked.

'No.'

They remained in the car. If at all possible, Henry liked people to come to him so he could get some sort of measure of them by the way they walked, held themselves, their build, body language – and also, tonight, so he didn't have to get any more wet than he already was.

He thought he had pushed it a moment too far, but then the man relented, flicked his hoodie over his head and jogged across to the driver's side of the Land Rover. Henry slid open his window.

'All right?' Luke said.

'Yes. Is this Britannia Top Farm?' Henry asked, and saw the cut across the bridge of the man's nose.

'No, this is Whit'orth Top Farm.' Luke sounded relieved.

'Good,' Henry said. 'I'm in the right place, then.'

Luke's expression changed. 'What can I do for you? I'm getting well pissed-wet here.'

'Can we come in? Maybe more conducive to a nice chat.'

'Bit late isn't it?' Luke whined. 'Won't it do in the morning? I'm off to bed now, officer.'

'No it won't do, actually,' Henry said. 'Need a chat. Time of day is irrelevant.'

'You got a warrant?'

'What? For a cosy chat?'

'So long as that's all it is.'

'Why would it be any different?' Henry asked, knowing already it would be.

'Whatever.' Luke turned and jogged back into the farmhouse.

Henry killed the engine and glanced at FB. 'Wing it.'

FB nodded enthusiastically. 'I think I'm going to enjoy this.'

They climbed out, went to the front door, then went in.

Henry went ahead down the short hallway, right into the living room, taking in everything with his experienced eyes, including the very jumpy figure of the young man standing in front of the fireplace, in which no fire burned and which looked as if no fire had raged in it for many years.

He also saw discarded beer cans and bottles, crisp bags, overflowing ashtrays, an Xbox and all the signs that there had been a few people around, including the pungent, unmistakable aroma of spliffs having been smoked.

'Bit of a do?' Henry nodded around the room.

'Nah, not really.' Luke shrugged, pretended to yawn.

'Just a few mates around?'

'Summat like that.'

Henry made an exaggerated sniff-up. 'Bit of dope smoked, too, by the smell of it.'

'Somebody had a joint,' Luke admitted. That did not bother him. Cops weren't concerned with folk smoking dope in their own homes any more. 'It's nowt.'

'Still classified as a criminal offence,' Henry pointed out.

'Whatever . . . arrest me then,' Luke said.

'I might do, actually. What's your name?'

'Luke.'

'Luke what?'

'Luke Wilder.'

'OK. I'm Detective Superintendent Christie.' He did not bother introducing FB because it was awkward in too many ways.

'What do you want?'

Henry walked further into the room, a little closer to Luke, who watched him with unease – recognizing him as the cop who had punched him in the face at the hospital. Henry walked up to him.

'Who hit you in the face?'

'No one. Walked into a door.'

Henry nodded. 'Do you know Annabel Larch?'

'Should I?'

'It's an easy enough question.'

'Uh – no, then. That it?'

Henry pursed his lips, wandered around the room, peering at various objects. FB remained by the door, playing the silent cop. Henry said to Luke, 'You're a fibber.'

Luke instantly went red and his mouth tightened up.

'Listen, Luke, I'm a bit concerned about this girl, Annabel, you know? The young lady you don't know. I'm concerned for her safety, plus the fact I'm after some very nasty people who attacked me and my car, which was not a wise thing to do.'

'What's that got to do with me?'

'I hit one of those nasty people in the face, Luke.'

'Well, it weren't me. I haven't set eyes on you before.'

Henry smiled. 'OK, that said, I have reason to believe that Annabel Larch is here.'

'No she ain't.'

'You completely certain of that?'

'Yeah.'

'Has she been here at all?'

'No . . . like I said, don't know her.'

Henry stopped by the settee and picked up a short outer coat that had been dropped by the side of it. He held it up and recognized it as the one Annabel had been wearing when she fell battered and bloodied into the Cock and Magpie. He saw flecks of blood around the collar and shoulders, saw it was still drenched wet and dirty from when he had bowled her over out of the path of the car that had almost hit her. He held the article of clothing between his thumb and forefinger, letting it dangle ominously. He looked across to Luke who had gone very pale, yet remained defiant.

'Really?' Henry said.

'She isn't here,' Luke insisted.

'So you do know her?'

Luke's Adam's apple rose and fell very visibly in his scrawny throat. He shrugged to try and give the impression he did not care one way or the other.

'Suppose so. She must've left it behind.'

'How long ago did she leave?'

'Hour? Hour and a half?'

Henry continued to stare at him, feeling his own ring piece twitch as it did when he was on to something.

'I'm concerned about her, Luke.'

'OK, so what?'

'Is there anyone else in the house?'

Luke shook his head.

'In that case, if there's no one else to disturb, you won't mind me and my partner having a look around, will you?'

'Not without a warrant. This has gone well beyond a cosy chat.'

Henry sighed. 'If you think I need a warrant to search for someone who I believe is in danger, then you don't know your common law, Luke.' Henry turned to FB. 'You fancy having a stroll around the outbuildings, boss? I'll do the house.'

It was a big, extensive farmhouse, long and low with a living room, a further sitting room, expansive kitchen, dining room and ground floor toilet. The first floor consisted of six bedrooms of varying sizes, box room to palatial. Everything was in poor condition. Wallpaper peeled damply. Plaster looked to have been affected by wet or dry rot in many places. The furniture was old, and even way back, must have been cheap.

Henry mooched around the ground floor, then went up the tight, creaking stairs, having passed the door leading down to the cellar without trying it.

Luke followed closely.

On the landing, Henry glanced up and saw a trap door up to the loft, thought about it, dismissed it. The hinges had layers of unbroken paint on them. No one had been up there in years.

He went into each bedroom, finally ending up in the main one at the front of the house, overlooking the yard. He walked over to the window, set low in the wall, and had to bend his knees in order to see FB walk across the yard to the stable opposite. Henry watched him reach the sliding door and begin to open it.

He turned and saw Luke hovering at the bedroom door.

'You seen enough?'

Henry shook his head. 'Nope.'

He looked at the unmade bed, seeing indentations in the mattress, the sheets screwed up, thrown everywhere, and did not allow his expression to change when he saw blood flecks on the pillows. He crossed the room, entered the en suite bathroom.

Lying side by side, supported by their elbows, Charlie and Jake watched the sliding door open wide enough for a tubby, oldish looking cop to step in, wearing a hi-viz jacket. He came in a few steps, then paused and sniffed the air. He turned on his torch, flicking the beam around the inside of the stable, across the opening to the hayloft, making the two men duck instinctively.

FB did not seem to see them.

But his nose had picked up the scent of something acrid in the air.

He inhaled, almost tasting it on the back of his throat.

He took a step forward and his right shoe crushed underfoot something about the size of a cockroach.

He stepped back, crouched down to see he had stood on a spent shotgun cartridge.

He picked it up between his finger and thumb and shone his torch on to it, sniffed it, then slid it into his pocket and stood upright with a click of his knees.

Then he stood motionless for a few moments, simply listening, hearing the rain drumming down on the stable roof, looking and smelling and trying to imagine that he might be standing in a crime scene, knowing there was nothing better a cop could do in such a place than simply stand still, take it all in.

From that position he stepped forward to the loose box ahead of him, flashing his torch again.

In the hayloft, Charlie rolled silently on to his side and brought up the shotgun.

Alongside, Jake pissed in his pants, emitted a tiny whimper, then mouthed, 'He's going to find them.'

Charlie placed his fingertip on Jake's lips and leaned right up to his ear. 'Shut the fuck up.'

At ground level FB moved from loose box to loose box, not rushing, then he turned away and made a diagonal path back to the sliding door, squeezing through and drawing it shut behind him.

Looking across the farmyard, he saw Henry emerging from the farmhouse and the front door being closed behind him.

'Anything?'

FB made a popping sound with his lips and said, 'Yep.'

He held up the crushed shotgun cartridge. 'Stood on this.'

Henry waited for more.

'How about you?' FB asked, surprising Henry.

'Yep.' Two can play at that game, he thought. 'Anyway, a used shotgun cartridge . . . y'know, we're on a farm . . . not that unusual.'

'The stable reeks of cordite. This has just been fired or I'm a Dutchman, Fanshaw-van-Bayley.'

'Anything else?'

'Fresh blood, lots of it, in one of the boxes, all up the wall. Someone's been sick in there very recently, too.'

'Right.'

'And I think there are two bodies under a sheet of tarpaulin in one of the stalls, although I can't be sure it's two. The blood trail along the floor of the stable indicates at least one person has been dragged from one loose box to another. What did you find, Sherlock?'

'Blood all over the en suite off the main bedroom and something not nice looking in the toilet itself, maybe a miscarriage – not pleasant. And he's the lad I hit in the face.'

The two men stared at each other.

'Oh, and best till last,' FB said, 'there's someone

hiding up in the hayloft. Saw a movement, heard a whisper . . . two people at least.'

'You remember that feeling you were talking about? I've got it big style now.'

'Plan of action?'

Henry was about to respond, had opened his mouth to do so, but the reply was cut short as the front windscreen of the Land Rover exploded into a million fragments. A spray of pellets from the shotgun fired by Charlie Wilder disintegrated the glass and the pellets and glass blasted into the faces of the two officers.

Thirteen

Each individual shotgun pellet and nugget of windscreen glass stung and hurt and bled in Henry's face. Even so, he knew how fortunate he had been not to have an eye shot out – or worse. He had taken the shot mainly down the left side of his face and it looked as if someone had dragged a rake along the skin.

FB had not been as fortunate. His injuries were similar to Henry's, but down the right hand side of his face. At least one pellet or sliver of glass had embedded itself deep into his right eye which was swollen up like a golf ball, closed and bleeding.

'How's it going?' Henry asked FB.

'Not good,' his boss gasped. 'Fucking eye is

so sore.' His head hung down as he spoke; he did not have the energy or strength to raise it.

Henry nodded, then looked up at the young man guarding them.

They were sitting in the loose box where Charlie had murdered Johnny, their backs against the blood-smeared wall, and both wore their own handcuffs. Their phones and PRs had been taken from them and smashed on the ground and their CS canisters had also been taken.

'What's your name?' Henry asked.

'Shut the fuck up,' Jake said, but with an uncertain quaver in his voice. He was armed with Charlie's shotgun, had been ordered to stand guard whilst the other two went to the farmhouse to discuss what to do. Henry noticed the lad's piss-stained jeans, the dark shadow around the groin area and top of his thighs. Jake rattled the shotgun in Henry's direction.

'We need to get to hospital, particularly him,' Henry said. He jerked his head at FB. 'He's going to lose that eye if he doesn't get it treated – and that'll be down to you, mate.'

'Like I said, shut it.'

'You're not a brave boy, are you?'

'Fuck d'you mean?'

'Already peed yourself. Shit yourself yet?'

Jake's face was a mixture of rage and embarrassment and Henry knew he had hit a nerve. Big question was how long and hard did he keep hitting it for?

'Did you kill either of those people?'

'Which people?'

'Annabel and the other person.'

'Johnny?' Jake blabbed, then clammed up.

Henry blanched and swore to himself, shocked by the name. Somehow Johnny had made it back here and was now dead for his trouble. 'Yeah, Annabel or Johnny. Did you kill either of them?'

'None of your business.'

'Oh, it is,' Henry assured him. He had a horrible taste in his mouth. He spat out a glob of blood and saliva which dribbled down his cheek. He grimaced at the horrible burning sensation across the left side of his face. If felt as if someone was fanning the flame of a Bunsen burner across it. 'It is my business, and you know something else?'

'What?'

'If you didn't kill them – and don't get me wrong here, I can't pretend you're not in deep, but not so deep I can't get you out of this.' Henry flinched, feeling the embedded glass and buck-shot in the flesh of his cheek and along his jaw line, and could only begin to imagine how FB was hurting. 'You do the right thing, lad, and I'll look after you.'

Jake sneered a harsh laugh. 'You're not in a position to look after me.' He pointed the shotgun straight at Henry. 'Know what I mean?'

Henry regarded him cynically. He was the type of lad who was a follower, three layers down from the leader. A weakling, but still dangerous for that. Henry could see he was dithering, but also knew that his and FB's time was short. Once the other two returned from their deliberations, things would really fall to pieces. Henry knew

209

he had to get under the lad's skin immediately.

'If we die now, you'll be to blame. Think of that, killing two cops on top of everything else. How does that grab you?' Henry said, trying to do a snake-charm with him. 'Then everything will get pinned on you. Those two down the end of the stable and us. Four murders . . . those other two guys will sacrifice you like a lamb. What's your name?'

'Jake,' he divulged.

Henry held himself together. A tiny breakthrough.

'Let us go, Jake. C'mon, son, let me take care of you.' Henry's eyes pleaded with him.

It was too late. Charlie and Luke slid back into the stable.

'They said anything to you?' Charlie demanded.

'No, no.' Jake shook his head vehemently.

Charlie looked at the two miserable figures of Henry and FB. 'I'm gonna enjoy killing two cops.'

Henry said nothing, just stared challengingly into his eyes. Then he glanced at Jake, who diverted his – and in that fleeting moment he felt a surge of possibility.

Charlie laid a hand on Jake's shoulder and pulled him a few steps away from the cops and the three of them had a hurried, heads-down, muted conversation, after which Charlie and Luke broke away to the far end of the stable, out of sight of Henry.

Jake stepped towards him.

'What are you going to do, Jake?' Henry said, just loud enough for him to hear.

Massive indecision crumpled Jake's face.

Henry raised his right eyebrow. The left one refused to move and he was sure there was a piece of glass in it.

'Fuck off,' Jake responded.

'Open the door,' Charlie shouted across the stable. Jake backed off to the stable door and shouldered it open.

Charlie and Luke then reappeared, dragging Johnny and Annabel. The police Land Rover had been reversed up to the stable and its back door was open. Henry watched this gruesome scenario unfold as the men, with the legs of each body tucked under their arms, dragged them across the floor, dropping the legs heavily before considering their next move. This consisted of pulling them up into a sitting position first. Henry's face showed his horror as he saw Annabel's head loll, her whole body just a bag of bones. It was easy for Charlie – although Henry did not yet know the name of this violent man, hadn't yet been formally introduced – to heave her up on to her heels, then throw her face first into the back of the Land Rover and fold her legs in after her, shoving her body in as far as possible between the bench seats.

Charlie was sweating heavily after this and placed his hands on his hips, surveying what he had done and what he had to do.

'My God,' Henry whispered in fear.

'What is it, what is it?' FB asked, almost insensible. 'What's going on?'

'You don't want to know.'

Jake glanced at them and Henry nodded urgently at him, but got no response.

'Oh God,' he said again. 'Not good, not good.'

It took both Charlie and Luke to heave the heavier body of Johnny Asian to his feet. He was only a slat of a lad really, but he was bulkier and taller than Annabel. They staggered comically with him, trying to balance him like a drunk, then they threw him face down into the Land Rover on top of Annabel and folded him in.

Henry then watched one of the most brutal, coldest things he had ever seen in his life.

Charlie grabbed the top of the Land Rover like a monkey swinging on the cross bar of a set of goal posts. He raised his feet off the floor, swung back and then flat-footed Johnny's body into the vehicle, kick after kick, making him fit.

Henry held back a retch and knew for certain that this man, whoever he was, was one of the most violently depraved psychopaths he had ever come across. If he hadn't known it for certain before, he knew now: he and FB would be the next victims. They would not leave this place alive.

Charlie and Luke gasped for breath, the effort of moving the bodies having exhausted them.

'I need a drink, I'm gagging,' Luke said.

'Yeah, me too,' Charlie agreed. To Jake he said, 'Think you can look after these two for another five minutes, then we come back and see if we can make them fit on top of these two?'

'Course I can,' Jake said bravely.

'Make sure you do,' Charlie warned him. His

eyes roved murderously over Henry and FB, then he and Luke ducked out of the stable door.

Jake watched them go, then turned to Henry.

'They come back in here, we're dead,' Henry said. 'And you are guilty of four murders, Jake. I'd say think about that now but you haven't got time. You need to act. Release us, we jump into the Land Rover and we're gone – and you helped us to do the right thing.'

'I don't know, I don't know,' Jake said, panicky.

'The handcuff keys are still in my pocket. Let me stand up and you get them, unlock the cuffs, then we all run.'

Then there was 'that' moment, the one Henry called the 'Sliding Doors' moment, after the film of the same name. The choice. The route. Decision time. The moment when life changes for ever.

'There will be no mercy for you if I'm dead, Jake boy.' Henry probed the lad's conscience even deeper. 'You might run, but you'll be found within hours and you know that because you've actually nowhere to go, have you? Armed cops will come for you and if that goes wrong, you'll be as dead as me.'

'Stand up,' Jake snapped, jerking up the shotgun.

Henry scrambled to his feet and held out his arms. 'Key's in this pocket,' he said, indicating his left hip.

'Don't you try to take this off me,' Jake said, shaking the gun.

'I won't – just do it.'

'Turn, face the wall.'

Henry did as instructed, finding himself nose up to a blood-smeared wall.

Jake walked up to him and forced him tight against the brickwork, placed the shotgun on the floor. He put the back of his hand between Henry's shoulder blades, then slid his other hand into Henry's jeans pocket, pulling out the hand-cuff key on its basic ring. Then he reached over Henry, manoeuvred him slightly and slid the key into the lock, releasing the ratchet on the right wrist, freeing Henry's hand.

He stepped quickly back, scooping up the shotgun, and Henry hurriedly unlocked the ratchet on his other wrist, then dropped the cuffs and bent down to help FB to his feet and unlock the cuffs that secured him with the same key.

'Come on pal,' he encouraged FB. 'We're going to get out of this. Where's your warrant card?'

'Eh?' FB said dully.

'Don't ask, just give it to me,' Henry said.

FB raised his face and looked at Henry, who clearly saw the damage done by the shotgun blast. Another inch to the left and Henry knew FB would have been a dead man. He fumbled in his jacket, found his ID and gave it to Henry.

The cops then looked up.

Jake stood there numbly, awaiting instructions: the story of his life.

'Land Rover,' Henry said.

Jake spun as Charlie and Luke came back into the barn.

Charlie instantly understood what was going on.

'You weak-kneed bastard,' he screamed and charged Jake, who reared back, terrified.

Henry grabbed FB's arm, hauled him sideways, then ran to the stable door, having to drag the chief behind him.

Luke blocked their exit.

Charlie threw himself into Jake and they started to grapple for control of the shotgun, but Charlie was the stronger of the two and he danced Jake back against the wall of the loose box.

Luke dropped into a cricket fielder's stance, crouching as though he was going to catch Henry and FB.

Henry released FB, dinked left in a feint, then powered into Luke and for the second time that night smashed his fist as hard as possible into Luke's face, just under his left eye, felling him instantaneously. Henry knew he would hurt his hand again – it had been like hitting a square of concrete – but he knew he had no time to dwell on it, or even shake it. He had to get himself and FB out of the stable.

He grabbed FB's jacket and ran out with him, glancing backwards just the once.

He saw Luke rolling on the floor, covering his face with his hands.

Saw Charlie and Jake fighting in the loose box, trying to wrench the gun from each other. Charlie was the stronger of the two. The one who fought without hesitation, or thought about consequences. He was the one who would put another man on the ground and then jump on his face without even the slightest shred of regret.

They fought over the weapon, face to face. The sinews in their necks were as tight as wound steel wire and the conflict seemed to drop into slow motion. Jake began to lose as the stronger arms of Charlie Wilder slowly rotated the weapon as if he was grappling with a rusted submarine hatch, twisting and wrenching slowly but surely until Jake could hold it no more and it snapped out of his hands.

Henry forced FB out of the door and as they reached the driver's door of the Land Rover, there was the blast of the shotgun being fired.

Henry ducked instinctively but did not look back. He ripped open the door and saw to his horror that there were no keys in the ignition. Even though his eyes told him and his brain understood the situation, he still reached in and fumbled around the steering column.

He swore, then to FB he said, 'We run.'

FB nodded and Henry steered him across the farmyard to the gate, this time looking back in fear.

'We need to move fast,' Henry told FB.

'I know, I got it,' he said, upping the pace of his lumbering.

'Otherwise we're dead.'

'Like I said,' FB huffed angrily, 'I fucking get it . . . I just can't see a friggin' thing.'

At the gate, Henry paused in the lane that ran by the farm. Going left would take them back towards civilization. Going right, he didn't have a clue.

Then there was the clatter of the stable door

opening and Charlie ran out. He had the shotgun open and was picking out two spent cartridges, throwing them aside and replacing them from the supply in his pocket. He snapped the gun shut, looked up and spotted the cops at the gate.

He raised the weapon and fired.

Henry had seen the process of unloading and reloading and just as Charlie closed the shotgun, he pulled FB sideways behind the stone gate post to give them some cover.

Henry felt the shock of the shot. FB spun and groaned.

'Shoulder, fucking shoulder,' FB shouted, feeling the new pain of shot in the joint.

Now Henry was not thinking, he was just reacting, drawing on the reserves of self-preservation fuel that are hidden deep in most people, but which rarely have to be plundered.

'I know,' he said, and dragged FB across the narrow track to a stile over the dry stone wall opposite. 'Got to get over this,' he said, and directed the chief to the narrow wooden steps which, to his credit, he climbed up and over, then leapt into the field beyond.

Henry followed, paused for just one moment to do something, throwing himself after FB, hitting and rolling on the soft, drenched grass just as Charlie reached the farm gate and loosed off another two barrels.

'Keep down and move,' he told FB.

Both men scrambled up the hillside, their feet slipping, not knowing what they were putting their hands into, but keeping low, hoping that the heavy rain and darkness would be their lifeline.

Charlie reached the stile and peered into the darkness, trying to spot movement, then, after reloading, blindly blasted the gun again hoping to hear a scream, which did not happen.

Luke staggered up behind him, cradling his face. Charlie looked contemptuously at him. 'If they get away, we're knackered.'

'So what do we do?' Luke snuffled.

'Hunt them down, that's what we do.'

Although Rik Dean had been dealing with what had initially been reported as a road traffic accident but had then turned into something more sinister, he had still managed to make it to the Tawny Owl for a planned evening with Henry and Alison and, of course, Lisa, Henry's sister, Rik's fiancée.

He hadn't expected to find Steve Flynn there. He didn't know him especially well, but was aware that Flynn and Henry had what could be delicately described as an uncomfortable past.

There had been no real reason for the get-together that evening, just a bit of socializing, and neither he nor Henry had expected to be dealing with stuff that turned up out of the blue. But such was the nature of the job, especially that of an SIO. People got murdered at all sorts of unsocial hours.

At Alison's instigation, Flynn had been invited to stay the night, which made Rik a little uncomfortable, too, because he knew – or at least so

Henry had whined to him on several occasions – that Flynn supposedly had the 'hots' for Alison.

The short time that Rik and Lisa had managed to spend with Flynn and Alison had been quite convivial, although Henry's non-appearance and intermittent phone calls were clearly annoying Alison, who was becoming convinced that Henry was just being pig-headed because Flynn had shown up. The two men were alleged to have put their differences to one side, but this obviously wasn't the case.

There had been a couple of moments when Rik thought that Henry might be right about Flynn and Alison. He had seen them having a deep conversation when they thought they were not being watched and they were very touchy-feely all the time. The way Alison looked at Flynn also made Rik furrow his brow. It was as though they shared a special something, a secret . . . a tryst? Rik did not like what he saw but didn't feel it was his place to challenge anything, because what did he know?

Rik had hit the sack with Lisa at midnight, assuming Flynn would not be far behind. He had not fallen asleep immediately, which he found annoying because of having to be in early next day to kick-start a full-scale murder investigation.

Lisa had snuggled up to him. Though he had thought she was out for the count, she surprised him by saying, 'Penny for 'em.'

'Eh? Uh? A mindful of whizzing thoughts,' he admitted. 'Murder and mayhem amongst them; wondering what the hell Henry's got himself into over in the valley, though I expect he'll slink in any time now. And whether there is anything between Flynn and Alison.'

'They do seem close.'

'You noticed?'

'Couldn't miss.'

'Mm . . . I caught them having a heart to heart.'

Lisa sighed, stifled a yawn. 'Probably nothing. Just good friends.'

'Heard that one before.'

Rik hugged her tenderly and this time, for definite, felt and heard her breathing become regular and deep with sleep.

She disentangled herself and turned her back on him.

He closed his eyes, fell asleep, and next thing he knew his mobile phone was ringing and a worried Jerry Tope was on the other end of the line.

After that call, Rik dressed quickly, explained to a comatose Lisa that he was turning out, but did not give her details. He left the room, went down the corridor and stairs to the bar area.

Where he found Flynn and Alison.

Rik's throat dried up. 'You guys still up?'

They were sitting in the lounge area of the main bar and, to be fair, on chairs opposite each other with a small brass-topped table between them, next to the dying embers of what had earlier been a roaring fire in the grate. Their body language seemed to convey their comfort in each other's presence.

'Not interrupting anything, I hope?' he added with meaning.

Their total lack of guilty response, either verbal or visual, reassured him and made him wish he hadn't asked.

'Hardly,' Alison said.

They were both sipping whiskey.

'What are you doing up, Rik?' she asked.

'I need to turn out. I . . . er . . .' He hesitated.

'What is it?' Flynn asked.

'They . . . um . . . seem to have lost contact with Henry.'

Both shot to their feet.

'What?' Alison screamed. 'I've been trying to call him but I just thought he was in a bad reception area, or whatever they call it. What's going on? Can't they get him over the radio?'

Rik shrugged. 'I don't know. It seemed he went to revisit a job but then disappeared off the grid. And yeah, it's in a radio and phone signal black spot, but that's how it is sometimes. I'm sure he'll be fine. He is with FB and the two of them are pretty formidable if it has to be that way.' He did not want to share anything more with Alison because the information he had just got from Jerry Tope was quite upsetting if you read between the lines – and so were the lines themselves. All Rik wanted to do was jump in his car and get going and halfway there get a message that Henry was all right, no panic, and he could get back to bed. He was sure that was what would happen.

'Whereabouts?' Flynn asked.

'Rossendale Valley, Whitworth – a one-horse town.'

'Know it,' Flynn said. He was an ex-Lancashire cop. 'Right on the edge.'

'Yeah, next stop Manchester. Look, guys, I want to get going. I'm sure it'll be nothing untoward, but I'd like to make certain.'

Alison sagged. Flynn caught her before she hit the ground and eased her back on to her seat.

'Bloody fucking job,' she snarled.

'He'll be all right, I promise,' Rik said. 'I'll keep in touch, yeah?'

'Can I come?' Flynn asked.

Rik wavered, then shrugged. 'I'm gone in two minutes. If you're not in the car with me, I'm not waiting.'

'Understood.' Flynn bent to Alison. 'That OK?'

'Yes, go, but keep me informed. As soon as you hear anything, tell me. I'll have my mobile and the house phone with me.'

Flynn nodded. He dashed out of the bar, up to his room.

Rik said, 'This kind of thing happens all the time. Cops get out of range, go off doing stuff – it's what they do. Nothing to worry about.'

'Then why are you turning out?' she challenged him.

'Good point,' he conceded.

'Look, I know it'll take you the best part of an hour to get to Rossendale from here, so I won't start fretting for at least sixty minutes. But if you hear anything on the way, bloody well phone me!'

'I will.'

Flynn came back into the bar pulling on his

flying jacket. He pecked Alison on the cheek and the two men were gone. On dithery legs, Alison crossed to the front window to watch Rik's car throw up gravel as it left the car park in the torrential rain.

'How serious is this?' Flynn asked as Rik negotiated his way along the unlit, damp and slippery minor roads out of Kendleton, heading towards Lancaster and the A6. There was no straightforward route from Kendleton to Whitworth. From the village, situated far to the east of Lancaster, but also in the far north of Lancashire County, he had to motor down the tight lanes from Kendleton before even reaching a main road, in this case the A683. Once on it he had to turn left and then pick up the M6 southbound at junction 34, blast down that motorway before branching on to the M65 which would then take him across Lancashire, then on to the A56 over Moleside Moor and into Rossendale. It was a fair trek at the best of times, with no short cuts. The driving rain made it doubly unpleasant.

'I don't know,' Rik said, then explained the phone call he'd taken from Jerry Tope, a name which jarred Flynn. Rik also added cautiously that maybe Henry just had a burst tyre in some radio/phone non-reception area and was wrestling with that.

'Nine hundred and ninety-nine times out of a thousand, the cops are all right,' Rik said.

'Jerry's not usually wrong about stuff,' Flynn said.

'No – he's a brilliant analyst, and a grumpy git.'

'Yeah.' Flynn watched the rain. When Flynn had been a cop, he and Tope had been good buddies, which was more than he could say about himself and Henry. Flynn had quit the cops after facing an unproven allegation of theft, and it had been Henry who had made his life unbearable. Their paths had crossed a few times since despite Flynn now living and working in Gran Canaria. Even though Flynn had proved his innocence to Henry, they were still uncomfortable with each other. It didn't help Henry that he suspected Flynn of having a thing for Alison. Truth was, he did have a 'thing' for her, but only in the sense that they shared a non-romantic history that would forever bind them.

About Jerry Tope, Flynn said, 'He can put two and two together, that's for sure.'

'Talking of which,' Rik ventured, 'you and Alison?'

Flynn grinned. 'Just friends. Really.'

Rik glanced at him. 'I believe you.'

'Besides which, for some unfathomable reason, she seems to love Henry. If she didn't, I'd be in like a shot.'

Henry forced FB on, stumbling and slipping through the field, FB blindly trusting Henry who tugged and directed and cajoled him, even though he could tell his boss was hurt and exhausted.

'We need to keep going,' Henry insisted, gasping for his own breath. His adrenalin had flushed out of his system and he was struggling to keep going.

'I got to rest,' FB panted. 'I'm not that fit.'

'Nor am I. Let's stop here.'

FB flopped into the grass.

Henry sat next to him. His heart pounded like he had never felt it before. He settled on his bottom, not caring how wet he was, and peered back down the hill. From the height they'd reached there was a good view of the valley below in which the straggling town of Whitworth snaked. He could see the street lights on the main road and side roads, and beyond that, on the other side, the rise of moorland that was Brown Wardle Hill.

It wasn't as if they were miles from anywhere and if he could have flown like a crow, he would have been at the main road in less than a mile.

He shaded his eyes with his hands to cut out some of the ambient light to see if he could spot Charlie and Luke coming after them, but saw nothing.

He caught his breath, then did a quick check of what equipment they had left. All means of communication had been taken from them and smashed by Charlie. Their extendable batons and CS sprays had also been taken and all Henry could find was his Maglite torch in its holder on his belt. FB also had his.

'How are you doing?' he asked FB. 'I think we might be OK.'

'Not good, to be honest.'

Henry took a chance, turned on his torch and

shone it over FB's face. He shuddered when he saw FB's right eye, which was bleeding profusely. He leaned over and shone the torch on FB's shoulder and saw that his jacket was saturated with blood from the wound he'd got when Charlie had blasted them at the gate.

'Hell,' Henry said.

FB breathed raggedly. 'I'm absolutely knackered, Henry.'

'I know. We need to get down into Whitworth and get a phone. You up for that?'

FB nodded. 'I'll do my best, but I've got a real tight feeling across my chest and up into my left arm. I feel like I'm going to burst open, like a bloody alien's in there.'

'That would be the heart I never thought you had,' Henry quipped.

FB found a chuckle inside him and called Henry something very rude indeed.

Henry turned the torch off, then heard the shouted words that stuck terror inside him and made him realize what a huge mistake he had made to think that a psychopath would give up.

'There they are!'

Fourteen

There was the flash and bang of the shotgun being fired again from a position much lower down the hill. The flash silhouetted the two figures behind the gun, maybe a hundred metres distant, diagonally away to Henry's left. Fortunately the distance and the weather rendered the discharge ineffective, and it also gave away their position to Henry, just as he had stupidly given away his and FB's position by using the torch. Henry knew that he and FB only had a very short space of time to get moving again before the brothers would be upon them.

He grabbed FB's good arm, flung it over his shoulder and, rising unsteadily to his feet, staggered as he took FB's weight.

Once moving, though, FB tried gamely to push himself along and make things easier.

They went up the hill, linked together as if in a drunken three-legged race. At the crest they tripped over a low barbed wire fence and came to a man-made, very flat piece of land, once part of a quarry, which looked as if the actual tip of the hill had been sliced off like the top of a boiled egg. This part of the quarry had long since been abandoned and the area was now a few flat acres of scrubland with rocky outcrops.

After a quick pause, Henry urged FB on and they hobbled out of step with each other until they reached the other side of this mini-escarpment where Henry stopped abruptly, something not right.

'Why we stopping?' FB demanded. 'I was just getting going.'

'I think we've come to a straight drop down,' Henry said, scrutinizing the landscape ahead. It was all just black, nothing to help him focus. 'I think we're on the edge of a quarry. It's too dark to see properly.'

'Used or unused?'

'No idea.' Henry looked back over his shoulder and dimly saw the two shapes of his pursuers coming over the lip of the hill on to the flat top. He thought this must be how an antelope felt being hunted down by African dogs. They just kept going until their prey collapsed with exhaustion, then tore it apart. 'I think we've got to go down, boss. They're right behind us.'

'OK,' FB said immediately, at which point Henry suddenly realized that FB was putting his absolute, literally blind, faith in him.

Henry disengaged himself from FB, turned sideways and felt down the side of the quarry with his foot. 'Not quite straight down, a bit of an angle, maybe, but I can't tell how far the drop is – might be ten feet, might be a hundred.'

'We need to find out.'

'Yeah.'

Henry sank to his knees, reversed himself and then started to descend carefully, finding footholds as if he was easing himself into a swimming pool.

'Not too bad.'

FB did the same, lowering himself over the edge.

At exactly the same moment, they lost their footing on the slippery gravel side, pivoted and began to tumble.

Henry was suddenly in a sickening, uncontrollable world of spinning, pounding, crashing and bashing. He cracked his head. He banged his knees. He twisted his ankle. The wind was knocked out of him as he hit a rock that jutted out. He put out his hands to try and stop himself rolling, but his forearms bent and flicked and he continued to roll, and the best thing he could do was cover his head, wait to hit the floor and die.

Then he smashed into a huge, quarried boulder which stopped him rolling, and was immediately crushed by FB who rolled into him with a thud and a groan.

Both lay there battered and exhausted by what had turned out to be an almost fifty foot drop, only stopping when they hit a sandstone boulder on a ledge that jutted out around the inside of the quarry. Had they rolled off this ledge, they would then have plummeted another fifty feet straight down into a half-flooded disused quarry and would undoubtedly have met their deaths.

FB moaned.

Henry said, 'Still alive then?' He winced at his own pains, cautiously touching the new wounds to his head from bouncing down the slope.

'No thanks to you.'

Henry was on his back, looking up the slope, and could just make out the two figures of Charlie and Luke peering over the rim. He swore. Relentless bastards.

A flash and a blast: Charlie firing the shotgun down at them. Henry heard the splatter of pellets against the boulder, just above where his head lay.

'Got to move again, boss.'

'Yeah, yeah.'

FB rolled on to his hands and knees.

Henry got to his feet, trying to work everything out, although the spin dryer drop and the bangs to his head and body had disorientated him slightly and given him wobbly legs. He took a pace forward, then another, then drew back quickly with a gasp.

'Yep – we've definitely fallen into a quarry. Two steps this way and we'll be flying through the air again.'

Bang!

Leaning over the edge above, Charlie had reloaded and fired again.

Henry felt the whoosh of shot splatter into the ledge to his right.

He flattened himself to the side of the quarry and pulled FB with him.

Charlie switched on a torch with a powerful beam, searching for the two men. He was lucky straight away and lit them up with their backs to the stone, now easy targets for a straight shot down the quarry face, with their own faces tilted up.

Henry heard a scream of victory.

'Move, move,' Henry yelled and pushed FB along the ledge. The torch beam followed them. Henry knew that Charlie must be reloading now and in a moment would fire again. They scrambled along, keeping tight to the quarry face, afraid the ledge would either crumble away or disappear and they would be pitched into oblivion, or shot like ducks in a fairground.

Henry then fell forwards on to his knees, into

a large hole in the quarry face, followed by FB. They had accidentally tumbled into a circular mineshaft drilled horizontally into the quarry face and hillside, maybe ten feet in diameter. Charlie fired again.

But they had found safety of some description.

'What are we gonna do?' Luke asked Charlie, standing on the edge of the quarry. They were breathless, their chests heaving, and drenched.

'Looks like they've gone into a mineshaft,' Charlie said. 'If they get ten feet in and lose sight of the entrance, they'll get lost. We need to get back to the farm.'

Luke wiped rain and blood from his face. 'Then what?'

'Then I got an idea.'

Henry and FB ran into the hole in the rock face. Twenty feet in there was a three-way split; left, right, straight ahead. Beyond that, although neither was to know this, the tunnel branched out in even more directions, like a spider diagram, deep into the hillside for many hundreds of metres, an unmapped maze of underground corridors.

It was the primitive flight response that drove Henry and FB on, desperate to get out of the line of fire and the torrential rain and get some respite for just a while to regroup their thoughts.

Henry led, turning a couple of corners. FB clung to him until Henry finally said, 'That'll do,' and stopped.

He twisted, found his torch and turned it on, noting that the beam flickered uncertainly at first, though after a whack on the palm of his hand it came on brightly. He frowned at this, but knew that sometimes the connections in these torches could be a little unpredictable.

He flashed it around the tunnel, getting a sense of the new environment.

He did not like what he saw.

The shaft was basically circular and had been drilled unevenly into the rock and the floor was fairly flat. The sides and roof were rough and water dripped constantly and ran in streams down the sides. Underfoot it was wet and muddy.

Without the torch it was complete blackness. Not even a chink of light from anywhere and already Henry was wondering about the wisdom of running in here. Fright had driven him in, but common sense should have made him stop six feet in, not keep running.

He shone the torch at FB, who had sunk on to his haunches and leaned against the wall, injured, beyond tired, and miserable.

Through his good eye he had followed the path of Henry's torch beam. 'I'm not keen on this place.'

'Nor me . . . but I think we'll be OK for ten minutes, then we'll check and see if the coast is clear.'

'You remember the way out?'

'Yeah . . . yeah.' Henry's first word had been confident, the follow-up one less so. He peered back along the tunnel in the direction they had come from, then tried to remember if it was a left or right turn. 'Be fine,' he said. 'How are you?'

'Fat, old and wounded.' FB coughed and wiped his mouth. Henry's torch beam was on FB's face and he did not like the fact that his boss's spittle seemed to have flecks of blood in it. 'I am in so much pain,' FB said.

'I know. We'll get out soon,' Henry assured him.

'What the hell did we just walk into?' FB asked.

'A psychopathic nightmare, then a mineshaft.'

The brothers raced back down the hillside to the farm, leaping the wall via the stile and going through the gate. The police Land Rover was still there, reversed back to the stable door, the back door open, the bodies in the back.

Charlie ran through the stable to where he had left Jake's body. Luke followed.

They came to a jarring halt and looked at him, another victim of Charlie Wilder's terrible rage.

Charlie smiled and remembered his dream from the morning again, those last moments of sleep in a prison cell. He saw the pixelated face of the person he had killed with a shotgun in the dream. Recalled it had not mattered who the victim was. Just that it was a victim.

Jake lay sprawled grotesquely on the floor of the loose box, half his face blown away.

Charlie continued to smile.

His pride and recollections were interrupted by Luke.

'We need to clear this up.'

'Yeah, you're right. We need to clear it up and I need to get back down to Johnny's sister's house and get that tag put back on.'

'Yeah, but how?'

'Call the guy up, tell him to get down there now.'

'He lives over Accrington way, doesn't he?'

'Tell him to get his skates on, then.'

'OK, OK, OK.' Luke held up his hands, found his mobile phone and the number in the menu and pressed dial as he walked around the stable, waiting for it to be answered. He cursed when the signal went, and shook the phone.

In the meantime Charlie picked up Jake's legs and started to drag him towards the Land Rover, leaving a trail of slippery blood, brain and bone.

Luke had circled to the back of the vehicle, concentrating on getting a signal. His eyes flickered towards the inside of the Land Rover, then back to his phone, and then he realized, understood what he had seen. The hand holding the phone slowly came away from his face just as it was answered.

'Hello, hello,' the voice at the other end of the line said, but Luke was staring into the Land Rover, horrified.

Charlie was still struggling to get a proper grip of Jake's legs and his back was to Luke.

'Charlie.'

'What?'

'Charlie – look.'

'Look at what?'

'This,' Luke said.

Uttering a 'tch' of annoyance, Charlie dropped Jake's limbs with a thud and joined Luke at the back of the vehicle.

Rik and Flynn arrived at Rossendale Police Station forty-four minutes after leaving Kendleton, which was good going against the heavy weather. Inside they found the patrol inspector under a lot of pressure: the whole of the valley had kicked off and been at each other's throats for the last four hours, and on top of that a thoroughbred racehorse had just escaped from a field and been mown down on the bypass, causing a dreadful accident. On top of that, the chief constable and a detective superintendent hadn't been seen or heard of since he had waved them goodbye some while earlier.

He looked ashen when Rik and Flynn entered his office, where, much to their surprise, stood a weary looking Jerry Tope, who had also turned out from his home near Preston.

Jerry's mouth sagged open when he saw Flynn, but Flynn merely acknowledged him with a wry smile and a wink.

The inspector rose from behind his desk and said, 'Sir,' to Rik.

'Where are we up to?' Rik asked briskly, forgoing any niceties.

'OK, last thing I know is that the chief and Mr Christie were looking at this large-scale map of the Whitworth area trying to find Britannia Top Farm—'

'Which is actually Whitworth Top Farm,' Jerry interrupted.

'Yes, OK,' the inspector said. 'Then they went and I haven't heard anything since. And—' he tried to look pained and as if this was an excuse – 'I've been busy.'

'Two cops not in contact,' Rik stated coldly. 'Priorities?'

'I know.' The inspector's head dropped as he wondered what it would feel like to have it chopped off.

Rik regarded him stonily, then looked at Flynn and Tope.

'What do you think, guys?'

'Let's go and follow the trail,' Flynn said.

'You don't need to come along,' Rik said to him.

'I think I do,' Flynn said in a tone that brooked no further argument. So that was settled.

'I've got a double-crewed car on its way back from the custody office in Burnley after literally just dumping a prisoner; I diverted them to Whitworth.'

'Good – at least that's something,' Rik said, unable to keep a tinge of sarcasm out of his voice. To Tope he said, 'Are you all right to go in your own car?'

'Uh – it's a Smart car, not great on farm tracks.'

'Here.' The inspector tossed a set of keys to him. 'Have my patrol car. I'll jump in with a mobile if I have to.'

'Have you got a PR?' Rik asked Tope, who nodded.

Flynn said, 'I haven't.'

'Fix him up with one.' Rik told the inspector. 'I need to make a call.'

After heaving Jake's body into the back of the Land Rover, Charlie drove it on to the track outside the farm, then waited for Luke to get the old Range Rover out of the barn behind the farmhouse that was used as the garage. When the cars were ready to roll, the brothers then went quickly through the farm, turning off lights, locking doors and securing the premises, before jumping back in the cars and setting off down the track. At the point where they could have turned towards the main road, Charlie went sharp right on the lane that led up to Britannia Quarries. When the tarmac petered out and became a track, they kept going up towards Jackson's Moor where they knew there was a deep, flooded and unused quarry.

On the rim of this, Charlie stopped and climbed out of the Land Rover, leaving the engine running, but in neutral and the handbrake off.

Luke drew in behind and the two of them simply pushed the police Land Rover over the edge of the quarry and watched it bounce down the almost perpendicular slope, hit a narrow ledge and somersault over into the deep water. For an agonizing minute it floated, then with an enormous gulp it sank quickly and joined numerous other stolen vehicles dumped there over the years.

They climbed into the Range Rover and without a word drove back towards Whitworth.

237

Henry was astonished at how utterly cold it was underground. He wrapped his arms around himself and squatted on his haunches next to FB, feet in the mud, a chill wind whistling around them. He had turned off the torch to preserve battery life and was reluctant to switch it back on.

Next to him, FB was also on his haunches, shivering terribly and, Henry suspected, lapsing into shock from his injuries.

Henry could hear FB's ragged breathing and the scraping noise his lungs made as he inhaled and exhaled, his teeth chattering. He knew he had to make a move now.

'Boss?'

'What?'

'Let's get back to the entrance. They're not going to be there now but we need to get moving while we can. Think you can stand up?'

Henry reached out blindly and slid his arm under FB's armpit and was shocked that he could actually feel the way the man's body was almost convulsing as he shivered with the cold. He tried to help him to his feet but, although FB tried his utmost to stand, his legs had lost all power and it was like lifting a dead weight.

'Ugh, Jeez,' FB said, sliding back down into a crouch. 'I can't do this, Henry . . . I can't . . . my chest feels like it's going to explode and my left arm is tingling all the way down to my fingers. I feel really ill – and I've been shot twice – I'm sorry. I know it's no excuse.'

Henry was just glad FB could not see his expression.

'We have to get out of here now,' Henry said firmly.

'No, no, not me,' FB said hoarsely. 'You go and get help.'

'Boss,' Henry whined.

'No, no I mean it. Leave me here and get help, OK? That's a fucking order.'

Henry closed his eyes despairingly.

He turned on the torch, had a look at FB's face and had to physically stop himself from emitting a squeak of horror. He switched it off, stood up and removed his stab vest and hi-viz jacket. A blast of icy wind hit him and he tried not to think about how cold it was as he wrapped the clothing around FB's wide shoulders.

'Right,' he said, 'which way?'

'That way, you fucking buffoon,' FB said, tugging on Henry's leg. 'The way we came.'

'Oh yeah.'

They were in Whitworth less than ten minutes later, Rik and Flynn leading, Jerry Tope following in the cop car. They flew along the roads, ignoring the flashes of the speed cameras, even though they knew there was nothing they could do to prevent themselves from receiving notice of fines in the near future.

None of the three was familiar with the area. They had all done the majority of their coppering in and around the west of Lancashire, rarely having to travel east, which they viewed as a wild, untamed and uncivilized world.

Flynn read the road map and shouted directions.

These weren't too complex geographically and they soon found Cowm Park Way, then the road that ran past the Cock and Magpie and up to the moors.

Henry picked his way carefully along the tunnel, using the torch sparingly, progressing mainly by touch and feel and, he hoped, a half-decent sense of direction assisted by the wind in his face. He assumed it would be blowing in from the entrance, but when he reached a three-way junction he was immediately enshrouded by doubt. Straight ahead? Left or right? In his mind's eye he tried to recall the journey he and FB had taken on their plunge into blackness. Straight in from the ledge, then left . . . was it? Christ, they hadn't even gone that far, just a matter of yards. This, he thought, must be like flying a plane in thick fog. Problem was the only instrument that could help him out – other than his own five senses – was flickering and about to let him down.

Surely he had to turn left.

He turned left.

Rik bounced his car to a stop outside Red Pits Farm and peered through the gate posts at the sign that displayed the name of the farm.

'This isn't it,' Flynn said, leaning over.

'No, you're right.'

Easing out the clutch he let the car move carefully forwards. Behind, Jerry Tope also stopped and looked at the sign, then followed Rik along a track never designed or intended for normal cars to use.

The farmer who owned Red Pits peered through his bedroom curtains at what on that track was a procession of vehicles.

'More cars,' he said to his wife who lay half-asleep in bed. 'Summat goin' on up there, summat not good. Might as well go and start the cows,' he said. 'Not going to get any sleep tonight.' When the cops had gone by earlier he'd been up dealing with a sick calf.

His wife grunted.

The farmer, whose name was Pickersgill, closed the curtain and walked across the bedroom floor in his wellingtons, then tramped down to the huge kitchen where his sheepdog – Jessie – waited patiently for him, tail wagging.

He filled a pan with water – Pickersgill did not have a kettle – and placed it on one of the hot rings on the massive cooking range that occupied most of one wall of the kitchen.

He was wondering what could be going on at Whitworth Top Farm. He knew it had not been a working farm for many years and had gone to rack and ruin after a scumbag family inherited it, then started selling off the land, of which Pickersgill had bought a huge chunk for a knock-down price. He had nothing to do with them but had watched their comings and goings with a detached interest. Fortunately, as scummy as they were, they kept themselves to themselves, so it suited him.

Next his mind moved to Abel Kirkman who

lived on the next farm along the lane. What a
tragedy had taken place there, but Pickersgill
wasn't surprised. Abel was a good farmer but a
hothead, and had married a shagger.

He sighed and was so immersed in his thoughts
that he didn't take much notice of Jessie sniffing
at the back door, her ears flat, eyes showing their
whites.

'What's up, gal?'

She whined and gave a little yelp, still concentrating on the door.

Frowning, Pickersgill went to the door, unlocked
and opened it, staggering backwards in shock at
the sight of the blood-soaked figure of a young
woman who crashed in, her red hands reaching
for him like a zombie.

They drove on further to Whitworth Top Farm
and both vehicles drew into the spookily empty,
unlit farmyard.

Rik and Flynn jumped out in the rain and
walked over to the front door of the farmhouse.
Tope climbed slowly out of the police car and
headed to the stable.

Rik pounded on the front door.

'No sign of life here,' he commented, continuing to bang. He glanced around the yard, seeing
Jerry Tope testing the stable door.

'Right place, you think?' Flynn asked.

'Who knows . . . shhh,' he said, cutting himself
off, holding up a finger. 'Hear that?'

Flynn frowned.

'Listen – from the inside.'

Both men tilted their heads to the door, though their concentration was interrupted by Tope, who had taken it upon himself to use an old pitchfork to lever the stable door open. It gave with a crack and Tope leapt back with a yelp of surprise.

Rik banged on the door again with his knuckles – rat-tat-tat – whilst peering through the frosted glass panel in the door, but seeing only darkness.

Then: 'There! Hear that?'

He banged the same rhythm, rat-tat-tat.

And from somewhere within the house came an exact echo: *rat-tat-tat*.

He glanced at Flynn, who said, 'I heard that.'

Rik stepped back, said, 'Bollocks to this,' and flat-footed the door. But it was heavy and secure.

It took a joint effort by him and Flynn to burst it open, step into the vestibule, then into the hallway, with Rik calling, 'Police. This is the police,' and brandishing his warrant card ahead of him.

He stopped suddenly, holding out an arm to keep Flynn still.

There it was again, the banging noise. With Flynn at his shoulder, he walked along the hallway and came to the cellar door under the stairway, behind which someone was banging.

Rik and Flynn looked at each other.

Rik drew back the bolt, then slowly opened the door and found himself at the top of steep and narrow cellar steps on which two wide-eyed and terrified women perched, shivering and scared.

Before he could say anything, Jerry Tope

skidded into the house, a worried expression on his face.

'Rik, you need to come and see this – now.'

Rik placed his feet carefully on the stable floor, looking at the blood on it and smeared on the walls of a loose box. The discarded, used shotgun cartridges and the broken remnants of two police radios and two mobile phones, crushed and kick-scattered across the stable.

He bent down and picked up a broken piece of a mobile phone, his heart beating hard as he plotted the implications of what he was seeing here.

'Fuck,' he said, his eyes combing the walls and floors.

He placed the broken phone down, stood up slowly and saw something on the floor of the loose box.

He swallowed, knowing instantly what it was.

He walked carefully over, stepping as if he was walking on very thin ice, then picked it up – a piece of laminated card – and looked at Flynn and Jerry, angling his find so they could see it clearly.

Henry Christie's blood-smeared warrant card.

Fifteen

'Where the hell are they?' Rik demanded of himself, of everyone.

Flynn and Tope looked blankly at the DCI.

'Shit, shit,' Rik said desperately, wanting to run around in a circle. 'Where's the Land Rover?'

No one had any answers. He threw up his arms.

He tried to call Burnley comms on his PR and his mobile, but could not find a signal.

'Right, right,' he said, trying to reach a decision. He looked at Tope. 'You stay here,' he told him. 'I need to get to a phone.' They had found a landline in the farmhouse, but it was dead. A look of horror crossed Tope's face which said, What, me? Out here? Alone?

However, he managed to control himself and say, 'OK.'

Rik had seen the look of fear. 'I'll be as quick as I can. I need a phone or a signal, either will do. Steve?' He looked at Flynn. 'You stay here too?'

'Can do.'

Rik flicked his fingers at Tope. 'Car keys.' He wanted to move as quickly down the lane as possible but despite the urgency of the situation he did not want to rip the bottom out of his own car on the track. He didn't have such qualms about a police car. Tope tossed the keys to him. 'Be careful, you guys,' he said and ran to the inspector's car, jumped into it and reversed out of the farmyard.

He did 'ground' it several times, but it kept going, so he wasn't too concerned, but he had to slam on when a man stepped out unexpectedly into his headlight beam and put up the equivalent to the police number one stop signal.

Rik cursed, but wound down his window.

'All right?'

'You a copper?' the man asked.

'Yes.' Rik didn't have time to be sarcastic – he *was* driving a cop car after all.

'You need to see this, then,' the man said dourly.

Annabel Larch did not understand why she was not dead.

By rights she knew she should have been, but it was only when she had heard the words, 'She's dead,' spoken fearfully by Johnny that she knew she was alive and realized that the only way she could stay that way was to play dead.

She thought she was dead for certain, could not believe her terrible misfortune when, after she had duped Jake to get away and initially escaped Charlie's clutches, she and that useless cop had stumbled across Johnny being attacked on the farm track and Charlie had dragged her back into the Range Rover. Then, following Charlie's failed attempt to get at Johnny in hospital (foiled again by the same dumb cop, apparently), he had returned to the farm where she had been locked in the bedroom, pumped up, violent, ready to do her harm.

It had been the most terrifying moment of her life when Charlie had come back in through that door.

His eyes had been on fire when he used the word 'betrayal'.

That first punch to her guts had been hard and dreadful, aimed at destroying the actual living thing that was proof of her and Johnny's love – or, as Charlie called it, betrayal.

The baby.

Even on that first blow, she instinctively knew that severe damage had been done inside her.

Charlie had then set about beating her up very badly and strangling her into waves of unconsciousness, then allowing her to breathe again, gulping for air, then putting the pressure back on her windpipe, stopping the blood and air to her brain until she passed out. She did not waken instantly, but when she did, Charlie stood towering over her. He had then set about punching and kicking her about the head and body, aiming long, accurate kicks into her stomach.

Suddenly he stormed out of the bedroom, leaving her curled up on the floor, gasping and bleeding, with a vicious burning sensation in her lower abdomen. This was when she realized the miscarriage was happening.

She had hardly even noticed Luke step into the bedroom as she pulled herself pitifully across the floor. Luke had not tried to stop her and only as she clambered on to the toilet did she see the trail of blood she had left behind her. She felt a griping, twisting, wrenching contraction in her stomach then which made her howl in agony.

She knew she had lost the baby.

Luke had subsequently taken her over to the stable where he had tied her to a ring in the wall and where, overcome by weakness, stress and loss of blood, she had passed out.

She stirred fleetingly on hearing Johnny's words – 'She's dead.'

She drifted in and out of consciousness, but

was aware of a scuffle, then the blast of the shotgun and a heavy weight falling across her like a log, but she wasn't totally sure what had happened. It was only when Luke dragged her across the stable into another loose box that she opened her eyes and found herself looking into the also open, but dead, eyes of Johnny.

And the horror wasn't over.

She wasn't certain of the passage of time as she faded in and out, but then she was aware of being dragged bodily across the stable floor again, lifted and then dumped into the back of a van or something. The same was done with Johnny's body. He was thrown in on top of her and once again she found herself nose to nose with the young man she had fallen for, who was now dead because of that liaison.

Then – the passing of time was vague – there was more shouting, shots being fired, running, more shouts and then silence.

Her head cleared and her survival instinct kicked in.

The fools thought she was dead. They hadn't checked – wouldn't know how to check – and had treated her limp body as if she was a corpse, and she had survived long enough to be dumped in the back of the van.

Even in this state – she was certain she could feel herself bleeding internally still – she knew this was her last chance to live.

Using every speck of strength left inside her, and despite the horror, she wriggled and pushed and forced her way out from underneath Johnny, rolled out of the back of what she saw was a police Land Rover and stood up on shaky legs.

More horror almost overcame her when she saw Jake's body in the loose box and she nearly fainted again – but she ran out into the farmyard and staggered away.

'Long time, no see,' Flynn said to Jerry Tope.

'Mm,' the DC muttered. 'Why are you up here?'

'Inquest.'

It clicked with Tope. 'Astley-Barnes?'

'Yep.'

'Hell of a job.'

Flynn nodded. 'How's Marina?' he asked.

Jerry gave him a dark look that said, Don't go there.

They were standing just inside the stable door, looking across at Rik Dean's car. The two girls from the cellar steps were huddled in the back of it. Flynn had sussed that their language was Portuguese. Although he had been living in the Canary Islands for a long time, his grasp of Spanish still wasn't great. He knew that Portuguese and Spanish were similar in many ways, but different in many too, so he hadn't tried hard to make conversation.

'This doesn't look brilliant,' Tope said.

'No.'

It was idle chatter.

'Where the hell are they?' Tope asked.

'Dunno.' Flynn pushed himself away from the door jamb he had been leaning against, stepped

249

out into the driving rain and walked to the farm gate, looking across the lane, over the wall where the stile bridged it to the steeply rising field beyond. He hunched down and walked to the stile, peering into the darkness, knowing nothing, but working through everything he'd learned over the last hour and a half or so.

For the life of him, he couldn't see anything but death's head.

Then he stepped on something: another used shotgun cartridge, which he picked up and scrutinized. The same as they had found in the stable.

He swore and looked up into the field – nothing. Then he turned away but as he did, his eye caught a glimpse of something tucked into one of the rungs of the stile where it was joined to the upright.

He reached out and took the item and a smile creased his face as he said, 'You really are a sneaky bastard, Henry.'

Then he looked up and saw the headlights of two vehicles coming towards him on the farm track. Far away, beyond these lights, he could see flashing blue ones.

'Where's the nearest dog patrol?' Flynn demanded.

'On the way from Preston; could be thirty minutes,' Rik said.

Flynn's face tightened. 'Let me go and look up the field in the meantime,' he insisted. 'I'm sure that's where they've gone.'

'You can't be certain.'

'I know – but why else would Fanshaw-Bayley's

warrant card be slotted into the stile?' Flynn waved his find at Rik. 'It's a paper chase – and we need to follow the clues, as it were. Henry's card in the stable, the chief's there . . .'

The two were standing in the middle of the farmyard, the driving rain beating down on them. Two more police cars had arrived, blocking the farm track, and more were en route at Rik's insistence, coupled with the weight of authority carried by the deputy chief constable, who had been alerted to the situation and was also turning out. Other 'circus acts' were also on the way – crime scene investigators, other detectives and more – as Rik took control of a situation that made him want to crap.

It was clear to him that the woman who had stumbled in at the farmer's back door was a key witness, but she veered from hysterical to almost comatose, was in severe pain from injuries and possibly might have had a miscarriage. Rik had struggled to get much sense out of her and had seen that his first priority was to get her to hospital, hence his call on the treble nine from Farmer Pickersgill's phone, followed by frantic calls to Burnley comms. Only when she was stable and being properly treated could he even countenance questioning her properly, though he wanted to wring her neck and, cruelly, tell her to get a grip.

He did establish she was called Annabel Larch, a name he instantly recognized. She also continued to repeat, 'Johnny's dead, Johnny's dead . . . Charlie, Charlie . . .'

In his brief conversation with the farmer he also discovered that two officers in a Land Rover had stopped earlier and asked for directions to Britannia Top Farm, but the farmer had put them right – after a bit of verbal messing with them, he admitted: it was Whitworth Top Farm they were after.

'Been like Piccadilly Circus,' the farmer had grunted. 'Up and down t'lane all neet long.'

He also told Rik he had seen the police Land Rover drive back down the track closely followed by another car which could have been a Range Rover, not long before Rik had turned up.

'They could have driven away, be checking up on something, if what that farmer said is true,' Rik explained to Flynn.

'And they might not have . . . Look, I'm not going to spoil anything by trudging up the field, am I? Just give me a decent torch.'

Rik's mind was racing with everything and trying to make sure he did it all right. Even if Henry and FB turned up safe and well, he knew he had to treat this whole farm as a serious crime scene – which it obviously was. He would rather look stupid at having overreacted than not reacted at all.

He looked at Flynn through the heavy droplets of rain coming off his forehead. 'Right – do it.'

'Good. Torch?'

'Boot of my car.'

Flynn went to Rik's Vauxhall, found the torch in the boot and headed for the field. Rik watched him go and turned to the equally drenched Jerry Tope who said knowingly, 'Annabel Larch.'

'Yeah, I know – and Charlie.'
'Charlie Wilder?'

The torch beam flickered pathetically. Henry groaned, turned it off and leaned back against the side of the tunnel, ankle deep in thick mud. His left turn had proved useless and he had stumbled fifty yards before realizing he had gone wrong, that this was not the way out.

A tremor coursed through him: dread and disbelief. How had he let FB and himself get into such a stupid situation? Almost in tears he pushed himself away from the wet tunnel wall and turned right, now having no clue whatsoever where he was headed. He knew that quarry workings like these were rarely mapped and once abandoned – as this one seemed to be – were usually forgotten about. He also knew they could go on for a long, long way.

And people, stupid people, got lost in them.

At the best of times they were dangerous places. They flash-flooded, they collapsed, they accumulated noxious gases.

Only fools entered them unprepared.

Or maybe people who were running away from certain death.

Possibly that was just about excusable.

He trudged on, the water from the roof dripping on him, having to slurp his feet through thick sludge. His hands were stretched out in front of him like feelers and their length was about all he could see; even his fingers were hard to distinguish. This was the first time he had ever been in total blackness and it was a sensation that was horrible.

He tripped, slammed down on to one knee, hitting a chunk of rock hard. His hands slightly broke his fall, but they sank into the mud, making a slurping noise when he drew them out.

'Not good, not good,' he mumbled as he dragged himself upright.

He stood there still, cocked his head and listened.

A swish of chill air brushed his face.

But he could also hear something else, something that disturbed him. A rumble of some sort. He blinked, wiped his face with a muddy hand and tried to listen again. He could not identify the noise – but he did not like it. It sounded dangerous.

Life in a tunnel, he thought.

'Henry? Is that you?' he heard FB's weak voice call somewhere ahead of him. A feeling of elation made his heart pound. A moment in history, he thought. The first time he had ever been pleased to hear his boss.

'Yeah, yeah.'

FB's torch came on. He held it underneath his chin, uplighting his double chins and face, giving his eyes deep shadows and exaggerating the swelling around his right one.

Henry went to him, then FB turned the torch off and everything was black again.

'Take it we're lost?'

'Looking that way,' Henry admitted forlornly.

'You're a wanker, you know that,' FB said,

returning to his default position of insulting Henry at every possible opportunity. Henry smiled at FB's bravado, because behind the words his voice was weak and pathetic.

'I agree,' Henry said. He turned on his own torch and ran the weak beam across FB who was sitting in mud, leaning his back against the tunnel wall, visibly shivering like a person with Parkinson's disease. He looked awful and Henry's heart went out to him.

'Are we going to get out of this?' he asked Henry.

'Course we are.'

'Well, I think I'm shit out of luck.'

Henry had to agree with that statement, too. He was sure they would get out but was not so certain they would both be alive and kicking.

Henry cocked his head again, listening. Somewhere, deep in the hillside, he could hear that rumbling sound again.

Flynn scrambled over the stile and began the slippy-slidey wet climb up the hillside through the deep grass. He pushed on, but did not over-rush, and used the torch beam like a searchlight to criss-cross his way.

It was hard to say if anyone had actually been up the field recently and part of him knew he was doing this simply for something to keep himself occupied. Although he had been a cop for a good few years, there was no way Rik would allow him anywhere near what was obviously a serious crime scene back at the farm. The professionals were on their way and Flynn had probably contaminated it enough already. Rik was undoubtedly glad to get him from underfoot because once you were not a cop any more, or working for the police, you were of little use to them.

Some of the grass looked as if it had been flattened by someone walking through it, but it was hard to say for certain.

Still he pushed on until he reached a low, barbed wire fence which had seen better days. He ran the torchlight along it, then saw another used shotgun cartridge, which he picked up and sniffed. It smelled fresh.

Flynn put it in his pocket, his face grim, trying to imagine what had happened here.

He straddled the wire and in so doing spotted something skewered on to one of the barbs. Flynn picked it off and shone the torch on to his find.

It was a small piece of card, folded into quarters.

Flynn opened it: one of Henry Christie's business cards.

Flynn walked on until his instinct told him to stop. He swayed and stepped back as he realized he was on the rim of a vast, dark hole and had almost tripped and fallen down a precipice into one of the biggest quarries he had ever seen. This huge crater was starting to become visible with the very slow approach of dawn.

'Let's give it another go,' Henry urged FB. This time he wasn't going to leave him behind. He helped him slowly to his feet, FB groaning in agony as he moved.

'My chest really hurts,' he complained.

'I know, but I think it's best we move.'

'You think anyone'll find us here?'

'I'm counting on someone being able to follow a paper trail,' Henry said, bringing FB up to his feet. Both men wavered unsteadily.

Suddenly their feet were covered in water above their ankles as if they had stepped into a fast flowing stream. Henry turned on his torch again and looked down, saw that they were in fact in a stream that had appeared from nowhere, was flowing quickly, gathering momentum.

The water rose and in a few seconds was halfway up their shins.

'It's flooding,' Henry said, suddenly understanding what the ominous rumbling sound was. 'The rain – the tunnel's flooding.'

'I heard you first time,' FB said.

Henry grabbed FB's upper arm. 'Let's move.'

The water level continued to rise quickly. The force of the flow increased as the two men splashed through the tunnels, feeling the power of the flood push against the backs of their knees. They fell, recovered, found their feet, pushed on, Henry refusing to let go of FB in spite of his own growing weakness and exhaustion.

They reached a junction and, using FB's torch, Henry saw it was again a three-way intersection and assumed this was the point he had reached before, where he had chosen to go left and had ended up lost.

He saw that the water also split here and the power of it lessened as it flowed into the junction, which gave him some relief.

This time Henry chose to go right and bundled FB ahead of him into that tunnel.

More police cars and personnel had arrived at the farm by the time Flynn ran back and collared Rik just inside the stable, where a lot of police scientific activity was taking place.

Rik listened, though he was distracted by the weight of being in charge of all this; to Flynn he came across as being a man on the edge of panic.

'He's got to be up there somewhere,' Flynn insisted.

'Yeah, I agree,' Rik said, 'but until it comes light I don't see us doing much as regards a search. I'll get the teams together and ready to go as soon we can see properly.'

Flynn saw the logic in this. It would be easy to miss something up there and was also potentially dangerous to searchers. He said, 'I think it's a good sign, though. Every chance Henry and FB managed to escape from whatever happened here. Henry left a trail to follow and there may be other stuff I've missed.'

'All the more reason for us to get it right when we start searching. There's a Support Unit team on the way and they'll do the search, but not before daybreak,' he reiterated. 'I know we want to find him – them – but daylight is going to be our best ally.'

'I get that,' Flynn said, beginning to feel like the proverbial spare prick. 'What can I do in the meantime?'

'I don't know,' Rik said. 'I really don't know. Just keep out of the way, I guess – and I mean that in a nice way.'

Flynn nodded, seeing Rik's stress, but still asked, 'Anything from the techies yet?'

'More blood. Looks like at least two people have been killed or wounded here – killed, probably, I'd say, based on what little I could prise out of that Annabel, who struggled to put two words together. But you know what I say? Think murder, then work back.'

'Where is she now?'

'Rochdale A&E. She was in a real mess, half-strangled, beaten up; horrible other stuff.' He stopped and looked at Flynn. 'The farmer down there says he's sure the police Land Rover drove back down the track, you know?'

'But not necessarily with Henry at the wheel.'

'I know, that's what I'm thinking.'

'Bodies in the back of it?' Flynn ventured.

'Shit,' Rik said angrily. 'We can't have been far off spotting it, we must have almost crossed paths.'

'Such is life, can't beat yourself up about it,' Flynn said, then pointed to Rik's car in which the two prostitutes were still sitting. 'What's happening to these ladies?'

'I'm going to get them taken to Rossendale

259

nick, give them a brew, warm 'em up, then speak to them. Comms are trying to contact an interpreter.'

'And what about this Charlie Wilder individual?'

'I'm going to go and knock on his door – now. I'm meeting an ARV on Wallbank estate in twenty minutes – but his tag still says he been at that address all night.'

'OK. I'll stay here, go with the search team when they land.' He glanced at the sky. 'Believe it or not, dawn is coming.'

'Thanks, that's good.'

After some car shuffling, Rik and Jerry Tope climbed into Rik's Vauxhall and started off slowly down the lane. A police car with the two prostitutes in the back followed and they set off, leaving Flynn to kick his heels some-what as he waited for the searchers.

The house on Eastgate, Whitworth, was a council semi, nothing special or unusual. The type of house Rik Dean had knocked at many times. It was all in darkness, no vehicle in the driveway.

Rik walked to the front door with his ballistic vest over his windjammer, Jerry Tope behind, similarly attired.

The double-crewed Armed Response Vehicle was on the road and the two AFOs stood by the car. Two more AFOs had already raced to the back of the house.

Rik banged on the door repeatedly until a light

came on upstairs; then came the sound of muted footsteps and the door opened a couple of inches on a security chain.

A young woman looked out of the gap.

Rik stuck his warrant card up to her face. 'Police. I'm looking for Charlie Wilder.'

'Why,' she sneered, 'can't you bastards just let him be? He's only just come out of prison.'

Through the crack Rik could see she was dressed in her night things. 'If you do not open this door in the next ten seconds, I'll be forced to kick it down and I'll be coming in mob-handed.' He did not have the time or patience to mess about, explain anything or be messed about.

His eyes and her only visible eye locked defiantly into each other.

'Open up, lass,' Rik whispered dangerously.

She swore, closed the door. Rik heard the chain slide off, then the door opened again.

'Who are you?' Rik asked.

She sneered but did not reply.

'Where is he?'

'Upstairs, back bedroom,' she said, shaking her head as if a big mistake was being made here. 'And he's been here all day.'

'Is he alone?'

'Yeah.'

'Is he armed?'

'Like, with what? No, OK? Not as far as I know . . . maybe his hand's on his cock.'

'Bitch,' Rik said and beckoned in the ARV crew from the front of the house.

'You do not need guns, you know?' the woman said derisively. 'No guns in this house. At least I don't think there are.' She pulled her thin dressing gown around her tightly.

'In that case, you go up and wake him and bring him down to us.'

'No way, not me. Your job, that.'

'Who else is here?'

'Just him and me.'

'You sleep together?'

'Fuck off.'

Rik jerked his head at the armed cops. 'Back bedroom.'

He opened his eyes and found himself looking up the barrels of two Glock pistols held and aimed by two armed police officers in dark blue overalls, ballistic vests and goggles.

'Jeez, what the—?' he said and one of the officers dragged the quilt off, exposing his body, naked but for a pair of boxers and an electronic tag on his ankle.

'You get out of bed very, very slowly and do everything I tell you without fucking about,' one of the officers instructed him forcefully. 'You get out, you get down on your hands and knees, then down on your stomach and spread your arms and legs – understand?'

'What the hell are you on about?'

The AFO pushed the Glock right up into his face. 'Do it now! Say nothing, just . . . do . . . it.'

'What's this about?' he demanded, almost laughing. 'You are such idiots.'

Rik loomed into his vision behind the AFOs. 'Are you Charlie Wilder?'

'Might be.'

'Are you Charlie Wilder?' he demanded.

'Yeah, you fucking know I am.'

'You're under arrest, suspicion of robbery and murder.'

He screwed up his face. Then lifted his leg and pointed at the tag. 'In case you haven't noticed, I'm tagged and curfewed for the next six months. I got out of prison this morning and other than getting my hair cut in Preston, then travelling back here, I've been here all freaking day, you chumps.'

'We won't tell you again, Charlie: get out of bed and get on the floor.'

The rain abated slightly and the sky brightened almost imperceptibly as dawn slowly encroached.

Flynn moved away from the police activity around the farm buildings and walked through the gates, crossed the track and leaned on the stile where he had found FB's warrant card. It was now in an evidence bag, as were Henry's warrant card found in the stable and the folded business card that Flynn had found at the top of the hill, overlooking the quarry.

Flynn's 'just do it' instinct was to swing over the wall and go looking again, but he knew that could be reckless. He had been up there once and to do it again might be silly and construed as police obstruction. He knew he had to wait

263

for the arrival of the Support Unit and they would carry out a properly planned search whereas he would just thrash about haphazardly.

'Where are you, Henry?' Flynn asked the wind. 'What's been going on here?'

Suddenly Flynn stood upright, peering into the gloom up the field, his senses sharp and alive.

He was certain he had heard something.

He was right.

A dark shape was pounding down the hillside.

Flynn tried to focus in.

The shape grew larger, more distinct. It was a man, and at the very last moment the whiteness of his desperate face appeared from the darkness.

Henry Christie.

Sixteen

The dawn did arrive. Slowly, unwillingly. The heavy rain abated as the skies lightened to dull grey from black, but the thick clouds remained stubbornly overhead, going nowhere, hanging there as ugly as the faces of gargoyles.

Shrouded by a heavy blanket, a towel wrapped around his neck, Henry Christie stood quietly amongst the group of onlookers consisting of the deputy chief constable, an assistant chief constable, other high-ranking officers and members of the ambulance and fire services, as well as Rik Dean, Jerry Tope and Flynn.

Henry's facial shotgun wounds had been treated by a paramedic who had also checked all his other injuries and insisted that he should go to hospital. Henry scowled at the very notion and opted instead for four extra-strong ibuprofen tablets.

Sitting in A&E was the last place he wanted to be.

He stood in the group at the top of the hill on the lip of the quarry, looking down to the ledge that had saved him and FB from tumbling to their deaths a further fifty feet into the quarry itself.

As daylight came, the huge extent of the quarry was revealed to Henry's eyes. It was a massive, sheer-sided bowl a mile and a half across and of varying depth. The quarry had been abandoned years before, the stone worked out, and would forever be a scar on the already harsh landscape of the moor. Fencing and some walls surrounded it, danger notices abounded, but all were in a bad state of repair, virtually useless.

'You OK?'

It was Rik Dean asking Henry.

Henry grunted, not really having it in him to form a reply. He was wet, cold, dirty, close to complete exhaustion, but above and beyond all that, he kept going because he had left a badly injured man in the tunnel.

So, no, he wasn't OK.

'Silly question,' Rik chided himself.

A few minutes earlier Henry, with the others,

had watched members of the local mountain rescue team secure ladders and a pulley system to the quarry face and then go down and enter the tunnel from the ledge. They had worked quietly and professionally, just a group of volunteers, true heroes, skilled at rescuing others from hills, mountains, caves and potholes. Henry watched six of them enter the tunnel and disappear, sick to his stomach with an overpowering sense of dread because he truly believed this was not a rescue.

This was an operation to find and recover a body.

They had entered the hole with a folding stretcher amongst their equipment.

He felt Rik's reassuring hand between his shoulder blades – a blokey form of comfort. This jarred him and he glanced at Rik, tried to raise a smile, but could not manage anything other than a scowl.

'I've known him for over thirty years,' Henry said, 'and I left him behind.'

'Henry, you couldn't have carried him. You left to get help.'

A deep, juddering sigh made his chest vibrate. 'He might be OK.'

'If he is, then OK, and I'll do a jig with the Bacup Coconutters.' The words spoken were, on the face of it, light-hearted. In tone and meaning, however, they were filled with deep gravitas.

Henry took a sip of the sweet tea someone had given him in a polystyrene cup and closed his eyes as the hot liquid travelled down his throat and warmed his chest.

Rik's mobile phone rang, now able to pick up a decent signal from the present location on the hilltop. He spoke a few words, then held out the phone to Henry. 'It's Alison.'

Henry blinked, swallowed, took the phone and detached himself from the group.

'Babe,' he said.

'Henry, love.' Her voice fractured.

He had to hold himself together as he said, 'You OK?'

'Course I am . . . it's you . . . what's really happening? Have you been hurt? I've been so worried and Rik is just useless.'

'Sorry,' he said inadequately. 'I'm OK.' He glanced up as a murmur flitted through the group of people assembled on the quarry lip. 'It's a long story.'

'When will you be home?'

'Soon as I can.' The line became silent as the two of them struggled to find words to say. Then Henry said, 'You'll be there for me, won't you?' He raised his face skywards as tears cascaded down his face like the rain of the night.

'Henry? Yes, of course I will. What do you mean? I love you. Just get home.'

'Thank God,' he gasped in relief. 'I thought—'

'But let me fucking tell you this, Henry Christie,' she cut in furiously – and despite himself, he could not prevent a grin from coming to his face: here it comes, the lecture. 'This kind of thing is not going to happen again.'

267

'No, you're right, it isn't.'

He glanced over and saw that everyone had moved closer to the edge.

'Love you,' Alison said softly now.

'I love you, too – but I need to go. Something's happening.'

He ended the call, threaded his way through the little crowd and handed Rik the phone, then went to the front.

Two rescuers had emerged from the tunnel, discussing something urgently, transmitting on their walkie-talkies and speaking to two paramedics who had just shimmied down the ladder to join them on the ledge. Then they turned back to the tunnel entrance.

Every organ in Henry's body seemed to go on hold. He watched, zoning everything out, his face not betraying his inner terror.

Four rescuers manoeuvred their way out of the tunnel, the stretcher between them with a bulky body on it, covered and strapped to it.

Henry swallowed and threw down his tea.

'It's the chief,' Rik said unnecessarily.

Course it's the chief, Henry heard a voice in his head scream angrily. *Course it's the chief. How many other bodies are there in there?*

But he remained silent, the blood pounding in his head.

The paramedics went to the stretcher as the rescuers placed it down. They leaned over the body, quickly checking for vital signs. It was something that did not take long, because there were none.

They stood up, looking up to the people on the quarry lip, and shook their heads.

Henry had just emerged from the shower in the male changing room at Rossendale Police Station, a newly acquired towel wrapped around his middle. He was looking hypercritically at his reflection in a full-length mirror on the wall, checking the injuries, dabbing his face with a blood-flecked paper towel. The paramedic had been right, he did need hospital treatment, but it could wait.

Rik Dean was bringing him up to date. 'Forensics confirm it is possible that two people were shot dead in the stable.'

'Two people were shot dead,' Henry said, wincing as he touched an open wound. At a rough guess he would say he had half a dozen pellets and about the same number of windscreen crumbs embedded in the side of his face. 'What about the hookers?'

'They're still with us in the waiting room. Looks like they're from Brazil, Portuguese speaking; ended up in the UK under false pretences. Expected to be working as child-carers, ended up giving blow jobs instead. Working for a guy called Hassan. We have an address and we're on to him.'

'Good. What else?' Henry asked.

'Annabel Larch did have a miscarriage – down the toilet in the farm.'

Henry tutted sadly, recalling the blood in the toilet bowl. 'What a shame.'

'She's going to have surgery and she's not in

a position to be interviewed, maybe won't be for a few days yet.' Rik was leaning on a row of lockers. 'She was hysterical when I saw her.'

'Wasn't that happy when I saw her, either,' Henry commented.

'As regards the farm itself, baseball caps and surgical masks recovered from a cupboard. One of the masks has blood in it, like one of the wearers had a nose bleed or something.'

'Or got smacked in the face?' Henry suggested.

Rik frowned at that. 'Mm, maybe. However, it looks like there's a good link between the Wilders and the armed robbery/murder in Rochdale yesterday afternoon. GMP are making noises about interviews.'

'They can wait.'

'I told them to back off.'

Henry breathed out slow and long. 'And the prison officer?'

'Well, could be Charlie on a revenge spree. Still, early days re that.'

'So,' Henry turned to Rik, started counting on his finger and thumbs. 'Charlie Wilder gets out of prison. He runs over and kills a prison officer who upset him. He later commits a nasty robbery in Rochdale. Then he finds out his girl has been cheating on him whilst he's been banged up, gets cross – which he seems to do quite easily – and tries to kill the boyfriend, who is a member of his gang. The boyfriend escapes from police custody, then gets blasted for his trouble. I stumble in like a prick, taking the chief constable along with me. Charlie kills another gang member,

Jake, who was about to do the right thing. Meanwhile he's beaten up Annabel half to death, so badly she loses a baby. We just about escape but get lost in some friggin' mine workings and the chief constable of Lancashire Constabulary is now dead.'

'Fair summation,' Rik said, stone-faced. 'Objectively speaking.'

'Charlie Wilder is a true psychopath,' Henry said, vividly remembering watching him kicking the bodies into the back of the Land Rover. 'But at least he's in custody; the other brother, Luke, is still out there.'

'Yes, though the question of the electronic tag needs to be addressed.'

'They'll have found a way to get it off and back on,' Henry predicted. Then he paused and glanced down at his stomach and the tummy shelf just below his man-boobs. He looked at himself in the mirror again, not liking what he saw under the injuries.

'You didn't kill FB, Henry – we don't even know how he died yet. Could be a heart attack.'

Henry blew a mini raspberry fart. 'Yeah I did.'

'Look, at the end of the day—'

Henry interrupted fiercely. 'A phrase I detest, "at the end of the day". What exactly does it mean?'

Rik rolled his eyes, then stepped up to Henry. 'Let me lay this on the line, OK?' He arched his eyebrows in an expression designed to brook no argument. 'Robert Fanshaw-Bayley was the chief constable, right? But the key word in that is

271

"constable". He was, bottom line, a constable. High up the tree, admittedly, but still a constable, Henry. And you know what that means? It means he's sworn to protect life and property, and that's what he was doing. Just as you were, because even though you're a detective superintendent, you are still a constable. And when you protect life and property, sometimes you put your own life on the line. It's the nature of the game. Mostly you end up OK, sometimes you get a smacking, sometimes – rarely – you get killed.'

Henry listened to the lecture, unimpressed.

'I robbed him of his right to die with dignity, surrounded by his family. He died in a flooded underground mineshaft, shot in the face, shot in the back. He died a shitty horrible death. That's what I dragged him into. A gung-ho adventure that needn't have happened.'

'You were concerned about the safety of a member of the public, Annabel Larch. You were doing your job,' Rik insisted.

Henry slumped heavily down on a bench and dropped his head into his hands, wanting to cry and bawl. Into his palms he said, 'Who's informing his wife?'

'The dep.'

'Right . . . it should be me.' He withdrew his face from his hands, stretching and distorting his features. 'His family need to know he died a hero's death. I know it sounds corny, but they need to know that.'

'Then you go and tell them.'

'I will – but not yet.'

'Why not?'

'Because I have a job to do. I'm going to put that evil bastard Charlie Wilder behind bars for the rest of his natural life.'

'Henry, leave that to us, the team. You're too deeply involved. You need to trust us to do that job.'

Henry shook his head as Rik pleaded. 'I'll do it by the book; no need to worry on that point.'

Rik's phone rang. He answered, said, 'OK', then hung up. 'Alison's here with that change of clothing.'

Holding her felt good and right and he held tightly. For a long time. And she clung to him, tears streaming down her face, until eventually they separated. She blew her nose, then said, 'Let me have a look at your face.' She pushed him down on to the chair in the inspector's office and tilted up his chin. He was a mass of cuts, bruises and swellings, lumps all over his head.

'I look like the Elephant Man on a bad day,' he said tastelessly.

Alison had been a nurse in the army and had treated many wounds like Henry's, and many much, much worse ones. She had brought her own first-aid kit along and wasn't afraid to look under the dressing and plasters the paramedics had put on to his wounds.

'It's a mess, but not serious, as such.' Once before she had treated a shotgun wound to his shoulder following a blood-soaked confrontation in Kendleton when Henry had found himself in the middle of a violent stand-off between visiting gangsters at war in the village. 'There will be scars and they won't be pretty. You might need plastic surgery if you want to look as gorgeous as you did yesterday.'

'Oh bollocks,' he groaned. 'Just what I need – a facelift.' He then looked into Alison's eyes and suddenly she was overwhelmingly more important to him than anything or anyone else in the world. She had come into his life soon after the death of Kate, his wife, and he knew he had found someone he wanted to spend the rest of his life with and when he died he knew he wanted her to be with him, holding his hand.

Today, that desire had become so much more vital.

He had ummed and aahed about asking her to marry him and had then done it, so they were officially engaged, with a ring and all that; then he had prevaricated about setting a date and about retiring from the police so he could live and work full time at the Tawny Owl. He knew that, practically, there was nothing stopping him making those moves. His house in Blackpool had been sold, the money banked; his two daughters had more or less flown the coop; all he needed to do was shake off the shackles of being a cop.

'Look, when I've sorted this mess, I will retire and we can get married, both sooner rather than later.'

'Henry, you don't—' she began, but he stopped her with a finger on her lips.

'It's what I want and what you want – I hope?'

'You know it is.' Her eyes glistened.

'Then let's do it.'

'Seriously?'

He nodded. 'I can be out of the job in a month; maybe we can pull a wedding together in three months? The only thing is, I just wonder if you'll be able to tolerate me around you all the time. I'm pretty high maintenance. I need a lot of lurving.'

'Don't I know it.' She gently cupped his face in her hands, careful not to press too hard on his injuries.

'No more call-outs, no more not knowing where I am, because I'll be right next to you, annoying you intensely.'

'Yes please,' she said.

'And with continued irony, I need to get on with some things first.'

'I know.'

Henry looked over to Steve Flynn who had been hovering close by, but out of earshot. 'Get him to drive you home, will you?'

He had been arrested and conveyed to Burnley Police Station. He had been acquiescent and manageable, but retained a self-satisfied smirk throughout the journey and the custody booking-in process.

The handcuffs were taken off him only when he was standing in front of the custody sergeant.

Jerry Tope had been asked to go with him and oversee his detention. He explained to the custody sergeant why Wilder had been arrested and the sergeant asked Wilder if he understood that. He said, 'Yes, but it's all crap.'

He was offered the chance of speaking to a duty solicitor, which he declined. He was also asked if he wanted someone else informed of his detention. He said he wanted his brother Luke told, and laughed at that. Although he was only dressed in his boxer shorts – he had been conveyed in the police van with a blanket over his shoulders – the sergeant still authorized a strip search and that his underpants be seized for forensic examination. A note was taken that he was wearing an electronic tag on his left ankle.

Jerry Tope watched and listened to all this, frowning.

He watched the strip search, which was carried out by a gaoler and another PC.

He let it all happen and laughed grimly as he bent over to expose his arsehole. He was then given a forensic suit and slippers and trapped up in a cell.

Jerry Tope made his way to the CID office and logged on to a spare computer.

'You said you were going to do this by the book,' Rik said. He was trying to keep up with Henry as the detective superintendent walked quickly across the car park at Burnley Police Station. Henry had driven over from Rossendale in his battered Audi coupé, Rik following in his own car. Rik had seen the look of determination in Henry's eyes and was feeling apprehensive about his sudden desire to go face to face with Charlie Wilder.

Henry reached the entrance to the custody complex, paused and turned to Rik.

'I am,' he promised. 'I'll make sure the custody officer logs it in the record that I am accompanied down to the cell and that everything that takes place there is witnessed and recorded.'

'I'll be there, too,' Rik said. 'We cannot jeopardize this by not complying with PACE.' He was referring to the Police and Criminal Evidence Act, the law that governs the way in which police deal with suspects.

It was Henry's turn to roll his eyes. 'Don't you trust me?'

'Frankly, no.'

Henry tapped in the entry code on the keypad – he knew by heart the keypad combinations for every custody suite in the force. The door buzzed and he pushed it open and stepped into Burnley Custody Office.

He waited patiently to see the custody sergeant who was busy booking in another prisoner.

The problem, often, with computers in divisions was that they were often slightly older than those found at headquarters and therefore were slower to function and crashed a lot.

The one Jerry Tope had logged into in the CID office was such a computer. Log-in took ten long, agonizing minutes.

'Could have made a brew by now – and drunk it,' he'd said to no one, because the office was empty. His fingers drummed on the desk as he waited to get into the system. Eventually he was in, typing furiously, but his searches seemed to take for ever and it took him over forty minutes to do what could have been done at his own computer in five – or less. When he found what he was looking for, he sat back in the rickety office chair (chairs in divisions were also poor cousins to those at HQ) and bunched both his hands into fists.

'Boss, I know what's happened,' the custody sergeant said to Henry, 'but don't do anything silly down there.'

'I won't, sarge,' he assured him, now firmly believing that everyone thought he was going to beat the prisoner to a pulp.

I may just have to prove them all right, he thought wickedly.

He and Rik followed a gaoler down the cell corridor to number four. Everything then slowed down for Henry as he watched the key being inserted in the lock, turning, heard the mechanism click and the door start to open outwards.

Behind him he was vaguely aware of someone coming quickly along the corridor. He glanced. It was Jerry Tope, waving a sheet of paper. Henry ignored him and turned back to the gaoler as he slowly drew open the heavy cell door.

Inside, the prisoner stood in the centre of the cell floor with his back to the door. He did not turn.

Henry stood on the threshold, his heart

thudding, adrenalin gushing, that bitter taste in his mouth, the tightness in his bowels.

'Turn around,' Henry said.

The prisoner did not react.

Henry heard Jerry shout, 'Boss?' but didn't look.

All Henry wanted to do was see the face of the man who had brutally murdered at least two people, maybe more. He was relishing the moment, savouring it, the words already practised in his head. He would tell him that he would never, ever see the outside world again. It was Henry's promise to those dead people.

'Turn . . . around,' Henry said again.

The prisoner turned slowly, a devilish grin on his face, mocking, laughing at him.

Everything drained out of Henry as Luke Wilder stepped up and sniggered harshly into his face.

Seventeen

Henry's eyes darted from Rik Dean's face to Jerry Tope's terrified countenance and back again to Rik.

The three men had taken over the detective inspector's office at Burnley nick – and none of the three of them had ever experienced such ferocious and unbridled anger from Henry Christie, and that included the man himself.

He was shaking with it, boiling, about to explode as he strutted to and fro across the office floor, his fists clenching and unclenching. Rik and Jerry stood there, heads bowed and shamefaced like school kids parading in front of a dangerous headmaster.

Henry stopped in front of Rik.

'You arrested the wrong man,' he said, trying unsuccessfully to keep his tone level.

'I–I—' Rik stuttered.

'Boss?' Tope ventured bravely.

Henry didn't even acknowledge him because at that moment his eyes were drilling like laser beams into those of Rik, who was sure that his retinas were being melted.

'Am I right, or am I right?' Henry demanded.

'Er, well, er . . .' Rik flustered. He was going to marry Henry's sister later in the year but suddenly the idea of having Henry as a brother-in-law did not seem quite so appealing. 'Well,' he attempted to explain, 'we got one of the bad guys. That's a result.' He almost cowered under his hand as he expected Henry to slap him hard.

'But not THE bad guy. Not the one who should be in a cell.'

'Boss?' Tope tried again.

Henry held Rik's gaze until his own turned to one of scorn. He shook his head sadly and looked slowly at Jerry. 'What?'

'Easy mistake to make,' Jerry said. 'Or should I say . . .'

'Say what?'

'Easy to be fooled.'

'Why would that be exactly?'

'They're brothers, they look similar, their ages aren't a million years apart, they know enough about each other to pull the wool over anybody's eyes for a time at least – they could con anyone. The photos we had were not brill and DCI Dean—' here he glanced at Rik – 'hadn't actually seen any of the photos, to be fair.'

'Thanks Jerry, but I'll fight my own battles,' Rik mumbled tightly.

'Just saying,' Tope sighed, slightly offended.

'Look, Henry, I made a mistake and I'm sorry. He had a tag on, I jumped to a conclusion. And we did search the house, it's not as though we didn't do that.'

'How thoroughly?'

Rik screwed up his face and shrugged. 'At least we got one of them.'

'But not the complete psycho one. Fuck!' Henry's face was hurting badly now and because he had almost blown his stack and his blood pressure had risen, each wound on his face was now seeping a greasy mix of antiseptic cream and blood, like oil paint. But his shoulders fell defeated and not a little despairingly. He closed his eyes, then opened them and looked at Tope. 'So why exactly were you racing down the cell corridor, waggling a piece of paper?'

'Er . . .' His expression now looked pained. 'Because I'd worked it out that maybe it wasn't Charlie in the cells.'

'How?'

'After he was booked in I went through GuardSec's database again, the company responsible for tagging and monitoring prisoners, and I saw that Charlie's tag was fitted around his *right* ankle. It just nagged me when we arrested Charlie – sorry, Luke – then it came to me. I also got some better mugshots from the system and it was obvious that we had Luke in custody, not Charlie. If we'd had that information prior to the arrest . . .' He left the rest unsaid. 'That's why he was so compliant – to keep us busy with him.'

'Ya-di-ya-di-dah!' Henry waved him off. 'Balls-up in anybody's books.'

'Henry,' Rik said, now having had enough of being treated like a clown.

'OK, OK,' Henry relented. 'But the next job is to hunt Charlie down, bearing in mind that because someone else was arrested we thought was him—' he glared at Rik – 'he's way ahead of us and could be anywhere, even out of the country.' Henry plonked himself down at the DI's desk, feeling the anger drain from him. He actually didn't want to let it go, because he knew that it would help him keep going. He sighed heavily and touched one of his pellet wounds with a fingertip, felt the bulge under his skin, then looked at the blood on his finger. 'That said,' he speculated thoughtfully, 'I know people like Charlie Wilder. Guys like him are home birds. They don't have the gumption or resources to spend their lives on the Costa del Sol.' He raised his eyes, feeling a headache coming on. 'Need coffee,' he said. 'Need more pain killers, too. Need a bacon sarnie. Jerry?'

'I'll fix it.'

'Right. We start at Johnny's sister's address, and we lean on her first. My guess is she doesn't even have a clue what Charlie did to her brother; when she finds out, she might be a good help. While we do that, I want the Wallbank estate locked down, every nook and cranny and property searched, with consent or without, I don't care. We get search teams in, firearms teams. I want two ARVs patrolling the place as of now. In the meantime, Jerry, get me that food, somehow – and also get Charlie circulated extensively, APB and all that shite, media, other forces, ports, airports.' He turned to Rik. 'Get the search team on their way and set up a couple of checkpoints on Wallbank so no one can get on or off the estate either in a car or on foot without being checked. I just hope he hasn't gone yet because I want that bastard caught and in the cells.'

*   *   *

283

Roy Philips, the long-standing local PC covering Whitworth, had been posted there for many years. He was content with his lot, knew he did a good job and was liked by the community, but not the criminals within it. They usually ran scared of him, gave him a wide berth when possible.

Philips had lived through the many changes in policing that went with the job. Originally he had served at the old red brick police station on the main road in Whitworth, which gave way to a new one, which was then closed in its turn. He then had to trudge all the way to Bacup to parade on duty (he lived in Whitworth) and then come back on to his patch. When Bacup nick shut down he then had to travel even further to Rossendale Police Station in Waterfoot, again to drive all the way back to his beat.

But he did not mind, just so long as the bosses in the upper echelons of the force realized what a complete and utter mess policing had become, not only in the valley, but right across the force.

When he paraded on at Rossendale early that morning he could see first-hand what an absolute nightmare had occurred since he had gone off duty the previous night after Abel Kirkman had blown his head off.

The sense of the loss of Fanshaw-Bayley pervaded the station and it was clear there would be a mass of police activity in Whitworth that day as the hunt to track down Charlie Wilder got under way, though Philips himself did not expect to be directly involved as such. He was told to continue his normal duties, but obviously to be on the lookout for Wilder. That suited Philips in a way, because he had a lot of work to do as regards finding relatives of Abel Kirkman and informing them of his death, as well as finding relatives of Abel's wife.

He was expecting a tear-filled, angry morning.

As the parade room emptied, Philips hung back and waited a few moments before sauntering to the front and looking at all the information pasted up on the wall and interactive whiteboard about Charlie Wilder and the night's events.

'You know him, Roy?' The question was asked by the sergeant.

'Yes I do,' Philips said. 'I locked him up for the assault that got him sent down two years ago.'

He remembered it well. Charlie had been a nightmare to deal with; violent, uncooperative, threatening, following his drunken attack on a man he had never met before, during which he had killed the man's dog. It had been a pleasure to get him sent down, and even back then Philips marked Charlie as someone who could easily kill others. He felt no remorse, had no conscience about almost killing a man who had done nothing to him, and actually killing his dog.

What surprised Philips was that before the incident he didn't know Charlie Wilder, but subsequently he learned that he and his brother Luke had gravitated up to the village from Rochdale and that he had never done anything wrong in Whitworth itself until that fateful night when he had a big drunken fallout with his girlfriend about babies, or lack of them.

Philips continued to examine Charlie's mugshot, mulling it all over, including the fact that he had shot and killed at least two people overnight, one of whom was Johnny Goode, and that he had used Johnny's sister's house as an address for the Probation Service.

Philips knew Johnny's sister well.

He had known Johnny, too, a strong lad with a bit of character; he had a nasty streak, but Philips judged him as essentially harmless. Philips had arrested him for stealing from vehicles about six months earlier, a minor offence for which he got a caution. He had taken him back to his sister's house on Eastgate, where he lived.

Philips squinted.

'Sarge, does Johnny's sister know yet that he's been shot dead?'

'I don't know. I've told you everything I know.'

'OK, ta.' Philips collected his patrol car keys and set off back towards Whitworth thinking he might put off trying to find Kirkman's relatives for an hour or two. He fancied doing a bit of bobbying first.

He drove into Whitworth along the A671, a road he knew well, had travelled many times. He turned on to Cowm Park Way and then up to the quarries past the Cock and Magpie. He knew the police Land Rover had disappeared and it was imperative that it was found soon if there were dead bodies in the back of it. He knew the quarries were a dumping ground for stolen cars and knew the location of the favoured disused flooded quarries into which most of the cars were pushed. If the Land Rover had been dumped, there was every chance it was in one of these big holes in the ground. A quick check would not go amiss.

The heavy overnight rain made it hard going for Philips's Astra, but not impossible, and he found what he was looking for at the second disused quarry – two fresh sets of tyre tracks in the mud but only one set leaving.

Philips was a good cop and prided himself, after many years of local coppering, on doing a bang-up job. This was why he did not contaminate what he found with his own tyres or footwear. Instead he backed off, called in his find and then spent some time stringing cordon tape around the tracks, fixing it on, around and under rocks and stones, of which there were plenty. Then he walked around to the far side of the quarry to look down into the water which he knew was over forty feet deep. Occasionally it was clear but not today. It was murky and muddy and he could not see two feet into it, but he was sure he had made a find.

He had been told that a CSI van was en route to him and he should await its arrival. He was subsequently told that a diving team had been turned out, too.

Henry was weighing up the pros and cons of conducting an urgent interview with Luke Wilder. This was where, if life was at stake, an interview could be authorized by a high-ranking officer and conducted with a suspect, but without their legal representative being present.

287

Luke had clearly stated that he was going to say nothing at all, a claim that Henry believed. Also, knowing as he did that the opportunity to save lives had possibly passed now, and that the endangered people were already dead, such an interview could go against Henry when the whole thing came to court.

He could imagine a defence barrister looking down his nose and saying, 'So, superintendent, you conducted an urgent interview with my client knowing full well that the people in the back of this police Land Rover were already dead, hm? So you could hardly have believed that this interview would save lives, could you?'

Henry would probably struggle to justify it and anything he had managed to obtain by interviewing Luke might be thrown out as inadmissible. It might not be a serious problem for later, but it could be jumped on by a sneaky barrister to cloud the waters of a criminal trial.

He decided to wait until Luke was properly represented – because even though he had decided not to have a solicitor at the moment, there was no way Henry would allow anything to progress further without Luke having one, due to the extremely serious nature of the case.

Then he would tear the little bastard limb from limb, verbally speaking.

Instead, he decided to go back to Whitworth, knock on Johnny's sister's door and let her know that the man she had allowed to use her home as a probation address had actually killed her brother in the most violent and brutal way imaginable.

Henry thought she would have at least some idea where Charlie was – and he was going to use every emotional dirty trick in the book to get under her skin.

If nothing else, it was a good starting point, he thought.

One of the CSI vans that had been at Whitworth Top Farm turned up for Roy Philips about thirty minutes after he had called in his discovery at the flooded quarry. He explained to the two crime scene investigators what he had seen and done, then left them to do what they had to do with the tracks and footprints. He drove off the moors, back into Whitworth, and headed for the Wallbank estate for a cruise around, because you never could tell. Many a wanted felon had been captured by eagle-eyed cops simply mooching around, although few cops had the luxury of this pastime in these days of targets, cutbacks and league tables. Philips thought that was a shame because he had always believed that mooch-patrol was an integral part of being a cop.

Wallbank was not a particularly large estate.

From the air it was basically an oval shape with one road dissecting it all the way through – that was Wallbank Drive – and Eastgate and Westgate formed arterial avenues around the perimeter, with a few other streets and cul-de-sacs.

Behind Westgate was Spring Mill Reservoir and beyond that was the huge expanse of Rooley Moor. Next to Eastgate was the micro-valley of the River Spodden which separated the estate from the main road, the A671, which ran north–south through Whitworth itself.

Philips drove down Cowm Park Way, turned on to Hall Street, then on to Wallbank. He drove slowly, acknowledging one of the armed response vehicles that had been deployed to the town to be on the lookout for Charlie Wilder.

Despite the fairly early hour, Wallbank was busier than usual. Obviously news of the night's events had filtered through and folk had been drawn out in the hope of seeing something exciting.

Philips cruised, getting nods from the small clusters of people dotted around who were, in the main, teenagers.

He was well known on the estate and in turn he knew a lot of people.

Eighteen

After dumping the police Land Rover with the two bodies in the back into the flooded quarry, Charlie got into the old Range Rover next to Luke and they drove down to Whitworth.

'What are we going to do, man?' Luke asked, trying not to sound desperate, glancing at his brother for guidance. Luke had entered a state of deep panic now but could see from the grim, determined expression on Charlie's face that he was revelling in the whole shit-storm.

Charlie's nostrils flared, and a cruel smile came on to his lips.

It did not take an idiot to work out he had just become the most wanted man in the country and if there was one thing Charlie Wilder wasn't, it was an idiot.

'You'll be OK,' he told Luke, 'but I've got to run.'

'Man!' Luke cried.

'No, I'm going to go . . . just haven't worked it out completely yet, but I do know I need time and I also need to find out where that bitch Annabel has got to. I've got to assume she's gone to the cops and that must mean she's been taken to hospital, yeah?'

'Seems right, yeah,' Luke agreed.

'My grand plan, therefore, little bro, is this: you become me for a while and hope that works. Worth a try, anyway. That will buy me some time, which I intend to use well.' His smile, somehow, became even more cruel. 'First off, we need some fresh clothes.' He looked down at his blood-stained, drenched and muddy self. 'Might not get as far as I'd like if I walk around like this,' he chuckled. 'Suggestions?' He turned to Luke.

'Yeah, I have, actually.'

Luke drove down to the southern end of Wallbank and parked the car behind a small block of flats on a cul-de-sac called Fern Isle Close.

Seeing Charlie's puzzled expression, he said, 'I know a guy who can help.' He pointed to one of the first floor flats. 'Lives there.'

'Who is he?'

'Billy Stone, local drunk, but a good guy . . . lives there alone.'

'And . . . the plan goes how?'

'You crash at his place for a while and I'll go get a change of clothing from Monica's. I'll get some of Johnny's, they should fit you.'

'Right,' Charlie drawled doubtfully, 'and what are you going to tell her about Johnny? She's not going to be right pleased to find out he's dead, is she? She's not just going to hand over his clothes, like.'

'I won't tell her he's dead, simple,' Luke shrugged. 'I'll just wing it.'

'OK, I get that,' Charlie said. 'Get the tag too and get on the phone to that guy, get him to meet us here instead.'

Knocking up Billy Stone wasn't such an easy job, even though he only lived in a cramped, one bedroom flat. Eventually he came to the door in his tatty boxer shorts.

'What the fuck do you want?' he asked, annoyed and tired and still under the influence of drink. His breath stank.

'We need to come in, Bill, mate,' Luke said.

Billy's dog-red tired eyes registered the state of the two men and without hesitation he stood aside and gestured for them to enter, then checked either way outside before closing the door.

They assembled in the kitchen and Billy asked, 'What the shit happened to you two?'

'Long story, Bill—' Luke began.

'One you don't need to know,' Charlie cut in, talking with a voice that sent a shiver down

Billy's weak spine, especially when Charlie revealed the sawn-off shotgun he had managed to conceal from view up to that point.

'Bugger,' Billy said quietly, now rueing the moment he had answered the door and cursing his first instinct to help someone who looked as though they were on the run from the law.

'It's all right, Bill,' Luke assured him. 'You're not going to get involved in anything here.'

Billy Stone was a fifty-year-old lag now. Most of his life he had been unemployed, drawing dole, stealing and being an alcoholic. He had been married twice, both the women also alcoholics, and his second marriage had been bigamous (for which he'd done six months inside). Now he lived alone in a simple world of beer, betting on the dogs with money he did not have, watching TV in pubs and thieving to keep his head above water. It was an existence he controlled and he had only himself to blame for his spiral downwards, but he also had only himself to fend for and this suited him. Although he liked a bit of company, he wasn't interested in becoming embroiled in anyone's business but his own.

'You sure of that?' Billy asked Luke.

'Yes – sure.'

'OK, what's happening?'

'Hey – this is my brother, Charlie. Just let him take a seat here while I pop out for ten minutes. Then I'll be back and we'll be going – how does that sound?'

Billy's 'OK' was dubious.

293

Luke then left. Charlie and Billy regarded each other.

'You look like you need a brew, mate,' Billy said.

Luke got back into the Range Rover, did a quick circuit of the estate to check for cops, but it looked all clear. He drove to Johnny's sister's house, parked outside and dashed to the door, pounding hard to bring Monica to it in her night things.

As she opened the door to him, he forced his way in past her, then in the hallway he spun and said, 'I need a change of clothing, Mon. Need some of Johnny's stuff, jeans, jackets, trainers, shit like that.'

Monica stared at him open-mouthed. 'What's happened? Where is Johnny?'

'Johnny's OK. We just need to get some fresh clothes, yeah?'

'I said, where is he?' she demanded, grit in her low voice.

Luke stepped up to her and gripped her face in his fingers, distorting her features. She whimpered as he brought her face close to his. 'Johnny's all right,' he said, feeling the tension inside him drawing his own skin tight across his skeleton. 'I need a change of clothing, OK? Do not ask anything else. It's better you know nothing, OK? If you want to help Johnny, you'll just do this.'

She reared her face out of his grasp. 'You'd better be telling me the truth. He'd better be OK.'

'He is, and I'm telling you the truth; now let's get some gear.'

She scowled at him, but led him upstairs to the

294

box room at the back of the house that was Johnny's tiny bedroom, just large enough for a single camp bed, no space for a wardrobe, so his clothing was scattered untidily in one corner of the room.

Luke stuffed an ASDA carrier bag full of clothing and trainers, then ran out of the house, but not before grabbing Charlie's electronic tag which was on the fireplace in the front room.

'Back soon,' he shouted at the front door.

'What about Johnny?' Monica asked again as she came down the stairs.

Luke stopped 'Johnny's OK. He just won't be home tonight, but I'll be back later, so make sure the door's open. I'll explain it all when I get a chance.' He looked tenderly at her, then suddenly grabbed her face again. 'Just do as you're fucking told, OK?'

Once more she tore herself from his vice-like grip.

He pointed a warning finger at her, then was gone.

Two minutes later he was back at Billy Stone's flat to find there was a mound of bloody clothes on the kitchen floor and Charlie was in the shower. Billy was sitting at the kitchen table, smoking and drinking whiskey.

'Thanks for this, Bill.'

'Whatever,' he said, unimpressed. 'I best get no shit from this.'

'You won't,' Luke promised, but even as he looked at the soggy pile of clothing, a thought came to him which was interrupted by the ringing of his mobile phone.

He answered it, listened a moment and said, 'Fern Isle Close . . . yeah, far end of the estate . . . two minutes.'

Luke then dumped the bag of fresh clothes and the tag on the table in front of Billy and went back outside just as a car pulled in and Dibney arrived with his very special tool kit.

'Time of day do you call this?' he moaned.

'Serious time,' Luke said, and led him up the outer steps to Billy's flat.

Charlie had emerged from the shower fresh, clean and naked in the kitchen and was already sorting through Johnny's clothing. Billy was inspecting the tag, rotating it as though it was a valuable antique.

'This is double money,' Dibney said.

Charlie pulled on a clean pair of underpants and turned to Dibney, then grabbed him by his jacket and slammed him up against the fridge, rattling the few contents inside it.

'You'll get paid, just put the tag back on, eh?' He tossed him aside and turned back to the clothes.

'But put it on me,' Luke said, shaking a leg.

'On you?' Dibney said, brushing himself down after being ruffled by Charlie.

'On me.'

'Fine,' he said, and had it fitted within five minutes. A few minutes after that he was on his way home with £400 in his pocket, counted from a wad of cash that Luke had in his jacket.

Luke and Charlie regarded each other.

'Well, man,' Charlie said.

'Yeah, I know.'

'Didn't go as planned.'

'No.'

'Anyway, you go and get your head down if you can. I'll do the same here for an hour.' Charlie glanced at Billy Stone. 'If you don't mind, that is?'

'Like I have a choice.'

'Nah, you don't.' Charlie turned back to Luke. 'Let's just hope that whichever cop turns up knockin' doesn't know me or you. Chances are they won't, otherwise this plan'll go to rat shit.'

'And what are you going to do?'

'Finish up my bizzy here, then go on the road.'

They shook hands, hugged and didn't say another word. Luke gave Charlie the keys for the Range Rover, which he had parked between some lock-up garages nearby, then he jogged back across the estate to Monica's house and went to bed to wait for the knock on the door.

It came sooner than expected and two cops hauled him off to Burnley nick.

As he patrolled the estate, Roy Philips was very tempted to knock on Monica Goode's door, but he was a decent enough cop to know that it could possibly spoil some of the plans – to which he would not be privy – that might already be in motion, so other than doing a couple of drive-pasts he kept his distance, continuing to roll slowly around the estate, eyes open.

On his third drive-past of Monica's house, Philips saw an Audi coupé pull in outside which he recognized as the one belonging to Henry Christie, although the man who climbed slowly out of the driver's seat looked nothing like the detective superintendent who had been with him at Abel Kirkman's farm yesterday afternoon.

Philips was shocked by Henry's appearance. Although he had heard what had happened overnight, the extent of the effect on Henry had not really been explained, nor the fact that the pristine Audi that Philips had seen yesterday had received such a battering.

Philips pulled in behind and got out of his car. 'Mr Christie?'

Henry turned slowly, his face a terrible mess, looking to Philips as if someone had scraped a cheese grater down the side of it.

Philips could not help but blaspheme at the sight.

'Morning to you, too, Roy,' Henry said affably. 'How you doing?'

'I'm . . . good. Christ,' he said again. 'You ran into Charlie Wilder.'

'Could say that.'

'I'm so sorry about the chief. How did he . . .?'

'Die? Not totally sure yet until the post-mortem.'

'I heard he got shot.'

Henry pointed at his own face. 'He got the other half of this – the worse half.' Henry shrugged ineffectually. 'And Charlie pulled the trigger.'

'I know him; I got him sent down. I pegged him as a dangerous individual back then.'

'Oh yeah – a tiger prodded with a shitty stick.'

'Erm, you want me to come to the house with you? I know Monica too.'

Henry shook his head. 'I want a one-to-one with this lass.'

'Understood.'

'Oh, by the way, well done – hopefully – for finding the Land Rover.' Henry jerked his thumb at Monica's house. 'Her brother's in the back of it, I think, plus another lad. Could have been me and the chief, too, if we'd played our cards right.'

'So, so sad about the chief,' Philips said again.

Henry's head dithered nervously, affected by Philips's words. 'Don't go there. I've boxed it away until I collar Charlie Wilder.'

'OK. I'll just—'

'Keep patrolling, and don't go near him if you see him. Oh, and don't forget Abel Kirkman's relatives either – something else I need to get sorted out. Can't forget it just because of what happened after, can I?'

'I won't, boss. I'm assuming a lot of cops'll be descending on Whitworth very soon.'

Henry nodded. 'More than in the rest of the county put together and if Charlie's here, then we're going to flush him out and if he comes out shooting, that'll be just too bad for him.'

Henry walked up to Monica's house and Philips got back into the police car.

He banged hard on Monica's front door, noting its flimsiness, the damage done to it, even jemmy marks by the lock. The pleasures of living on a council estate, he thought cynically.

When there was no reply, he banged again and again until he was pounding remorselessly with the side of his fist like a mad man until the door opened and she stood there scowling at him, her eyes registering his face with a little shock – but only for an instant.

Henry held up his blood-smeared warrant card in a clear plastic evidence bag. 'Detective Superintendent Henry Christie,' he announced himself. 'I want to talk to you – and don't even think of closing the door because I'll tell you this, love—' here he bent close to her face and growled softly, not caring if he was intimidating her – 'I'm in no mood to piss around.'

He saw her swallow, then wordlessly she opened the door fully and allowed him in.

In the living room, he turned to face her.

'You know what's going on?'

'No,' she said sullenly, 'why should I?'

'You're a gangster's moll by all accounts,' Henry put to her.

'You are so wrong, whatever your name is.'

'Henry Christie.'

'What are you doing here? The cops have already been and made an arrest. There's no one else here except me.'

'I want to know where Charlie Wilder is.'

'Why should I know that?'

'Because this is his address according to the prison release details.'

She shook her head as if he was stupid. 'If

you don't know how that works, you're an idiot. He needed an address, this was it. End of.'

'All right, I'll have that. So where is he?'

'Actually, I don't know. He came here yesterday afternoon, but I wasn't even here, so I haven't seen him at all, actually,' she sneered.

'But he left his ankle tag here.'

'His business,' she shrugged.

'Where's Johnny, your brother?'

She shrugged. 'How should I know?'

'When did you last see him?'

'Yesterday morning, I think . . . I'm not his keeper, y'know.'

What Henry was about to say next was interrupted by his personal radio: 'Superintendent Christie, receiving?'

Keeping his eyes locked on to Monica, Henry fished the PR out of his pocket and answered, 'Stand by . . . I'll give you a shout back.' He recognized the voice calling as that of Jerry Tope.

'It's urgent, boss.'

'Two minutes,' Henry said with finality. He did not want to lose the momentum of the conversation with Monica. He said to her, 'Sit down, love, we need to talk.'

Jerry Tope had been working hard on the stuff Henry had delegated to him with regards to circulating Charlie Wilder's details. As he did it he was furious with himself over the issue of identifying Luke Wilder, but tried not to beat himself up too much because it was just the way his mind worked and he couldn't change that.

301

The problem was that Tope looked at information, intelligence, reports, whatever, played with it, mulled it over at his own speed and then found the nuggets of gold from that process, which often took a while.

Normally it did not matter too much. He was an intelligence analyst, and the key word there was 'analyst'. A word, he would argue, which in itself suggested a certain laid-back approach, a plodding quality to what he did. He usually sat in an office at headquarters, poring over stuff, but was seldom operational, on the coalface as it were, and more rarely in at the kill when an arrest was made.

This, he told himself, was why it had taken him a bit of time to realize that the electronic tag on the ankle of 'Charlie Wilder' was on the wrong leg. He instinctively knew something wasn't right when Rik Dean arrested the man who was believed to be Charlie, but Tope had needed to sit down and work through it at a computer, with a nagging sensation in his brain which was confirmed when he discovered that the tag had been put on Charlie Wilder's right ankle, not his left.

By that time, Henry Christie had come face to face with Luke in a cell.

'Damn, blast and bollocks,' Jerry had cursed after the event.

So after he had completed the required circulations regarding Charlie, he went back on to the security company's website, hacked illegally into its database and went on to the GPS system that the firm used to track the movements of the tags, just to have a look at where 'Charlie' had been.

The system was very accurate.

Tope shot upright, grabbed his PR and called Henry, who he knew had gone back to Whitworth.

Roy Philips could not bring himself to leave Wallbank, his urge to find or assist in finding a murderer keeping him drifting slowly around the estate – just in case.

It was as he drove slowly along Westgate that he saw something slightly unusual.

A man walking along the footpath who, Philips knew, was rarely out of bed before noon – and after that he would usually be in one of the many pubs or clubs in Whitworth. A man Philips usually found staggering home drunk at midnight. Morning was very unusual for him. In fact the only time Philips had ever seen this man out in the morning was when he picked him up from a gutter, drunk, and drove him back to his flat.

The sighting seemed all the more odd when the man, who was walking towards Philips, spotted the cop, stopped guiltily, pirouetted and began walking the other way, as if the cop in the car wouldn't notice this very suspicious manoeuvre.

The other strange thing was the supermarket carrier bag he held in his hand, which appeared fairly light, yet bulky.

Billy Stone, Roy Philips said to himself, what are you doing out here at this time of day, boyo?

Stone walked on, head down. Philips did not

need to accelerate to draw level with him and within a couple of seconds he was lowering his window.

'Mornin', Billy,' he called. Stone glanced sideways once, then continued to walk. Philips kept alongside him. 'What are you doing out at this time of day?'

'Why, is it a crime?' He shook his head, mumbled something else, kept going, upping his pace slightly.

Philips was intrigued by the bag. 'What've you got in there, mate?'

'Nowt.'

'Doesn't look like nowt to me. I want to have a look. You stop walking right now, Billy.' He swerved in and stopped.

Billy Stone suddenly burst into action. He swung the bag through the open car window and into Philips's face, and ran. The bag burst open across Philips's knees to reveal it was packed with wet, dirty clothing. Philips picked up a T-shirt; he held it up and saw that, as well as being wet, it was also bloodstained.

Philips threw the split bag and contents across into the front passenger footwell, then set off after Stone, transmitting on his PR as he did.

Billy Stone ran as if he had been shot in the leg. He wasn't a man designed for speed, and his gait was rather like a painful lope and not terribly quick. Philips followed him on to Westgate Close and Billy ran into a garage colony that was a cul-de-sac with lock-up garages on either side. Philips smiled patronizingly, knowing he had the man trapped, because at the far end was a six-foot high concrete wall and unless Billy Stone was a hurdler, there was no escape on foot.

Philips was right up behind Stone when he reached the wall, where he stopped and turned, already exhausted, to face the front grille of the police car, his hands on his knees, looking as though he was going to heave.

As Philips climbed out of the police car, one of the armed response vehicles entered the cul-de-sac behind him.

Henry had done a lot of damage to Monica Goode within just a couple of minutes. But the truth was, he did not care. He had hurled the bloody fate of her brother straight into her face, no finesse, sympathy, empathy, using none of the skills he would normally have employed when delivering news of a death And his idea of using emotional blackmail had simply been replaced by a sledgehammer approach.

He wanted to give it to her smack between the eyes because he suddenly found he did not have the time, patience or inclination to coax anything out of her. He wanted to see her raw reaction there and then, which he got as he watched her world crumble. At the same time Roy Philips shouted up that he was chasing a suspect on the estate, but Henry turned the volume down on his PR once he heard that the man being chased was not Charlie Wilder.

'So that's it, then?' he concluded.

'Yes, yes . . . I don't know where Charlie is,

and that's the God's honest truth. I swear on Johnny's life.'

'But Luke came back here earlier and took some of Johnny's clothes – and the ankle tag.'

'Yes, but I don't know where he took them or why. He wouldn't tell me, and he threatened me, too.'

'Clearly he didn't go far?'

'No, he came back soon after and got into bed, Charlie's bed, and told me to shut my face.'

'Shit,' Henry said, half-listening to the chase that was going on. 'I'm going to be back,' he told her, 'and we are going to have a very long talk, you and me.'

She nodded, tears streaming down her crumpled face. 'Where is Johnny? Do you know?'

'I don't – but I do know he is dead . . . and for that, I'm sorry.'

His instinct almost made him reach out to her, but instead he turned and went out. As he walked down the garden path, he upped the volume on his PR and called Jerry Tope when there was a lull in the chase, which seemed to have reached a satisfactory conclusion, someone having been caught.

'Jerry? What do you want?'

'Possible location for Wilder, based on that electronic tag.'

'Really?'

'Yes. Sometime last night, between Charlie and Luke leaving the farm and us arresting Luke at Monica's house, the GPS shows that the tag went from her address to another address in Fern Isle

306

Close, then back again. This is presumably where Luke fitted it on his leg, somehow.' Tope gave Henry the exact address.

'You can be that specific?'

'Well, only up to three metres. I've checked the voters' register and a guy called William Stone lives in a flat there.'

'PC Philips interrupting on that,' the local cop cut into the conversation.

'Go ahead, Roy,' Henry said.

'I'm on a garage colony on Westgate Close, boss. You need to get round here and see this, urgently – I've got that William Stone here now.'

'Less than two minutes,' Henry said, sprinting to the Audi.

He swerved on to the garage colony, slamming on to stop behind a Ford Galaxy – the armed response vehicle – parked behind Roy Philips's car. Philips was holding a man by the concrete fence at the end of the cul-de-sac. Henry walked over.

'This is Billy Stone,' Philips said, giving Billy a little shake. 'Lives at the address on Fern Isle Close.'

'What happened?' Henry asked, bending his knees slightly to look up into Billy's sagging face, seeing a vivid map of broken capillaries spread over a slightly bulbous nose and, like a spider's web, across his ruddy cheeks. The classic look of an alcoholic, one who drinks a lot of cider.

'I saw him walking,' Philips said. 'Odd at this time of day, but even odder that he wouldn't stop for a chat. He had a plastic carrier bag in his hand which he wouldn't let me look in and he did a runner, but he wasn't hard to catch, were you mate?'

Stone raised his head miserably, still trying to catch his breath, his lungs rasping.

'The plastic bag's in my car; unfortunately it burst when he threw it at me. Have a look, boss.'

Henry took a few steps back to Philips's car, reached in through the driver's door and pulled out an item of clothing. With a finger and thumb he lifted it up, then unfolded it between his hands.

A Metallica T-shirt. Splashed with blood.

Charlie Wilder's Metallica T-shirt.

As if he had ice spreading through him, Henry suddenly became cold.

Billy Stone watched him worriedly.

Henry came up to him. 'I take it you were disposing of this stuff for him?'

'Look, sir,' Billy pleaded, 'I don't even know the guy, he just came round with his brother a few hours ago. Honest, I don't even know him. I know Luke, yes—'

'What are you doing with his clothing?'

'I'm just . . . I'm just . . .'

Philips gave him a shake to get him to spit it out. 'Just what, Billy?'

'We know what you're doing, Billy,' Henry said. 'You're an accomplice – to murder, now.' Billy's eyes opened wide. 'But what I want to know is this: is he still in your flat?'

'Have you ever killed anybody?'

DCI Rik Dean stood in the open cell doorway,

looking into the insolent eyes of Luke Wilder. Luke was sitting on the edge of the cell bed, his elbows on his knees, his face resting in his cupped hands.

Jerry Tope stood a couple of feet behind Rik with a sheet of paper in his hand.

The faces of the detectives were serious.

'I'm not talking,' the prisoner said.

Since his true identity had been discovered, Luke had been put through the custody system again, though this time he refused to divulge anything, his name, address or date of birth.

'That's fine, Luke, don't have a problem with that.'

Luke yawned to give the impression he was bored rigid with the situation. But he was getting weary now; he wanted to sleep and his resistance was waning. That did not bother him too much because he knew that the law required the police to let him have eight hours of uninterrupted rest. They had no choice but to let him sleep, which would give Charlie even more time to do what he needed to do and then scarper.

'So, coming back to my question: have you ever killed anybody?' Rik asked. Luke gave him a lopsided grin.

'I don't mean, were you a passenger in the car that ran over and killed that prison guard yesterday morning, which I know you were and I will prove in due course. I know Charlie was driving. I know you were the passenger – but that's on the back burner for an hour or two.'

Luke blinked, outwardly showing nothing.

309

Inside, his guts churned sickeningly. 'Saying nowt.'

'That's fine, Luke. This isn't a formal interview anyway, it's not on the record, it's just an information sharing exercise, but I still need to know something: to the best of your knowledge, have you ever killed anyone? You know, actually directly killed someone?'

Rik saw Luke's nostrils dilating as he wondered where this was leading.

Eventually Luke said, 'No.'

'Good,' Rik said. 'Because have you ever thought what it might be like to snuff out a life? Take everything from someone? Take them from their family. Take them from their future . . . destroy a family . . . you know, stuff like that?'

'No.'

'Good. I mean, we know Charlie has. He's a psycho and he loves it, but you, I don't see that. Not to that degree. Charlie kills and you just watch, eh?'

No response, other than a yawn again.

'I mean, to knock someone around, show you're a man – that's one thing, isn't it? But to leave them dead, that's a whole different agenda, isn't it?'

Luke pushed himself to the back edge of the bed, leaned against the cell wall.

'Isn't it, Luke?'

'Whatever.'

'The thing is this, Luke. Before I tell you the next thing, I want you to know that if you help us, we can help you – and that's a promise.' Rik turned to Tope, stepped back and allowed him to take up position at the cell door with the sheet of paper in his hands.

'Luke, we just want you to know something,' Tope said. 'We know that you and your gang – which incidentally now only numbers two – carried out an armed robbery at a convenience store in Rochdale yesterday afternoon. As you know, the store owner was shot dead—'

'I didn't—' Luke began to protest.

Tope held up a finger. 'Let me finish, I hate being over-talked. During that robbery, the daughter of the store owner was brutally assaulted – by you, Luke Wilder. We know that – but what you don't know is that she died of horrific brain injuries one hour ago, because you kicked her to death.'

Luke's chin dropped.

'You took everything away from that young girl and destroyed a family, you and Charlie.' Tope gave Luke a quick nod, stepped back, and Rik took his place.

'So you *have* killed someone, Luke – but here's the crux: I want you to have a think about all this and then, when you're ready, speak to us and tell us all you can about Charlie, where he is and what his plans are, OK?'

With a bright smile, Rik slammed the cell door shut.

He and Jerry walked side by side down the corridor towards the custody desk.

Rik started counting. 'One . . . two . . . three . . .'

On 'six' there was a pounding from Luke's cell.

Rik said, 'Owe you a quid – I was certain it would be on three.'

Nineteen

Earlier, Charlie had given Luke five minutes to get back to Monica's, then reloaded the shotgun with the last two cartridges he had left. That didn't bother him because that was all he would need. He had no intention of getting his head down.

Billy Stone watched him slide the ammunition into the barrels and click the weapon closed. 'Safety catch?' Billy asked, even though he knew nothing about firearms.

'Hacksawed off,' Charlie said, holding up the gun and showing Billy the rough saw marks. He placed the gun on the kitchen table and asked Billy if he had a big coat of some sort. Billy opened the pantry door on the back of which swung his few coats. He picked a parka type and handed it over.

'Nice one,' Charlie said, slipping into it, then sliding the shotgun down the left sleeve to see if he could hide it there – more or less – and if there was room to let it slide out into the grip of his left hand. It was just a bit tight as it came through the hole. He looked at Billy. 'Need to cut it. Scissors, please.'

Billy rummaged in the cutlery drawer and found

a pair of blunt ones. Charlie held out his left arm, the palm of his hand facing upwards to expose the seam running up the inner side of the sleeve.

'Four inches should do it.'

'Me, cut it?'

'Yes, you.'

Billy's hands shook as he took hold of the sleeve and snipped at the stitching to loosen it. He stood back to admire his handiwork as Charlie slid the shotgun up and down the sleeve into his hand and back again, nodding with satisfaction.

'Nice, that, just the job.'

'Cost me, that did, that coat,' Billy said, knowing he was being brave and cheeky, but when Charlie peeled off a twenty from his roll of notes – the take from the convenience store robbery – he was glad he'd asked.

'Thank you Billy. Just one last thing.' Charlie pointed to the pile of discarded clothing. 'That lot needs to go, never to come back again. Know what I mean?'

'Right, right, right . . .'

'Any ideas?'

'Uh, my mate . . . he works down the mill in Hallfold, the one that does kitchen units. He looks after the furnace there. They could go on there.'

'Do it,' Charlie said, peeling off another twenty-pound note which Billy almost snatched from his hand. Then he held out another twenty and said, 'For your mate.'

Billy took this one cautiously, a puzzled frown on his brow. Charlie saw the expression and shrugged. 'Only money,' he said, but he knew that Billy, although he was nothing more than a drunk, had seen right through him.

Charlie Wilder was setting out on a course of action from which he would probably not return alive.

Fifteen minutes later, Charlie was parking the old Range Rover in a street about a quarter of a mile from Rochdale Infirmary.

Charlie Wilder found Annabel within just a few minutes of walking in through the front door of the hospital. Wearing Billy Stone's coat with the shotgun tucked down the sleeve, he went straight to the reception desk and said, 'Annabel Larch?'

The lady behind reception said, 'Unfortunately I can't really tell you anything unless you're her family.'

'I'm her brother,' he said, his face showing worry. 'I would like to see her and know how she's going on. I believe she's suffered a terrible assault.'

The lady sized him up – he gave her his best puppy-dog look – and she relented. 'Tell me your name, take a seat and I'll see if I can get a doctor or nurse to come and talk to you.'

'That's really kind.'

'You may have to be a little patient, though. She is being treated as we speak.'

'That's OK. My name is Johnny Goode . . . Larch is her married name.'

The lady nodded and picked up a phone.

Charlie wandered to a seat in the waiting area, pleased with his lies.

A few minutes later a nurse came through the

double doors from the A&E unit and glanced at the receptionist, who nodded in Charlie's direction. She came over to him with her hands clasped in front of her, as though she was praying. She reminded Charlie of a nun with her simpering, sympathetic expression. Then and there he wanted to blast her face off, but he gave her his best worried smile instead.

'Mr Goode?' she asked. He nodded and started to stand up. 'No need to get up,' the nurse said, placing gentle fingers on his shoulder, then sitting on the chair next to him. 'You're Annabel's brother?'

'Yeah.'

'I'm afraid we can't let you in just at the moment. She's being treated by the doctor and is very poorly.'

'Did she . . . did she lose the baby?' Charlie asked, his voice cracking with emotion.

'I'm so sorry; she did.'

'Oh God,' he moaned. 'Such a tragedy.' The nurse's face changed then, because he'd said those words as though he was laughing. He realized his error, breathed heavily and said, 'That's really awful.' He hung his head and shook it so she could not see the look on his face. He wanted to laugh and dance and cheer, and then stamp on Annabel's dead body, because that's what it would be very shortly. 'Why can't I see her?'

'We're just getting her ready to be taken over to Bury General, where they have the facilities to care for her. An ambulance is on the way now; do you have a car?'

He nodded.

'Maybe you'd like to make your way over to Bury? I can give you directions. Once she's over there I'm sure you'll be able to see her.'

Again, Charlie had to hide the smile that swamped his face as he mumbled, 'If possible, I'd like to see her be put into the ambulance and then I'll follow it, if that's OK.'

'I'm certain that would be fine,' the nurse said understandingly and laid her hand on his right forearm, squeezed and gave him that smile again, the one he would have liked to smash off her face. That would have to wait.

She left him and he sat back to be patient.

If it was a long wait, then so be it.

The firearms team leader came out of the flat shaking his head, then trotted down the steps and walked up to Henry who was standing with his arms folded behind the police cordon tape.

'All clear,' he said. 'The place is empty and there's nowhere in it to hide even a hamster.'

'So he's gone?'

'Afraid so.'

Henry nodded numbly and said 'Thanks, sarge.' He inhaled, closed his eyes momentarily and then, literally dragging his feet, walked slowly back to his car, which was parked on Wallbank Drive amongst all the other police vehicles. He watched the firearms team climb aboard their personnel carrier and drive away.

He gave the Audi a sad visual once-over, sat in it, turned the engine on to generate some warmth and slumped back in the comfortable

316

leather seat, allowing exhaustion to engulf him. He tried some deep breathing to generate some energy, but it had no effect.

Without warning, as if he was being ambushed, his breathing actually became short and ragged, and his chest tightened up as agony arced through him. He doubled up, clutching himself with a groan, crossing his forearms over his chest, his fingers bunching into fists as the events of the night began to take their toll on his body and his mind. He writhed and ground his teeth as though he was struggling to free himself from a strait-jacket. He forced his fingers to open and unlock and grabbed the steering wheel to try and control this bastard of a demon that had invaded and taken over his whole being. A demon that laughed contemptuously at his failure, his lack of judge-ment, his utter incompetence. His knuckles turned white with the power of the grip as he tried to overpower this . . . thing that was intent on tearing him apart, this thing that had the face of Charlie Wilder; it then morphed into Robert Fanshaw-Bayley's face and finally became his own, as if he was staring into a distorted mirror.

In a parallel thought, he knew he wasn't having a heart attack, but that he was possibly on the verge of a nervous and physical breakdown.

The tears streaming down his face confirmed this and he emitted a long, awful wail as pain and despair racked his body and helplessness invaded his mind. For what seemed like an age he submitted to this inner carnage until, at last, it dissipated and he raised his eyes to look

317

forwards, through the car windscreen, as a realization struck him. His mind cleared and the pain in his body became just a background ache.

What am I playing at? he demanded of himself. *You complete and utter selfish twat, wallowing in self-pity. This fucking thing isn't over yet, not by a long* . . . (he pulled the gear lever down into reverse and the Audi shot backwards and hit the police car parked a few feet behind with a crash; then he selected drive, yanked down the steering wheel and put his foot down on the accelerator) . . . *chalk.*

He sped around on to Eastgate and reached for his newly acquired personal radio, which beeped at the moment he picked it up, indicating that someone was calling him via the mobile phone application within it.

'What?' he demanded.

He was driving with one hand, skidding the car around and back on to Wallbank Drive.

'Henry, it's me, Rik – we just heard about the raid. Me and Jerry are sat in comms listening to the op – sorry, he's not there.'

'What do you want?' Henry said.

'We have some information that you need, could be crucial.'

'Fire away.'

'We just spoke to Luke Wilder on the QT, gave him a bit of a Hobson's choice, I think – something along the lines of, "Grass on your big brother, or take a very big rap yourself."'

'Ahh, my tactics,' Henry purred. 'You're learning at last.'

318

'Knew you'd be impressed – but you won't want to hear the next bit, I don't think.'

'Which is?'

'Luke thinks Charlie's going to go for Annabel.'

'Well, funny you should mention that,' Henry said as he turned on to Hall Street and sped towards the main road. 'It just occurred to me, too . . . and I'm on the way to Rochdale Infirmary now.'

'What?'

'You heard. Get on to GMP now and tell them to get someone there and that they need to exercise extreme caution – you know why – and get on to our firearms team that's just left Wallbank and turn them round and tell them to make for the infirmary, too; I know it's cross-border, but unless GMP have a team within minutes of the hospital, then it has to be done. So tell them it's happening and make sure the high-ups are aware in Lancs and GMP. I haven't got time to do that.' The political ramifications of sending a Lancashire firearms team to operate in Greater Manchester, Henry knew, could be a real problem, but it was one he was prepared to deal with head on. If he ended up deploying a Lancashire team, then he would take all the flak quite happily.

He reached the junction with the A671, turned right and hurtled his battered car south towards Rochdale, the dark feelings that had almost overpowered him now buried deep at the back of his mind.

He had a killer to catch.

* * *

319

'She's still on A&E,' Rik informed Henry. 'But they're going to transfer her over to Bury General . . . hang on, Jerry's on to the infirmary now . . . Jerry?'

Henry heard some muffled noises. He was almost at the hospital.

'What about cops?' Henry shouted.

'GMP informed. They've got a patrol on the way, but no armed officers within striking distance. I've spoken to our deputy chief constable and he's on to GMP's chief now; in the meantime, our firearms team is only a few minutes behind you, Henry.'

'OK.'

'What, Jerry?' Henry heard Rik ask the DC. More muffled voices, then Rik said, 'They think the ambulance to convey her across to Bury is there now.'

'They think?'

'Best we've got,' Rik said. 'The shit's hit the fan with all this.'

An ambulance drew up in the emergency vehicle parking bay outside the A&E unit. Charlie could see it through the window and that the two paramedics seemed to be in no particular rush. The driver climbed out and sauntered around to the back doors of the ambulance and opened them, pulled out the ramp and then a stretcher, which he handled expertly. The other paramedic, a woman, entered A&E and Charlie lost sight of her.

He stood up and went through the double doors

into the corridor beyond and saw her walk into the emergency reception area of the unit at the far end of the corridor. Charlie hovered by a snack machine – the one at which Henry had earlier agonized whether he should have a Mars bar or not – pretending to choose something, and saw the male paramedic push the stretcher through the same doors into the unit.

Charlie was certain they were here to collect Annabel.

'Thank you, God,' he said.

He sauntered out and leaned on a wall near to the back of the ambulance from where he could see into the waiting vehicle.

He was still waiting twenty-five minutes later when there was a flurry of activity beyond the doors and a moment later the two paramedics came out pushing the stretcher, with a nurse walking along either side, one steadying a drip on a frame, the other consulting a clipboard. On the stretcher was the slight frame of Annabel Larch, a sheet drawn up to her chest, the drip being fed into the back of her right hand and an oxygen mask, linked to a bottle fixed to the head of the stretcher, covering her nose and mouth.

Charlie pushed himself upright from his lounging position at the wall.

The paramedics rolled the stretcher up the ramp, its wheels collapsing as it went into the back of the ambulance. The nurse with the clipboard gave it to the female medic. There was a quick discussion, then the medic climbed into the back of the ambulance and sat next to Annabel whilst her partner closed and secured the double doors of the vehicle.

Charlie hung back, waiting.

The nurses did not even glance at him as they headed back into the unit.

The male paramedic walked down the side of the ambulance to the driver's door, opened it and stepped up behind the wheel.

It was at this point that Charlie moved.

He ran along the side of the ambulance, opened the driver's door just as the paramedic was starting the engine. He looked at Charlie, suspecting nothing, so when the shotgun slid down Charlie's sleeve into his hands and was shoved into his face, his hands rose slowly. Charlie said, 'Out, now, and don't do anything heroic or I'll blast the fuck out of your face.' He juggled the shotgun to emphasize his promise.

'OK mate, OK.' He was an experienced medic and this was not the first time his ambulance had been hijacked. The guidelines were that all staff complied with any threats of danger and did not put themselves in harm's way.

'Out, now.'

He swung his legs down. Charlie took a pace sideways and then drove the butt of the shotgun into the back of the paramedic's head, flooring him instantly. Charlie did not give him a second glance. He climbed into his seat, slammed the driver's door, slotted the shotgun between his legs and put the ambulance into gear.

This had worked out better than he could have anticipated. He had visualized having to kill

Annabel in the hospital, but being able to drive her away and take his time with her somewhere was simply off the scale as far as Charlie was concerned. The fact that there was another paramedic in with her did not put him off. He was quite happy to deal with her however she wanted. He guessed she would be happy to run away.

'All right back there?' Charlie called through the gap in the cab wall. He looked over his shoulder at the shocked face of the female and smiled. 'We're going for a ride, girls.'

He turned back to face the front, but the driver's door opened and he was hauled bodily out of the seat and thrown to the ground.

Henry drove the Audi fast down Whitworth Road towards Rochdale, screeched into Mizzy Road, then left into Whitehall Street which ran along the front of the infirmary, parking his car illegally on a grass verge that also had double yellow lines alongside it.

He walked quickly towards the Accident and Emergency unit, not really taking too much notice of the ambulance parked under the canopy in the area reserved for such vehicles. He walked behind it and glanced with disbelief at the paramedic spreadeagled on the tarmac, bleeding from a massive head wound, and the driver's door just closing with a clunk.

He stopped – but only for the briefest of moments – trying to make sense of this, particularly hard in view of the way his mind was currently working, then sprinted down the side of the ambulance, saw that Charlie Wilder was in the driving seat and just about to release the clutch and engage the engine. Henry almost ripped the door off its hinges, reached in with a roar of pure rage and grabbed Charlie's coat, pulling him out of the seat, twisting painfully as he threw him down.

Henry saw the sawn-off shotgun skitter away from between Charlie's legs.

Charlie landed heavily on his hands and knees, his backside up in the air facing Henry, who could not resist.

He kicked him hard and accurately in the balls, hoping he had driven the testicles all the way up through his body and into his throat. Charlie leapt away with a scream, then rolled on his back, cupping his balls, rocking from side to side, groaning.

Henry walked to him, towered over him, his face thunderous in its ire. As the blood pounded through him, every scrape on the side of his face had started to bleed again, droplets of red rolling down his cheek, pushed out by every pulse in his head.

'Hello, Charlie,' he said, 'It's me again.'

This spurred Charlie into action. He was a tough street fighter and a kick in the balls was not going to prevent him achieving his aims. His right leg shot out and caught Henry on the right knee, hard. Henry felt it go slightly and he rocked back a couple of feet, by which time Charlie had flipped into a crouch and launched himself at Henry, smashing his shoulder into Henry's lower guts, pounding him against the side of the ambulance and wrapping his arms around Henry's middle.

Henry punched down hard on the side of Charlie's head, striking his ear which seemed to squelch sickeningly under blow after blow, then burst crimson, but Charlie held on remorselessly, trying to manoeuvre himself into an advantage, the blows not seeming to have any effect on him.

Suddenly he let go and dropped to his knees, confusing Henry.

It was a ruse and Charlie rolled away and scampered towards the shotgun.

Henry saw it, moved more quickly, and as though he was converting a try at rugby he kicked the gun away and it whirled off across the ground like a spinning top, well out of Charlie's reach. Then he fell on to Charlie's back with his knee right on his spine between his shoulder blades, crushing the man's lungs and forcing all the air out of them.

Henry pinned him there for a moment, gasping for his own breath.

He glanced at the paramedic, who had only just managed to get on to his hands and knees, his face covered with blood.

He could see the female paramedic's terrified face looking out from the rear of the ambulance.

He thought about FB, Johnny Asian, the horribly injured girl in the back of the ambulance, a dead baby, the murdered prison guard, the shopkeeper and the other lad, Jake, who had been about to help Henry and FB.

'Fucking let me up, you bastard.' Charlie

squirmed under Henry's knee, trying to look up at him. Henry released the pressure, but continued to hold Charlie on the floor with his hand at Charlie's collar.

Then Henry stood up and let him go.

'Should effin' think so. I've got my rights,' Charlie said, rising on to all fours.

Henry took a step back. He raised his foot and slammed it into the side of Charlie's head, knocking the whole of his head out of shape.

From that moment on nothing else in the world mattered to Henry other than delivering justice to Charlie Wilder in the only way he truly understood.

X